Man Walks into a Room

A NOVEL

Nicole Krauss

W F HOWES LTD

This large print edition published in 2008 by
W F Howes Ltd
Unit 4, Rearsby Business Park, Gaddesby Lane,
Rearsby, Leicester LE7 4YH

1 3 5 7 9 10 8 6 4 2

First published in the United Kingdom in 2007
by Penguin Books

A CIP catalogue record for this book is available
from the British Library

ISBN 978 1 40741 336 5

Typeset by Palimpsest Book Production Limited,
Grangemouth, Stirlingshire
Printed and bound in Great Britain
by Antony Rowe Ltd, Chippenham, Wilts.

You shall not discern the footprints of any other;
you shall not see the face of man;
you shall not hear any name—

—EMERSON, 'Self-Reliance'

PROLOGUE

JUNE 1957

Girls girls girls reads the sign on a chain-link fence and we whistle and cheer as the bus slams past, churning up a cloud of dust in the basin. An angry black fly buzzes against the window and someone tries to singe it with a cigarette. The stubble of sagebrush is endless, and Kohler says you wouldn't be more than a day dead before the coyotes would clean you. Right before we left Pendleton, Kohler got a tattoo of a girl who wriggles when he flexes, and he rolls up his sleeve for the sixth or seventh time today.

When we pass a road sign saying a hundred miles to Vegas we whoop again, leaning out and drumming the bus's flanks until the ribbon of asphalt twists off into the distance. Someone says he heard that the first shot they exploded over Bikini had a picture of Rita Hayworth taped to it, and that gets a few snickers. Kohler's been to Vegas and he talks about how we're going to check into the Desert Inn on our night off, play the nickel slot machines, see Shirley Jones.

At 15:13 we slide into Desert Rock, stretching

3

and jogging around on the tarmac to work out the stiffness. It's a hundred and ten degrees or hotter, the kind of heat that makes your head split. The shower of a distant rain cloud evaporates high in the air before a drop of it ever reaches the desert.

We're issued a fresh set of fatigues and afterward there are no immediate duties, so we find a patch of shade and watch as a few guys set out in a ragged band to investigate, joking and pushing as they disappear into the distance looking for craters.

At night the sky is pure astronomy.

We do nothing for days but wait, trying to lose time by sleeping or hunting lizards on the cracked desert floor. We are living on the bed of an ancient lake, someone writes home, there are fossils to prove it. We take a drive to a ghost town near Death Valley, standing at the crossroads dueling with our hands cocked like pistols. Occasionally someone plays a scratchy recording of Johnny Mathis or Elvis over the P.A. We drink to keep our blood from getting thick, water by day, beer by night. We watch the girl do a jerky dance on Kohler's biceps. The wind blows continually in the wrong direction, a strange wind that unsettles us, swirling the dust in restless eddies. We eat our meals with sand between our teeth. When the wind finally shifts, orders come through that the shot will take place at 06:30. We rise at 04:00.

The test shots are named for scientists or mountains, except for the one we've come for, Priscilla, suspended seven hundred feet above the ground in a helium balloon. A bulletin is sent out to civilians warning of damage to the retina caused by looking at the fireball as far as sixty miles away, but miners will still scrabble up to the top of Angel's Peak like it's the Fourth of July.

We ride the thirty miles out to Frenchman Flat in the back of military trucks, pinned with radiation badges, now colored a safe blue. Two thousand yards from ground zero the trucks come to a halt and we stumble down, half-asleep. We get down into the foxholes until we're eye level with the desert floor. A thousand of us are almost nothing on that endless flat, like ants from above, like something only a little unusual, not a species but a small event that doesn't think of itself as history. We are mostly quiet now, listening to the coyotes and the scratch of the desert until the bitch boxes start screaming orders through the thinning dark. Later some of us will be sent to Vietnam, and when we are sweating in our tents, crawling with spiders, our skin infected with fungus, we will remember this, the simplicity of it.

While we wait a caravan of trucks rumbles by with the frightened jostle of live animals. A thousand yards ahead we see them push out nine hundred pigs, herding them into foxholes and pens. Some of the pigs wear brand-new field jackets with liners to be tested for durability. A handful of rabbits for the scientists' continued efforts to record the effect of flash blindness.

There are fifteen minutes before countdown. Fifteen minutes for us to think about Vegas, of the time we shook Ike's hand, of drummers in the big bands like Krupa who could finesse a set of drums, make them talk without hammering at them, of the soft piano music in the clubs in California. Fifteen minutes for another Chesterfield, to absentmindedly notch little holes in the trench wall with our fingers. A thousand thoughts, a small cross section of a moment in America. Our helmets askew, not yet strapped on. The pants of the new fatigues still starchy. The sun rises in glory as if it had yet to invent the desert. Two minutes for the newspapermen to settle into their seats at Control Point, men in suits with tickets in their hatbands who would narrate this to no one.

A thousand men with their arms across their eyes like girls at the movies, listening to the lone, amplified voice count backward from ten. This is June of 1957, before the countdown becomes synonymous with rocket launches that will send astronauts beyond the earth's atmospheric vacuum.

And then a noise we've never heard before. Something like maximum volume. Even with our eyes closed we see a flash of hot white light from a bomb four times as big as Nagasaki, so bright there are no shadows. We count to ten and look and what we see is the blood coursing through our own veins and the skeletons of the men in front of us. The X ray of a thousand GIs, their bones like a desert slide show. The yucca trees stand out in relief, the mountains are aluminum.

The bitch boxes scream for us to stand up and we rise, stunned, moving without thinking except for the boys who are on the bottom crying and praying. We rise up and as we do we're slammed with a shock wave of hot air like it's going to rip our heads off. It knocks us back, and the ground pitches. We are too panicked to wonder about the logic of our orders. We obey because it's the only way to make it through alive.

The air is dark as a comic book doomsday. How can I explain that we took this personally?

Another wall, a moving flash flood of dirt and debris, pelting us with sticks and stones and other things we can't think about just now, some of us half-buried. There is a moment of strange calm, like a deep pause of respect before the singing of the anthem. Then we can no longer breathe. There is no air left as the pressure reverses and comes sailing back toward ground zero, calmer, sadder now as the detonation begins to collapse in on itself, a vacuum that threatens to suck everything in. We are fighting for air, every man for himself as the debris settles, and then we see it, the thing we have come for: a huge fireball going up on the back of the mushroom cloud like the devil mounting heaven. The most beautiful thing we have ever seen, boiling in its own blood, rising to forty thousand feet and spreading until it obscures the sun, spreading above our heads and raining down the remains of the

7

desert. We cannot think. There is no room left in our minds for anything but this.

Fourteen miles away, at Control Point, it blows the doors off the hinges. The Geiger counters have to be calmed like scared horses. Nearby, highway travellers pull off the road and stand by their station wagons dazed and blinking, scouting the sky for aliens. The blast is felt at Mercury and Indian Springs, heard as a rumble as far as California and Reno. In Utah a wave of heat blows through children's hair, flattening their T-shirts against their chests as they run and twirl under a flurry of ash.

When the silence finally settles we stand and march forward for the assault on ground zero. A thousand men, our film badges blushed scarlet, like girls who've just been kissed.

PART I

MAY 2000

When they found him he was halfway down the only stretch of asphalt that cuts through Mercury Valley. The two police officers saw him up the road, ragged as a crow. He looked at them blankly when they pulled up next to him, neither surprised nor grateful. They asked him questions that seemed to confuse him, and his gaze slipped past them to scout the desert. He didn't struggle when they frisked him. They opened his wallet and counted out twenty-three dollars and change. They read his name and address aloud to him but his expression registered nothing. The man before them in a filthy suit bore almost no resemblance to the bright, focused face on the New York State license; sun had darkened his features and dust had worn itself into the creases of his skin so that it was impossible to believe he was only thirty-six. They assumed he'd stolen the wallet, and though it was clear he was dehydrated and confused they locked his wrists together as they led him into the car. He sat rigidly in the backseat, at a forward tilt with his eyes fixed on the road. They called him Samson not because

11

they believed it was really his name but because they could think of nothing else to call him.

While they treated him in the emergency room in Las Vegas for whatever he was suffering, one of the police officers put in a call for a search on Samson Greene, d.o.b. 1/29/64. When it was discovered that Samson Greene had been missing for eight days, last seen walking out of the gates of Columbia University and down Broadway into the clear afternoon, things began to get interesting. Someone in the Twenty-fourth Precinct in Manhattan was able to connect the police officer to the social services agency where Samson's wife worked, and after speaking to three people he was finally put through to her. *Hello?* she said quietly into the phone, already informed of who was on the other end. *Is he alive?*

There was a short, confused discussion: what did he mean, they weren't sure if it was him, didn't his license say Samson Greene?, to which the police officer didn't want to reply, Lady, Samson Greene could be lying in a ditch somewhere outside Vegas having taken a knife to the chest from the man who's now a card-carrying member of the West Side Racquet Club, the Faculty of English at Columbia University, the Museum of Modern Art. *Are there any distinguishing marks?* the police officer asked. *Yes,* she said, *a scar down the back of his left arm.* She paused, as if Samson were lying in front of her and she was inspecting his body. *And a birthmark above his shoulder blade.* The police officer said he would call her back as soon as he knew anything,

12

giving her the number of the pay phone out of courtesy. She insisted on waiting on the line, so he left the receiver hanging off the hook while he went to check whether it was in fact her husband on the gurney. A nurse passing by picked it up and said, *Hello? Hello?* When there was no answer, she hung up. A minute later the phone rang but no one was around so it just rang and rang in urgent bursts, each ring separated by a brief, desperate silence.

Later they were able to reconstruct most of his journey from the receipts for bus tickets in his pockets, from the few accounts of witnesses who recalled having seen him – a waitress, the manager of a motel in Dayton, Ohio – confirmed by the ghostly flicker of his image caught by the wandering eye of security cameras. When they eventually played these tapes back to Samson he smiled and shook his head because he could not remember where he'd been or why he'd gone there. In a way that she couldn't explain, alone in her own sadness, those images made Anna Greene want her husband terribly, as she hadn't since they began to share a bed, a car, a dog, a bathroom. In one of them, the only one in which you could see Samson's face clearly, he was standing at the checkout desk in a Budget motel outside Nashville. He was holding open his wallet and his face was tilted upward, his expression as peaceful and absorbed as a child's.

While Anna was looking down from the plane on the rucked mass of Nevada cut by a glinting vein leading to Vegas, the neurologist, a Dr Tanner, was studying a CT scan of Samson's brain. By the time Anna arrived at the hospital, disheveled, wheeling behind her a small suitcase none of whose contents she could remember packing, Samson had been diagnosed with a tumor that, all those months lost in work or sleep, had been applying its arbitrary, pernicious pressure on his brain. The heat during the drive from the airport had been, even in May, almost unbearable. Now Anna was shivering in the air-conditioned hospital, her damp shirt clinging to her back. She couldn't understand, nor was anyone yet able to explain to her, how Samson had gotten to where they'd found him, some nowhere in Nevada. It was with great difficulty that she registered the words of Dr Tanner, who was sitting across from her now. *It's about the size of a cherry, pressing on the temporal lobe of his brain, most likely a juvenile pilocytic astrocytoma.* And in her own mind – clear, unthreatened by disease – Anna imagined the shiny dark red of a cherry nestled into the gray matter of the brain. Once, five or six years ago, they had pulled off the road in Connecticut to follow a painted sign that said *Cherry Picking*. They'd driven back through the early summer evening with two baskets and stained fingers, the windows open to let in the smell of cut grass. As she listened to Dr Tanner's voice and his patient, kind pauses, Anna sensed he was a happy man, one who would drive home in his soundproof car listening to classical FM, to his wife with her bright and easy laugh – a man who did not wake

14

each day to the misery he'd left slumped in the chair the night before. She felt envious of him, envious of the nurses passing in the hall who were happy enough to dress themselves this morning in starched uniforms, envious of the orderlies and the janitor pushing his gray mop along the linoleum floor.

Dr Tanner continued: *After the surgery we'll perform a biopsy and hope it's benign*, he said, a word, Anna thought, that seemed unkind as all euphemisms are, and as Samson had once pointed out to her. Dr Tanner turned the CT scan around and slid it across the desk to her, leaning forward in his chair to trace the atlas of Samson's brain with the cap of his pen. It came to rest on a yellow island in a continent of blue. *He seems, for the moment, to be operating on a kind of autopilot, an awareness educated enough to get him across the country alone. Whether or not some or all of his memory functions have been destroyed permanently, or whether the surgery will itself incur such damage, is impossible to predict.* Anna looked out the window to the hospital's landscape kept ever-green by the steady dose of water meted out by sprinklers. She was thirty-one years old. She had been with Samson for almost ten years. She thought of the time he'd had a toothache so severe he cried, and also, inexplicably, of the time he'd sent her flowers for her birthday but on the wrong day. She turned back to Dr Tanner and studied his face. *If you remove it and it's benign*, she finally said, *is there a chance he'll be all right?*, though by *all right* what she meant was *the same. I don't think you understand*, Dr Tanner said, his voice filled with the compassion that is sometimes confused with pity. *Chances are his memory will be obliterated.* He paused, a deep, medical pause, his fingers resting lightly on Samson's brain. *He probably won't remember who you are.*

What he remembered about opening his eyes was the clock on the wall above the door that read 3:30. He must have drifted in and out of consciousness for a while longer, because when he woke again the clock was gone and he was in another room with a window, the curtains pulled back to let in the sun. Later he tried to remember exactly what he felt and thought in those first hours, but unlike the sharp clarity of what followed, he could only recall the vague wake of the anesthesia. He wanted to remember those first pure moments without reference, when something had been removed from his brain and what filled its place, like air rushing into a vacuum, was emptiness. Though there was nothing else to call it, it wasn't quite forgetfulness. He tried to explain this to Anna once enough time had passed that he learned, again, what forgetting was; it wasn't like the amputation of an arm where the mind still feels an itch in phantom fingers. It was a complete eradication, the removal of both memory and its echo, and it was this that Anna couldn't understand, this lack of regret. But how can one regret what, to the mind, has never existed? Even *loss* is an inaccurate description, for what loss is without the awareness of losing?

Weeks later, on the plane back to New York, Samson sat next to Anna, his head shaved and bandaged over the incision, the large envelope with his CT scans resting on his knees. He had lost twenty pounds, and the clothes he was wearing – the only things Anna could find in the cheap stores near the hospital – were unfashionable and didn't fit properly. Out of the corner of his eye Samson saw that Anna was staring at him, but he was afraid if he spoke to her she might cry. He trusted her because she cared for him and there was no one else. When the plane began its descent into La Guardia, she covered his hand with her own, and as they touched down he looked at her hand, trying to make something of it. During the taxi ride through Queens, Samson pressed his forehead against the window and read the illuminated signs along the highway. When they crossed the Triboro Bridge and Manhattan rose against the night sky, Anna asked, 'Do you remember?'

'From the movies,' he said, and leaned forward to see.

The benign astrocytoma they removed from his brain had been preserved on slides, and stored in the hospital's pathology lab. The biopsy suggested that it had been slowly growing for months, maybe years, without effect. It was what they called a *silent* turnor, without the manifestation of symptoms that

18

might have alerted anyone to its presence. Before the moment Samson had put down a book in his office at the university and closed his memory with it, there might have been small falters, moments when his memory lapsed into blackness before returning seconds later. But if these had happened there was no way of knowing now. All the while, the turnor had been forming itself in his mind like a nightmarish pearl. That late May afternoon, school just let out, the shouts of students floating in through the open windows, it had finally gained enough mass that its gradual exertion of pressure became too much. Between two words in a book Samson's memory had vanished. Everything, save for his childhood, which days later in a hospital in Nevada he woke up remembering.

At first he couldn't even remember his own name. Still, there were things, like the taste of orange juice, that were familiar to him. He knew that the woman who stood by his bed in the red shirt was pretty, though he couldn't think of plainer faces against which hers stood out. These early signs were promising, and as the doctors tested him it became clear that not only had he retained a sort of intrinsic memory of the world but, more remarkably, he was able to lay down new memories. He could remember everything that had happened after the operation. The doctors seemed puzzled by this, and during teaching rounds they paused for a long time in

Samson's room. They continued to inject him with glucose, but as the days passed it was clear his memory loss wasn't an effect of the edema. His particular scenario – retrograde amnesia causing the loss of all specific memories prior to surgery, while the capacity to remember still functioned – was highly unusual. And while Samson seemed to have forgotten his entire auto-biography, he nevertheless knew that the flowers on the night table were called amaryllis and that the woman who stood by his bed, Anna, had brought them for him. And it was in opening his eyes to those obscure white blooms a week after his operation that something like a fragment from a dream dislodged itself and floated up to the surface of his mind.

It was the vivid color of the memory that star-tled him, a luminous blue. It was all around him, warm and smooth, and moving through it toward the glow of light he could hear muted sounds that seemed to come from a great, impassable distance. There was a felicity despite the slow pressure on his lungs that finally pushed him upward. He remembered that when his head broke through the surface of the water he'd been surprised by the chill of the air and the world that stood in perfect, microscopic clarity: the blades of grass, the night sky, the dripping faces of two boys illu-minated by the pool lights. 'Forty-three seconds!' one shouted, looking at his watch, then barreled down the diving board, leaped into the air, and clutched his knees, dropping into the water with a lucid splash.

In the days following his operation, memories from his childhood continued to appear in his mind with unnerving precision. It was as if the apertures of his eyes, confused by the outside world, had been directed inward and begun to cast, like a camera obscura, perfect images on the whitewashed walls of his mind. The hairline cracks of a sugar bowl on the kitchen table. The sun falling through the leaves casting shadows on his fingers. His mother's eyelashes. Anna had been overjoyed, squeezing his hand each time he described to her what he could remember. That's what she was at first, this woman who sat day in and day out by his bed, whose thin wrists he could encircle with two fingers: an audience for his memories. And although it alarmed him that she knew, like an informed agent, many of the years and places of those memories, he continued to narrate them to her because he sensed that she could help him. Again and again he described his mother to her, in the hope that Anna might find her and bring her to him. When he asked why his mother wouldn't come, she covered her mouth and looked away.

'I love you,' she whispered, and in halting sentences she began to explain, weak with apology. He could not absorb everything she was trying to tell him. When she told him that his mother had died he felt it like the clean break of a bone and a sound came from him that he did not recognize. When he was too exhausted to weep any more he lay in silence, all his being drained to the flat line of the heart stilled.

Anna remained hopeful, despite the doctors' warning that these recollections of his childhood didn't necessarily mean Samson would recover later memories. It sometimes happened like this, they said. As if the preservation of those early years was so crucial that they were kept under the protection of another faculty of the brain, so carefully guarded that they survived intact when, in a trauma to the brain, all other memories perished. And so it seemed to be with Samson, whose memories, beyond the age of twelve, faded away into the future like footsteps.

When the taxi pulled up to their apartment building, Samson got out while Anna paid the driver. He stood bewildered at his door, unable to absorb that this was the very street he had lived on for five years, that before that he had lived ten blocks south, before that downtown, and before that in California, and so on back through innumerable rooms with their qualities of light, their different views. His belief in his past life was polite: the kind one manufactures when in conversation with the faithful. And though he knew almost nothing about the woman walking toward him now, he wanted somehow to please her, or at least not to upset her any more than she already was.

As Anna put the key in the lock, he could hear the sound of a dog's excited whimpering and pawing at the other side of the door.

'That's Frank,' Anna said, fumbling with the lock. Samson saw that her hand was shaking and he was about to offer to help when the key slid into place and Anna pushed open the door. The dog jumped onto Samson, knocking him against the wall.

'No, Frank, calm down,' she said, giving the dog a gentle tug on the collar. Frank turned around to lick her hand. She patted him on the head and he sat, obedient under her touch, peering at Samson with curiosity. Each stroke pulled the dog's brow upward, widening his eyes and making his face appear comically surprised. Samson laughed and the dog shot out from under Anna's hand and regaled him with snorts and a flurry of paws. He had an urge to grab the dog around the neck and bury his face in its soft ears, to curl up next to him.

Anna switched on the lights and Samson and Frank followed her into the living room. Its walls were lined with hundreds of books. A few faded rugs covered the wooden floor, and the room was scattered with chairs and lamps that Anna was now turning on one by one. It was a pleasant room and looking around it Samson tried to connect it to the woman walking through it. It was like her somehow, it shared a certain coherence.

When the room was completely lit – *like a stage,*

Samson thought – she turned to face him. She had long, dark hair and a face that changed each time he looked at it. He'd overheard the doctors warning her not to expect anything of him, not to push him in the beginning to strain to remember. Not to look at him hopefully, expectantly, as she now was. He glanced from her to the books, the windowsills filled with plants, and when he squeezed his eyes shut he felt something flap up like a pigeon into the skylight of his mind. He opened his eyes.

'Did you read all these?' he asked. Anna's eyes swept across the shelves.

'You did,' she said.

Later, during long afternoons at the library, Samson would read of miraculous cases in which sight is granted to the blind. As the bandages were removed, their families gathered around them awaiting the epiphany, *so* this *is how it looks!* But it never came because to see is not necessarily to perceive. The shapes the newly sighted registered had no currency with their brains, never conditioned to conceive of space. The colors had no bearing on the world they'd constructed out of time and sound. Reading these accounts – the bated breath, the sudden flow of light, followed by the confusion and failure of recognition – reminded Samson of his first days home. Anna, the rooms of the apartment, their things: he could see it all. But nothing yet had the weight of significance. Although the memories of his childhood were clear, they seemed marked by an other-worldly quality, so that now each thing seemed almost an archetype of itself, not yet trailed by a procession of associations and experiences.

The second night Samson was home Anna was exhausted and fell asleep before him. He lay in the dark, breathing quietly so as not to wake her. There was a sound of cars driving through the rain and laughter from a television floating up from the floor below. He felt uneasy in their bed, but couldn't think of someplace else he longed to be. Though he couldn't remember the many years that had passed since his childhood, the bedroom he'd grown up in seemed part of a vanished world that had existed long ago. Despite his awkwardness and confusion, he felt not like a twelve-year-old but a man of thirty-six. It was only that he couldn't remember how he'd become whoever he now was.

He was grateful to finally be alone with his thoughts after the confused days since the operation, the slow awakening from oblivion to the facts of his situation. There was so much he didn't know – how his mother had died, whether he had been in love with Anna, whether he had been a good man – but he didn't yet have the courage or even the means to ask. He didn't yet know how to breach the distance between himself and another person in the form of a touch, a question.

He turned on his side to face Anna, careful not to wake her. It was the first time he was able to

25

really look at her, to study her without meeting her eyes that always seemed to want something. Although he was slowly beginning to understand his situation, he felt less as if he had forgotten time than as if time had forgotten *him*. That he'd fallen asleep in one life and somehow passed into this one along the axis of a consistent heartbeat, so that some memory of where he came from, of who he was, had stayed with him. Of all the things he had been asked to believe, the strangest of them was that the woman who slept beside him now was his wife.

Looking at her, slack and humid in sleep, Samson tried to recognize her. He studied her bare arms and the bent of her fingers, then closed his eyes and searched for these things. He pressed the blackness for something of her that might be left lingering behind like perfume.

He moved closer. He wanted to touch her in order to feel what *he* had been like. To step into the role of Samson Greene like a character in the movies who assumes the clothes and car, who steps into the shoes, of another man. As if with his palm on the curve of her waist, mimicking the gestures of Samson Greene, he could step into his past. There is such a thing as tactile memory, the sensation of cold, sharp, or smooth, and he wondered whether somewhere in him was not the feel of Anna.

He could smell her now, a faintly sweet smell. Her chest rose and fell as she breathed, the outline of her breasts pressed against her cotton shirt.

How many times had his fingers absently brushed across them, so that she had never pulled away in surprise? If he reached for her now without waking her, would her body submit to his hand or would it sense, somewhere deep in its own history of a thousand touches, the difference in this one? The intelligent body turning over on its side, away from him, unforgiving. They had not touched each other often at the hospital or since they'd come home. He hadn't reached for her and she must have felt how his body was strict and uneasy with her. He was more comfortable petting the dog. When she had begun to change her clothes before bed, he'd been embarrassed when she looked up and caught him staring. In the dim room the sight of her pale body had shocked him.

If he could memorize her now, tomorrow he could look at her remembering. Anna wanted that. He began with her face, the arch of her brows. How did they go? An image came to him of his mother, the way her eyebrows rose when she was surprised. He remembered a box of puppets he had played with as a child. He imagined threads attached to Anna's brow, her shoulders, elbows, fingers. If she moved now how would it be, if she got up and walked to the window? As she stood in the shadows of the streetlamps he would tug up the string attached to her right wrist until it brushed her cheek, collapse the string attached to the top of her head, lowering her face into her raised hand. His own hand hovered above her now and the desire to touch her body was so powerful he felt it might suffocate him. He began to float his palm down, but just before it reached her Anna rolled into him and nestled her head against his chest. Startled, he froze, his hand stalled in the air above the empty mattress.

His arm still raised, he slid off the edge of the bed. He felt foolish and ashamed and when he found that the bedroom door was shut, it seemed as if the room was closing in on him. He felt an overpowering desire to be outside. He turned the handle and slipped into the living room, his heart pumping as he moved toward the front door.

There was a noise in the kitchen and he halted, frozen in place. The dog turned the corner, his tags jingling. Frank cocked his head and looked at him.

'Shhh,' Samson whispered.

Frank hurried over, turned around, and sat at Samson's feet. They remained like that for a moment, both facing the door. Samson leaned down and petted him.

'Hey, fella.' Frank breathed in his face.

Samson switched on a lamp. The living room was littered with crumpled cocktail napkins and plastic cups from the homecoming party Anna had thrown that afternoon. She hadn't told Samson about it until the bell rang and people started filing in, complete strangers for all he knew, hugging him and pumping his hand, lining up to greet him while he sat pasty-faced in an armchair like some kind of demented Santa. Everyone seemed to hope to be the one he remembered, as if winning his recognition were a million-dollar sweepstakes.

Right away it was obvious that the party was ill conceived. A group of people stood uncomfortably by the crackers and cheese. A few kids hovered near their parents, nervous smiles plastered across their faces as if they'd been told they were being brought to see a sick man who should not, at all costs, be reminded that he was dying. Not only did Samson recognize no one, he also couldn't seem to recall anyone's name even after they'd introduced themselves, and so during the brief two hours of the party people took to announcing their names in loud voices before they spoke to him, as if he were not only amnesiac but deaf too. At first, once he understood that these friendly people hoped to share something with him, Samson had tried to be as cooperative as possible, smiling and holding a child on his lap. But soon the clamor of voices became too much and he began to feel overwhelmed and dizzy. The party came to a grim end when Samson locked himself in the bathroom and whispered to the kid who kept rattling the door to please go pee elsewhere because he was feeling sick.

'I'm sorry,' Anna had whispered through the door once everyone had left, 'I'm so very sorry.' Samson had unlocked the door and when he saw her eyes fill with tears he felt she might break if he didn't take her in his arms.

Now he walked around the empty living room, examining its contents as one might if left alone in a stranger's house. There was a photograph of him on the shelf, sitting on a low stone wall with a flash of red leaves behind him. He picked it up and searched his face for clues about what he had been thinking when the shutter clicked. He remembered how while watching a television show at the age of three, he'd been shocked when he'd caught sight of himself on the screen, sitting Indian-style on the floor with the other kids in the studio audience. The camera zoomed in on his face. He'd never told anyone about it. It was something he felt sure had happened; he had been in two places at the same time, and for many years he was faintly aware of the presence of that other self carrying on somewhere. But he never again came across any proof of it again, and with time the belief in his other self dwindled away like an imaginary friend, until he forgot about him altogether.

He lifted one photograph after the next, studying them. He found it was easiest if he thought of the man in them not as himself but a stranger. This wasn't difficult since he still hadn't gotten used to his own face. When he passed his reflection in the mirror he was overcome by a wave of nausea, the primitive reflex of an animal whose instinct suddenly fails him. He didn't know what he expected to see. His mind had not yet formed an image of himself.

He felt sick and nervous, and hurried back around the room turning all the photographs face-down. He began pacing around the cramped space as if he were the wild boy raised by wolves that he'd read about as a child, whose first night indoors was spent in panic, looking for a way out. He dragged his fingers across the spines of the books; there were hundreds, maybe thousands of them. Their orderliness disturbed him, and he pulled a few off the shelf at random. Not satisfied, he grabbed whole armfuls. Things fluttered down that had been lodged between the pages, movie stubs and newspaper clippings and a postcard with a lighthouse on the front.

He turned the postcard over. *August 18, 1994. Dear Anna, Today I finished the last page, and now I am thinking of you.* That was all he'd written. He must have put down his pen and looked out at the water, and then placed the card between the pages of his book and forgotten about it. He felt a sudden fury, that the man he used to be could so easily trail off in midsentence, that he could forget to finish a letter to his wife with impunity. A man who could go away and come back, who could write home or not, who could leave off from the page and disappear into the afternoon – and nothing would be held against him. A man who was not a freak, who was loved and recognized by dogs and children alike. He ripped the card into pieces and heaved open the window. He was surprised to feel hot tears on his face. He leaned out as far as he could and opened his hand, and as the shredded bits of the lighthouse fell through the air he stuffed his knuckles in his mouth and howled, a cry so high-pitched that it was almost soundless.

He watched the bits of paper settle on the sidewalk below. A woman hurrying on her way somewhere stopped and looked up. Samson leaned back into the shadows. The forgetting was beyond his control; it was said and done now, and even if he'd wanted to he could not wish the lost time back. It angered him to have so little choice in his own fate – to go to sleep in the liberty of childhood and wake up twenty-four years later in a life he had nothing to do with, surrounded by people who expected him to be someone he felt he'd never been.

When he returned to the bed, Anna had moved back to her own side. Looking at her in the dim light of the streetlamp, he was struck by her beauty. He lay down and closed his eyes. With sleep came forgetfulness. He felt at home there.

His days were filled with doctor appointments and tests. There were more CT scans and MRIs. By now he knew the ritual and would wait in his lead apron scanning the pages of *People* magazine until the technician came for him. He recognized a few of the celebrities, an old Mick Jagger, a fat Liz Taylor. 'Oh, she's been through a lot since you last heard about her,' the nurse joked when she found him studying her picture. He liked these magazines as he had liked comic books as a boy: he wanted to trade them and collect them all. He liked the bits of ephemera and the tales of celebrity lives that he picked up in their pages, and liked, also, to employ this knowledge to surprise people with his quickness. Once, when he called a prissy friend of Anna's a slave to Martha Stewart, she started to exclaim that it was all a hoax, that he was playing dumb and really could remember, and he had to race through his stack of magazines to show her the special issue on America's richest women.

Everyone in the Neurology Institute liked Samson, and for a little while he was himself a kind of minor celebrity, a one-in-a-million case. He was an easy patient, even-tempered and obedient, shuffling through the tests and swallowing what they gave him. Once as he lay still in the claustrophobic tunnel of the MRI machine, listening to the light FM they piped through his earphones, he felt – a feeling he couldn't yet articulate – the absurdity of his situation. He had no trouble completing the cognitive tasks the neurologists set for him and they concluded that his sense of language, his ability to understand abstract concepts, his intellect itself, remained remarkably intact. They determined that though he had no remembrance of the last twenty-four years, he still had the mind of an intelligent adult. Using primitive sketches drawn on the backs of loose paper, they demonstrated to Samson and Anna how the mind doesn't store knowledge it learns about the world chronologically, the way it does experiences. Samson could formulate ideas with such facility partly because his factual, or semantic, memories hadn't been wholly destroyed. The result was a peculiar inventiveness in his way of thinking, his tendency to make connections between remote things as if unimpeded by the banal standards of habit. It was a side effect of his loss of memory, a creativity that sprung from an advanced mind experiencing the world as a novelty.

For it was the simplest tests he always failed: *Where did you go to college? In what year did you*

marry your wife?, to which he looked at them helplessly, hurt by their insistence. Time and again
they made him recite the events of the days and
now weeks since his surgery, tracing the line back
until it dropped off into darkness.

It was a long, unyielding darkness, a lengthy
pause that could not be counted in years. And
just when it seemed that it might be interminable,
it ended and Samson emerged again on the other
side in the sharp, unforgettable light of childhood.

He had grown up in California, in Los Altos, not far from the Pacific. As a child he'd often driven to the ocean with his mother. There was a spot they liked a few miles north of Half Moon Bay. They would pick their way down the steep cliff path that ran between the brush and aloe, then walk along the water. Samson would run ahead and crouch down to examine a shell or stone like an archaeologist of past waves. Often they took their dog, a little black dog, with them. She ran alongside Samson and buried her nose in whatever he stopped to look at, or else she hung back, keeping pace with his mother. Afterward they would drive back in the late-afternoon light, Samson lying in the backseat with the warm, sandy dog while the trees and sky flashed past the open window.

He remembered these scenes clearly. At first they came to him one by one, small moments out of time like snapshots. Soon he began to string the individual memories together, but as he placed one after the next a wealth of new memories would well up between the two. Every day his childhood multiplied, grew more complex with the addition of shadows, objects, angles, expressions. If he unearthed a blue chair it had to be sat on, and quickly he remembered his mother peeling apples in it, or the dog ramming her paws between the legs to retrieve a tennis ball. With this sudden whirl of motion, the succession of still images began to move and gained momentum. He found he could run through the years then stop on a moment at random like a single image in a stereoscope. His bicycle leaning against the side of the house, a crown of rust around the bell, the rubber foot on the kickstand scratched from use. The wooden rungs of his jungle gym eaten green by rot, the drab canvas tent sagging under the weight of water. The covers of books he had read over and over with the crazed perseverance of a record-breaker. The clarity was startling and Samson wondered whether he was imagining these moments. Not that they hadn't happened at all, but that they had been embellished by details from elsewhere, fragments that survived the obliteration of other memories, vagrant data that gravitated and stuck to what was left to remember. But in the end he rejected this idea. The memories were too perfect: take one detail away and they collapsed into disorder.

He remembered playing handball with two boys against the garage door. They took turns swatting the rubber ball with their palms and each thud it made against the garage left a greasy smudge on the paint. He figured that if they could hit every spot on the garage door then it would be a uniform smudge, and so his mother might not notice or care. The hot July sun was on his neck. He aimed at the corners, higher and lower than he normally would have, and soon the boys began to yell at him for throwing away his shots. As a joke he threw the ball at the back of one boy's legs. The boy threw it back harder, pelting Samson in the stomach. He doubled over in theatrical pain, but as the boys approached him he uncurled and dashed past them to the hose. He turned it on with a flick of the wrist and as the warm, lazy water made its way through the green coil the boys began to back down the driveway. The water came just in time, and putting his thumb over the nozzle to increase the power of the spray, Samson aimed at them. He watched them disappear down the street shouting, the skin of their backs showing through their wet T-shirts, the water dripping down their legs leaving a trail on the dull asphalt. He spent the rest of the summer running from the boys with their water guns and buckets, running barefoot through the prickly grass, scrambling over fences, jogging through backyards, looking for the nearest pool he could leap into in order to rob them of the pleasure of soaking him first.

In his memory he was often running. He sailed past the houses on his street lined with dusty eucalyptus trees, past the Shreiners' tennis court where Mr Shreiner lunged to return the endless rounds

38

the ball machine steadily fired at him, past the Reids' gazebo strung with wisteria, the school yard, the rise of foothills. He flew past his mother, who lay in a lawn chair with a book folded on her lap. Sometimes it was at top speed so that he could feel the hard ground explode in his shins with each step and his lungs gasping for breath, and other times it was a leisurely jog, a pace he felt he could keep up forever, that might take him across the county, across the state line, or down to Los Angeles. *Where are you running to?* his mother would ask as he clattered down the stairs, punching his arms into the sleeves of his T-shirt. But already he was out the door into the marathon summer.

If he wasn't running or playing with the two boys he was completely still. Sometimes, exhausted, he would lie on his back for hours wherever he had stopped, reading whatever was within reach. *What happened to you?* his mother would say, coming home from work to find him lying on the kitchen floor, a carton of orange juice still open on the counter. And either he would keep reading or he'd roll over and hug her ankles then leap up and dash past her, over to the neighbor's pool or past Jollie Lambird's house, whom he'd had a crush on since the second grade, to see if just now she was on her way out the door. It was like this, running through his twelfth summer, that Samson's memories disappeared midstep into the void.

* * *

At first the doctors listened carefully as he recounted these memories. But within a week or two, once his case had been discussed and marveled at in grand rounds, it was filed away and the doctors seemed to lose interest. He was given over to the care of a neurologist called Dr Lavell. A colleague of Lavell's in Las Vegas, a woman he had done his residency with, had called him about Samson a few days after the surgery. In their first meeting Lavell attached electrodes to Samson's head and asked him to answer questions while watching his brain waves peak across a screen.

'What can you tell from all that?' Samson asked after Lavell had completed the tests.

'That you're a thinking man.'

'Anything else?'

'In your case, not too much. We already knew we had a highly functional mind on our hands.'

Lavell turned back to look at the screen. Finally he said, 'But it's pretty, no?' They both watched in silence.

'You know what I was thinking just then?' Samson asked.

'Tell me.'

'I was thinking, what if you could make out exactly what was going on in someone's mind just by watching those spikes?'

'The thoughts themselves? Now *that* would be something.'

'I suppose you wouldn't get many volunteers. Too intrusive.'

'I'd say. Only the very bold. Or the exhibition-ists,' Lavell said.

Samson grinned. From then on he came in to see Lavell once a week.

Samson was highly observant, nervously absorbing everything around him. He looked to others for signs of how he should act, and because he liked and respected Arthur Lavell, Samson watched him with particular care. Lavell was in his mid-sixties, bald except for a chaplet of unruly gray curls that reached his collar. His face was fleshy, as if his features were under the reign of some greater force of gravity pulling down the jowls and stretching the nostrils. There were dark pouches under his eyes. He had stubby fingers and one of them was cinched by a wedding ring that looked more like an artifact stuck on his finger than the symbol of any committed passion. Lavell wasn't the sort of man easily associated with passions; he had the phlegmatic movements of a bottom feeder. Samson had been told that over the years Lavell had spent more and more time in the research laboratory, and was known around the institute for his brilliant mind. An ambulatory thinker, he often walked out of meetings or grand rounds in pursuit of an idea. Sometimes he laughed aloud when no one else did, or fell asleep in his seat. But although Lavell was polite to everyone, and popular among the residents, he seemed not to reciprocate their feelings. Samson sensed he was somewhat ambivalent about people, more loyal to the organ of the brain than

41

the personality it produced. Perhaps this is why as the years went on he had practiced medicine less and spent more time in the laboratory, drawn out only by the most interesting cases.

And if Samson, in turn, was drawn to him it was perhaps for this very ambivalence. It was an emotion that in those first remarkable days, returned to his life, Samson understood. For despite the beauty of Anna, the charming photographs, the loveliness of his apartment full of the souvenirs of a life well lived, Samson could dredge up no feeling for his own life but that of vague admiration.

amson woke to the alarm and felt Anna wake, roll, and climb out of bed. Her bare feet across the wooden floor. A splash of water in the sink, the shower. He lay still under the covers as she dressed, preserving her as one sense, a series of sounds. Then he felt her standing above him, lowering her head toward him. As her lips touched his forehead he opened his eyes, long enough to register her face above him. Then he shut them again and waited for the sound of the dog in the hall, the key in the lock.

He had already been home a month, and he and Anna had improvised a makeshift existence. They avoided subjects they both knew were waiting like fault lines to split the ground beneath them. Instead they talked about things Samson still couldn't get his head around: the collapse of the Soviet Union, the Russians now being our big friends, the fact that nobody seemed to be very worried any more about the threat of nuclear war.

When friends called anxious to speak to Samson, Anna briefed him on who they were before he

43

reluctantly took the receiver. Eventually he stopped taking the calls, and listened from the other room as Anna spoke in weary, hushed tones about his condition: the tests showed no signs of the tumor's regeneration; he was still seeing the doctors; no memories had returned beyond childhood; she was a complete stranger to him; and he himself was different, not the same person at all.

She paced the floor as she spoke and sometimes she wept into the phone.

Sometimes on the street they ran into people he'd once known. Most wore a curious, pained expression, though others made more cheerful jokes or recounted funny things Samson had once done or said, great times they'd had together. As they walked away they promised to call soon, and some of them did and some of them didn't.

When he finally worked up enough courage to ask Anna what had happened to his mother, she paused and touched his face.

'She had cancer. It was five years ago.'

He didn't know what he had expected, but when he heard this, his mother's death finally emerged as a hard, sharp fact. Although he tried to be gracious about all he was being asked to accept, there were moments when that seemed too much to ask. That Soviet Communism had fallen, that Governor Reagan had become President, that John Lennon had been assassinated, were one thing. That his mother, the only immediate family he had, had ceased to exist, was quite another.

He broke down, shielding his face with his hands, and then Anna's body was against his, holding him.

'I know,' she whispered into his hair.

Minutes passed. When he disentangled himself and looked at her, her face was stark and unfamiliar.

'Did I get to say good-bye?'

'Yes. It happened very quickly. But you were there with her. You sat by her bed until the very end.'

It was all he could bear to ask. Soon he began to accept that his mother was gone, but he found it difficult to get used to the idea that Anna knew things about her that now he didn't: how she had aged, her last words. The thought of it made him feel guilty, as if he had abandoned his mother, appointing a stranger to remember her.

A few days later, watching as Anna put the leash on the dog to walk him, he asked, 'Was she early or late?'

'Hmm? What do you mean?'

'My mother. If you had to describe her habits, was she generally on time or late?'

'Always late. She was like that even when you were a kid, right?'

'What was her favorite color?'

He could hear the coldness in his voice. Anna studied him in silence.

'Is this a test?' She leaned against the door, holding his gaze before she answered. 'Blue. She wore it all the time because it matched her eyes. They were blue but sometimes they looked gray, and near the end she couldn't see very well. She had three different pairs of glasses but she could never find any of them. She was very proud and wouldn't take anything from anyone. Called you to tell you jokes, but sometimes missed your birthday.'

'Okay. Stop.'

'Your birthday: born prematurely, January 29, 1964.' She was speaking rapidly now, and for the first time Samson noticed a hint of a lisp, something in her speech left over from childhood. 'Nobody remembers your first words. The first day of nursery school you climbed onto the rocking horse and screamed when anyone came near you. You wanted to be an astronaut.'

'Okay, Anna. I'm sorry. I shouldn't have—'

'How about this: the first time you got a hard-on was just before your twelfth birthday. You went – yes, I remember now, you said you went swimming and then you were lying in the sun in your shorts. The dog was leaning against you.'

He stared at her, horrified. It was like making contact with aliens only to find they'd been watching you for years. His own mind may have been a clean slate, but whatever terrible and shameful things he had done or said and forgotten now, she would remember.

'I think I've heard enough.'

'I don't think so. There's much more, it goes

on and on, see?' She gripped his wrist hard and he winced. 'And what do you know about me? You want a test, here's a test: tell me what the hell you know about me.'

'I don't know.'

She threw his hand down. 'You don't know. *You don't know!*' she shouted, her voice breaking. 'And the most awful part of it is that *I still love you*. I've lost you and yet you're still here. *To taunt me.* Can you understand? Do you have any empathy at all for what it's like?'

A sob that seemed to come from someplace animal shook her body. Samson took her hand. He rubbed her knee and patted her back, but it only made her cry harder. He fluttered around her, searching for where to put his arms, placing a hand delicately around her waist, the other on her head, drawing her toward him until somehow he was holding her in his arms. He felt her tears against his neck, but her shaking subsided and her breath became steadier as he rocked her. He was surprised at how easily she fit herself against him, how warm and small her body felt.

'When did I meet you?' he asked quietly.

'It's been almost ten years.'

'You were only twenty-one?'

'Yes. You were twenty-six.'

'What did you like about me? In the beginning.'

Anna pulled away and looked up at him, surprised. 'You were – are—' She stumbled. 'No one else was like you.'

47

Samson was about to ask what he had liked about her, but he stopped himself, realizing how it would sound. He felt the warmth of her against him.

'Was I any good in bed?'

The question surprised him as much as it did Anna. She made a funny smile and lifted her chin. Up close her face lost all focus, and her mouth was warm and tasted of oranges.

Samson lay in bed for a while longer after Anna left for work. The night before, they'd slept together for the third time, and when it was over an instant coolness had spread through his limbs, and he'd ransacked the dark for his underwear and T-shirt. He had wished to draw a boundary around himself, to make an island of his mortification so that it wouldn't be sensed by the woman who had just made him groan with pleasure. She had lain still and narrow in the dark, but after a half hour passed in which they said nothing, he hadn't been able to stop himself from touching her again, easing his fingers across her stomach and up to the swell of her breasts, feeling her body tense and arch beneath his hand.

He got out of bed to go to the bathroom. He could still smell her on his body. Steam hung in the air from her shower, fogging the mirror. He traced his name with his finger then rubbed it out. His face was slowly beginning to cohere, the various features coming together to form a recognizable whole that no longer disturbed him when he saw it flash past in windows and mirrors. Hair was beginning to grow in around the red welt of scar tissue.

He opened the closet and fingered the silk ties hanging neatly on pegs, the pressed linen shirts, the fine wool pants. He chose a gray suit and a yellow tie with a pattern of small birds. It took him a few tries but finally he managed a clumsy knot. He had gained back the weight he'd lost, and the clothes fit him perfectly, but he felt uneasy in them, an imposter. He decided to buy himself new clothes as soon as possible. He put on the Las Vegas baseball hat Anna had brought to the hospital. The scar was hideous, stapled like rail-road tracks.

Anna had left the newspaper on the counter. He flipped through it. An article about cloning caught his eye, and he read it in full, mesmerized. They had cloned a sheep, there were two of them now, and the question was, would they soon be able to clone humans?

The dinner dishes were still on the kitchen table, as was the photo album Anna had brought out after dessert. It was open on the page they'd been looking at the night before – photographs of their honeymoon five years ago in Rio – when Samson had abruptly got up.

'Where are you going?' Anna had asked.

'For a walk.'

'Are you all right? Do you want me to come?'

'I just need some air,' he'd said.

Anna nodded. 'Take the dog.' Frank was already turning in excited circles at the door. Samson knew she'd said it because she was afraid he'd get lost or mugged.

He didn't go far; just around and around the block so many times that even Frank got bored. The pictures – dazzled shots on the beach, the two of them locked in embrace after embrace – kept flitting through his mind. For a minute, waiting for the light to change, he thought about not going back. It was a silly thought, but it was thrilling to think it.

When he returned Anna was sitting on the couch watching a late-night talk show. She was smoking a cigarette.

'I didn't know you smoked.'

'Once in a while.'

They watched a lithe, giggly, blond movie star joke with the talk show host about her years in high school as a fat slob.

'You used to smoke,' she said, an afterthought.

'I did?'

'You quit when you started teaching. You were very sexy. You would take these deep drags.' She imitated him, pulling hard on the cigarette, squinting, exhaling out of the corner of her mouth. 'There was a faded rectangle on the back right pocket of all your jeans.'

Samson imagined himself on a glossy black motorcycle with a teardrop tank, a cigarette dangling between his lips. 'Did I ever ride a motor-cycle?'

Anna looked at him strangely. 'No.'

She held her cigarette limpidly between two fingers. It surprised him how easily she handled things, how fluently she shared her life with the hundreds of objects that passed through her hands.

'How're you doing, Samson?' She drew her knees up to her chest and laid her head on them, looking at him.

'I'm okay.' He smiled weakly. 'How are you?'

'Lonely.'

'I'm sorry,' he said, reaching out to rub her ankle along the little ridges left by the elastic of her sock.

'You feel so far away.'

Samson nodded.

'Do you feel that way too?' she asked.

'Far? No. I don't know how to explain it. Like I'm . . .'

'What?'

'Present. In myself.'

'But you're not *you*.'

'I feel like I am.'

Her face contorted and he thought she might cry.

'*Please*,' she whispered, rocking her knees. 'It could still come back. It *has* to come back.'

'Anna—'

'No. Don't say anything.'

He put his hands on her knees and gently held them still.

'You know, sometimes I get the feeling that we're just a bunch of habits,' she said. 'The gestures we repeat over and over, they're just our need to be recognized.' Her eyes were fixed on the TV, as if she were reading subtitles. 'I mean that without them we would be unidentifiable. We'd have to reinvent ourselves every minute.' Her voice was soft, and Samson felt she wasn't speaking to him but to the man in the photographs.

She exhaled and dropped the cigarette into a glass, where it fizzled, and as she got up to brush her teeth she leaned in close and breathy as a nightclub and kissed his neck. The feel of her lips stayed as he watched the blond movie star leap up and show the audience the cheerleading routine she still remembered because though she had been fat she'd still been a cheerleader. The kiss stayed there with no place to go, no sensory reserve that could absorb it and file it away as a common act of intimacy, a thousand times received. He knew what Anna was asking: whether you could love someone without habits.

Samson washed the dishes, walked Frank, then headed out to an appointment with Dr Lavell at eleven. It was half past nine, and though he had time to spare he found himself hustling up Broadway anyway, keeping pace with the crowd. He was drawn to the window displays but felt it would be awkward to stop and look, to disturb the flow by standing still and forcing people to move around him. He tried to mimic the sense of purpose of these people bound for destinations, who could, at any moment, draw up an itinerary of their futures, who received curt instructions from the tiny telephones they listened to like walkie-talkies.

It was hot outside, and Samson was already sweating in his suit. He took off the jacket and held it crumpled at his side. When he got down to the subway platform it was a furnace, dead air trapped in subterranean vaults under the city, great generators of inner-city weather. He listened to the thunder of trains slamming in and out of the tunnels.

Inside the crowded metal car under the ultra-violet lights, the helpless passengers looked like a litter of baby mice. Samson found a seat next to a huge boy, the biggest boy he had ever seen, who was serenely explaining to an interested man just how he could break his arm in two places. Samson's eyes came to rest on a girl hunched across the aisle who was chewing the polish off red nails, the kind of girl who looked like she hadn't slept at home last night. If she looked up and caught him staring he would look away, but she kept her eyes on the floor. Samson watched her until the 116th Street stop and then she stood, glanced at him with a precise and practiced boredom, and got off. Samson closed his eyes and the train thundered on through the darkness.

He couldn't help staring. He told this to Lavell,

who quoted a famous photographer to the effect that staring is the best way to educate the eye. If someone referred to something Samson didn't know about, he often didn't ask. Later he might look it up. He was devoted to the information he could get from books or, even better, magazines. He filled his time reading everything he could get his hands on.

Lavell's office was located in an almost forgotten hallway of the Neurology Institute, terminating in the dead end of a broom closet. On the way Samson passed a woman in a hospital gown and socks with rubber skids who mimicked with unnerving precision the expressions and gestures of anyone who passed. He tried to look away, but out of the corner of his eye saw her look away too, caricaturing his dismissal.

Lavell had been at the end of the hall for so many years that his room, though spacious, had a cramped feel. The floor-to-ceiling shelves were stacked with books. Every surface not taken up by papers was cluttered with medical paraphernalia. There were plastic models of the brain with removable hemispheres, a ceramic phrenology bust mapped with L. N. Fowler's psychogeography: the regions of blandness, youthfulness, wit. A skeleton stood by the erasable whiteboard on which Lavell sometimes illustrated things for his patients. Scattered here and there were toys for children who came to him, locked in the anechoic chamber of autism.

'Who's that woman?' Samson asked, sitting in the chair the doctor motioned to.

'Who?'

'In the hall, like she's possessed.'

'Marietta? She has Tourette's, a very severe case. It makes her tic like that. She has an overpowering impulse to mimic whatever she sees.' Lavell lifted a stubby finger and rubbed his eyebrow. 'A colleague of mine, smart guy, wrote a case study of her. Whether the individual Marietta truly exists or if the impulses, so all-consuming, make her just a phantasmagoria of a person.' He listed the great ticquers of all time, enumerating them like Hall of Fame batters. He described an old medical book that began with the anonymous memoir 'Confessions of a Ticquer.' 'Have you considered writing anything yourself since your surgery? Keeping a journal, et cetera?'

Samson was aware of Lavell leading the discussion here and there, directing a flashlight on the empty mine shafts of his mind. But he enjoyed their talks; Lavell seemed to expect nothing from him. Samson felt he could say or do anything, could crouch on the chair and jerk around like a monkey, screech *Whoo! Whoo!*, and Lavell would not be moved to comment.

A tall Asian man with his hair standing on end opened the door of the office and squealed a quick-fire 'Hi! How are you? Hi! How are you?'

'Fine,' Lavell replied curtly, and turning his attention back to Samson, continued talking until the man softly shut the door and continued on his way.

'And how are *you*?' Lavell asked, leaning back in his chair.

'Oh, fine, I guess.'

'How are things with Anna?'

There was so much Samson wished to ask, for instance how many times a day did an average man of thirty-six masturbate, and how often did married couples have sex? He wanted to administer to Lavell a questionnaire about how a woman's body worked, about what to do to make her scream and moan and throw flowers at his feet. But he couldn't bring himself to do it. It was too mortifying, especially as it seemed highly possible that the questions would be answered with textbook pictures, reducing the whole erotic mystery to a series of movements as academic as a square dance.

Lavell leaned back, waiting. His chair creaked.

We did it! Samson wanted to shriek, but instead he coughed and answered, 'With Anna? The same, really. She was upset the other night.'

'Yes?'

'She asked me if I had any empathy for her. For everything she's going through right now.'

'Do you?'

'It's sad. Sometimes she'll get a certain expression on her face and it makes me feel awful. But I guess I'm having a hard time figuring out how I'm suppose to feel myself – it's hard to even *begin* imagining what it's like for her.'

'Interesting choice of words, empathy.'

'Why?'

'For exactly the reason you said. Empathy is the capacity to participate in, or vicariously experience, another's feelings. In order to do that, you need to draw on the memory of having experienced something similar – the very thing that is *impossible* for you to do.'

'That's true.'

Lavell raised his hands. 'So what did you say to her?'

'I held her. She was crying so I put my arms around her.'

'Good choice,' Lavell said.

Eventually the discussion turned to his childhood, as it often did. The memories returned in no particular order. Why one memory declared itself at any given moment, he didn't know. Knowing would mean understanding the order of the things.

And then their conversation surfaced again in the present, breaking up the sound of birds bickering in the trees outside, and apropos of nothing Lavell asked, 'Do you know what it feels like to be in love?' The word seemed out of place between his fleshy lips. Samson thought of Jollie Lambird, which embarrassed him, and he looked down at his shoes that seemed too shiny.

'I don't know. Maybe.'

'What about Anna?'

'Look, it's all a bit mystifying.'

'I should think so. One minute' – Lavell snapped his fingers – 'and the next thing, you're married. It would throw anyone.'

Samson pictured Anna as he had seen her this morning, hovering above him. 'She's lovely. Beautiful and kind and what's not to like? But why her and not someone else?'

'A decision you made, we have to assume, based on experiences with other women before you met Anna.'

'But who is she? I wake up in the middle of the night and she's lying next to me. Sometimes she holds her breath when she sleeps. Her head hits the pillow and in a minute she's asleep and then suddenly she stops breathing. Like she's just jumped into a freezing lake. Like the sudden revelations of her self-conscious—'

'Her unconscious.'

'Her unconscious, as if it's shocked her. Sometimes I want to pound her on the back to get her to start inhaling again, but just when I think she's going to turn blue the breathing starts up as if she never stopped, as if she weren't this close.' Samson held up two fingers with an inch between them.

'Close to what?'

'That place just beyond everything she knows for sure. The same place I woke up in.'

'You had a cerebral lesion. Don't you think there is a logic – a terrible logic – to your amnesia? The tumor destroyed—'

'I know, I know. A little to the left or right and

I might not have remembered how to go to the bathroom. I might have existed in some eternal moment, with no memory of the minute that's just passed. I might have lost my ability to feel. I'm lucky, sure. What I lost is, in the grand scope of things, almost . . . negligible. It's true that there's grief: it wakes me in a cold sweat thinking, Who was I? What did I care about? What did I find funny, sad, stupid, painful? Was I happy? All of those memories I accumulated, gone. Which one, if there could have been only one, would I have kept?'

'You were saying that Anna stops breathing when she's asleep. How at those times you think she's "this close" to something. To what?'

'Oblivion, I guess. Where I was when they found me in Nevada. And now I've come back from it and can never be the same again.'

'What was it like, this oblivion?'

Samson shrugged. 'I don't remember.'

'Do you ever think there might be people who would envy you?'

'They'd have to be crazy.'

'Okay, how about this: if you could have your memory back right now, would you take it?'

'Hey, whose side are you on?' Samson asked. To change the subject he told Lavell about the article on cloning he'd read that morning in the paper. As a boy, he'd always been drawn to science, to the discovery of miraculous things, the race for knowledge about the earth, human beings, the sky.

It fascinated him now too, the idea that perhaps in fifty, a hundred years they could clone everyone at birth. 'An extra,' he said, 'in case something tragic should happen.'

Lavell raised an eyebrow.

'Seriously. They could keep the Extra on some kind of farm out in the middle of nowhere, just letting him get exercise and fresh air so he'll be ready if he receives the call to duty. And then one day the call comes through – there's been a plane crash, or cancer, or a skiing accident.' Samson thought for a second. 'Anything but a suicide, because a suicide would mean it's a no go, the Original wanted out and so that's that.'

'The call comes through.'

'Yes, and now we have a problem, right, because the Extra doesn't know anything about the Original's life. All right, so maybe he's been reading about his life in installments they give him every month on the farm. Still, he doesn't know the intimate things.'

'The little names the Original whispered to his wife.'

'That sort of thing. So the cloning project looks like it's going to be a total failure, but then what do the scientists do?'

He held Lavell's gaze a beat like a performer, a stand-up, drumroll please.

'They develop a way to slide out the Original's memory like a safe-deposit box and pop it into the Extra. The whole thing, life experiences, all of them. And there you go. No one could tell this guy from the Original except for the fact that he doesn't have the same physical scars.' Samson sat back and folded his arms over his chest. He was pleased with the idea, pleased with the sudden ease of talking when the subject wasn't himself.

'An interesting proposal. Actually I know a doctor who's working on something like that. Not the cloning but the memory part. Transferring memories from one mind to another and so forth. A long shot if you ask me. But getting back to your scenario, I wonder, for argument's sake, what would happen in a case like yours where the Original's memory is damaged?'

Samson thought for a minute. 'In such a case I, the Original, would be forced to relinquish my role as key player, and the Extra would step forward and have his day.'

'To lose your memory would be to forfeit your position as the Original.'

'Right.'

The door of Lavell's office creaked opened and the gregarious Asian man poked his head in. His face broke into a broad grin when he saw them and he seemed about to say something but thought better of it and closed the door.

'He sings two Lionel Richie songs over and over,' Lavell said. 'Ask him to sing "Say You, Say Me" when you leave.'

On the way out Samson passed Marietta, who was watching television in the lounge, regurgitating

61

the histrionics of a soap opera in her endless
pantomime. The Asian man didn't want to sing
'Say You, Say Me,' but he belted out 'Hello' instead,
in a quivery falsetto accompanied by hand gestures:
Hello, is it me you're looking for?

The days passed. Each day Anna tore off yesterday's page from the calendar, and later Samson retrieved the page from the garbage. Eventually he might tie the pages in bunches like letters.

After he'd worn a pair of corduroys he found at the back of the closet for a week straight, Anna offered to take him shopping. She sat patiently on the wooden gym bench in the sports store while Samson paced the rows of gleaming white sneakers, looking for the style he wanted.

'I found it,' he said, bringing over an electric-blue suede sneaker. Anna wrinkled her nose. 'I want them,' he insisted.

'You'll look ridiculous.'

'Everyone has them.'

'Who's everyone?'

'Look around,' Samson said over his shoulder, bringing the shoe over to the sales assistant who raised his eyebrows when Samson asked him to measure his foot.

'You've got pretty big feet,' the assistant announced, adjusting the sliding ruler.

'They're huge,' said Samson.

He wore the new sneakers home, carrying the old shoes in the box, and refused to take them off all evening. He wore them around in his bathrobe, breaking them in. They were the only ones in the whole store, he told Anna, that weren't ugly.

While Anna was at work he wandered the city, riding the subway and getting off at random. He kept his eyes on the ground swabbed with old gum until the escalator spat him out into the hot, bright streets. He'd misplaced the map Anna had given him, the one she'd marked with points of interest, but if he got lost he walked until the city reorganized itself around him and he found himself somewhere he'd been before. There were certain places he always seemed to return to, squares or street corners, like refrains, points of convergence where the city doubled back on itself before escaping again around the corner.

It was high July, then August. The city perspired, water dripping down from rusty air-conditioning units, leaving dark circles on the street. Sometimes a bus would hurl past kicking up dirt that lodged in his eyes, buses whose signboards read *Limited* and never seemed to stop but rather sped past with their privileged, otherworldly passengers. Samson walked from the Upper West Side all the way down to the tip of Manhattan where he could see the Statue of Liberty through the greasy air. He picked his way along the West Side Highway, around the construction pits and piles of sand and rubber tubing, watching the gulls land on the rotting piers. If he found himself in a district of gritty neon storefronts he would go in and loiter in the cool air until the Korean or Pakistani shop-keeper eyed him and then he would pick up the nearest thing and bring it to the counter, dealing out his crumpled bills like milk money.

The city hurt to look at, all angles and glints of sun like shattered glass. The trees were pitiful, anchored in concrete. The dogs seemed to accept this, and no matter how many times they passed the same tree they would act as if they'd never seen it before and mark it as their own. Sometimes Samson would take Frank along, who, unlike Anna, had forgiven him everything. When they caught each other's eye, he felt that Frank under-stood him and did not feel it necessary to remind him of the many things they had once done together. Often Frank could not be bothered to go through the charade of fussing over the tree, and simply stopped to pee wherever he was. On these days he seemed to hold in disdain the other dogs that were slaves to the system.

One day Samson rode the Circle Line and caused a sensation among an outing of third graders when he took off his hat and showed them his scar. He told them he'd gotten it fighting forces of evil. They crowded around him and one fat boy gripped him around the knee. He told them he had jumped from a burning building, but later forgot and told them he'd jumped from a plane.

When it rained, puddles gathered in the gutter, water that was a chemical, acid green. At such times Anna, with her little sayings and the smell of her perfume and the hair bands she wore like rings on her fingers, was scratch, a blip, a stain on his anonymity.

He crossed Central Park littered with joggers and the shouts of children with miraculous ideas. He watched them in the playground, a small country governed by the ever-changing laws of games invented out of sticks and stones. They needed so little to get on. The distant city rose up through the trees.

He walked until he was exhausted and eventually he might sit on a bench. Once a man with a hood drawn around his face passed, pushing a supermarket cart stacked with unidentifiable things. *Sparesome change?* he hissed, throwing out a glance like a gnawed bone and then, without stopping to see if Samson would dig a hand into his pocket, answered himself, *Gawblessyou,* as if he was playing a part, but without conviction. He expected nothing; perhaps he would not even have taken any change had Samson offered. As the man passed, almost brushing his knees, Samson saw the rinds of dirt under his fingernails and his battered heels that poked out of the sneakers he wore like slippers. Samson did not remember seeing any homeless people in Los Altos, and he could not get used to them now, the woman who cried on Fifth Avenue, wearing nothing but a trash bag, the men who slept over the grates that blew warm, dirty air.

He thought: You come, you find a life ready-made, you just have to slip it on.

He watched people. Men and women hurrying home from work in possession of their own memories. They were a mystery to him, how easily they turned the corner, as if they could get home in their sleep.

At night, when Anna came home from work, she told him about the drifters who'd washed up in the agency, a three-hundred-pound black man who stalked the halls muttering about how he had to get out to feed the thousands of children he was convinced he'd fathered, or Ken from Japan who dove under tables for cover from imaginary bombings by Yakuza. Samson told her about his trip on the Circle Line or to the observatory deck of the Empire State Building, and for a moment they might have been the most ordinary couple in the world. But they weren't, and there didn't seem to be much point in pretending. He didn't want to make Anna sad, but when he caught himself trying too hard to play the role of her husband he became disgusted with his failure and fraudulence and retreated deeper into himself.

Mostly he tended the blankness in the center of his mind. His memory had abandoned him, and though he had searched within himself all these weeks, he could find no desire to have it returned. If it came back now, he felt he would turn it away, and the knowledge of this renouncement, a small act of defiance, gave him a feeling of liberty. He told no one of his resolution. He wanted to explain it to Anna but he didn't know how to, a covenant he had decided upon alone, a small, sharp rebellion against all that was beyond his control. Soon it became a secret so well hidden that even the doctors did not find it when they swept their searchlights across his mind.

The empty space was enormous, but he guarded its borders. Only when he lay in bed at night did he allow himself to cross it, the moonscape that stretched from his twelfth year to the day he awoke in the hospital. He moved through it like the scientists he saw on TV trudging through the tundra in Gore-Tex parkas. He moved like a man who knew the danger, the seriousness, of his mission. He moved through it backward and swept away his footsteps.

Not an Astronaut but an English professor. He should have guessed. It was the natural destiny of a book-hungry child, and yet somehow the sheer accumulation of knowledge it must have required unnerved him a little and he stayed away from the university until late August. Passing the iron gates one day, he finally approached a guard and asked for directions to the English Department. It was still vacation and other than the maintenance men and a few permanently roosting graduate students, the campus was deserted. When he found his way to his office he was surprised to see his name on the door and a note saying he was on medical leave. He felt disappointed, like an eager student who had dropped by on the off chance that the professor was puttering around the office in golf togs.

The office was hot and dust hung in the air. Posters for conferences in Berlin, Basel, and Salamanca hung on the walls, all of them with Samson's name listed among the speakers. Books lay open, facedown on the desk. He picked one up and flipped through the pages and in the margins he recognized his own neat handwriting. He closed it quickly and returned it to its place like a piece of evidence.

There was a knock on the door and for a moment Samson sat dumbfounded, wondering if he could hide somewhere.

'Who is it?'

The door opened and a girl poked her head around it. 'Professor Greene?'

'Uh, yes?'

'I saw you going up the stairs. I wasn't sure if . . .' She slipped inside and closed the door behind her, clutching her bag to her chest. She looked at Samson, waiting. 'You don't remember me, do you?'

Samson looked back helplessly.

'It's okay, I didn't expect you to. I'm Lana? Lana Porter? I was in your Contemporary Writers class?'

She was tall and lanky, with jet-black hair cut across her forehead and just below her ears like a pageboy. She wore a tiny diamond stud in her nose. She seemed frenetic, the sort of girl who has to eat constantly to maintain her metabolism.

'People have been saying all kinds of things. I didn't know what to believe.'

Her gaze fluttered across him then jumped back to the scar on his head. She studied it shamelessly, and for a few seconds it kept her still.

'What did they say?' he asked.

There was something refreshingly obvious about her, not only because she was tall and her angled

lines refused to blur into the background of furniture but because of her straightforwardness, as yet
unsocialized by a profusion of apologies.

'That you were a vegetable.'

'I see.'

'I didn't believe it. It would have been too awful.'
Lana took a few steps toward the desk and sank
into a chair, making up for this move toward rest-
fulness by sliding her feet in circles across the floor
as if to preserve the possibility of a sudden move-
ment in any direction.

'Is it terrible? To lose your memory, I mean.
I guess that's a dumb question. I can tell you now
– now that the class is over and you can't remember
it anyway – that every time I asked a question in
class I wondered afterward whether you would
think it was stupid.' She paused. 'I don't know why
I'm telling you this.'

'It's okay, people seem to.'

'What?'

'Seem to tell me things. It's odd, but since all
of this happened, the people who used to know
me seem to want to confess things. They want to
explain how things were between us. They get very
honest. There's a look of relief on their faces as
they admit things.'

'You can't really blame people. Think how weird
it is to see you.'

'I know. It must be strange not to be recognized.
I'm sorry.'

'You look the same except for that—' She thrust

71

her chin upward, gesturing at his scar. 'But as soon as you open your mouth you can tell something's different. It's eerie.'

'I *feel* eerie,' he said.

He looked at her and she looked back, waiting.

'You do construction work on the side?' he asked.

'What?'

'Your shorts. With the little loop for a hammer and all those pockets for, I don't know, wrenches.'

'Very funny. It's called *style*.' She grinned. 'That was a pretty good imitation of your old self, though.'

'Was it?' He narrowed his eyes at her and smiled back. 'Lana Porter. Sounds like a movie star.'

'You're thinking of Lana Turner.'

'Oh.' She crossed her legs, and he looked up, wondering if she had noticed him looking at them. 'So you used to call me Professor Greene?'

'No. I used to call you Samson.'

'But when you knocked just now, you called me—'

'I was being polite.'

He looked at her, this electric girl, and wondered what exactly it was about her he should have remembered.

She had a breezy way of talking that put him at ease. She didn't wait for him to struggle to find the right questions, but instead told him about her summer break, what little of it she had, since she had to take a couple of classes in order to spend the next semester at the film school at UCLA and still graduate on time. How she'd been assigned 'The Swimmer' again in one of her literature classes – when he looked confused she explained that it was a story he'd taught in class – and how the other night, curled up in her bed, the only place she could read anything, she'd finished the last page and started crying. She told him about how she'd cried a lot since coming to New York two years ago, from Cleveland, Ohio. She cried through the whole first week, when the pay phones on the street swallowed her quarters and left her with the flat, senseless dial tone, a sound she believed – according to a theory she was forming about the city's volume – came from other parts of the city, from the electrocardiograms of dead people. She cried when she passed the skinny guitar players underground who also played the drums with their feet for a hat full of change and a couple of dollar bills. And she cried when they handed her back her Columbia ID with the photograph they'd taken of a girl who'd been crying because she couldn't ever go back to the suburbs of Cleveland anymore, not in the same way.

As she spoke he tried desperately to imagine it all. Something about her appealed to him, and he wanted to be able to picture the brief stunt of her teenage history, to follow it as if through a telescope lens.

She told him how she'd decided to cut her hair,

which was blond and reached her waist, how she had to pay the hairdresser extra money to convince him to do it because he said it was a crime to cut it, people kill for hair like that, and how afterward he got down on his hands and knees to collect it because he realized that he might be able to sell it for a wig. She left the money on the counter and walked out, leaving him crawling around on the floor. She walked down Amsterdam Avenue and tried not to keep touching her hair, which sort of threw her off balance every time she ran her fingers through it, like when you think there's another step but there isn't and you come down hard on the ground. The next day she dyed it black with some stuff she bought at Rite Aid. For a while the new haircut made her feel better, made it feel that it wasn't her, Lana Porter, who had left her high school boyfriend, who was taking the year off to try to push his band out of the basement to maybe make it big in Japan, left her bedroom with plush wall-to-wall carpet, left all her popular friends who had never been as smart as she. With the new haircut people looked at her differently, which she was glad for because she couldn't anymore be the same person she had been all along; she had to give something up to make room for all of it, for the dumb, ecstatic city. She stopped crying after that, and now she only cried once in a while, when she least expected it or when she finished books that she especially loved.

She seemed not to inhale when she spoke so that the words tumbled out in breathless disorder, and Samson sat waiting to hear more. But then she glanced at her watch and announced that she had better go, she had work to do in the library.

Samson volunteered to walk with her, explaining that there were some books he wanted to check out. He followed her across the green, through the cool halls of Butler Library, and she showed him how to look up call numbers on the computer. He hunted and pecked at the keys with his index fingers, but couldn't understand how to move the cursor with the thing called a mouse, rolling it around in sudden, spastic strokes. He wanted to match her openness, to be as casual and easily present as she seemed, so he told her how Anna had wanted him to take a computer course at the Y. He'd gone a few weeks ago and sat among the jangly society women with their manicured nails poised on the keyboard and the geriatrics who waited until the teacher came by to turn on their computers. Though they were promised that learning to navigate cyberspace would change their lives, Samson felt he couldn't bear a baptism in the twenty-first century with such a group and walked out in the middle of class. When he told Anna what had happened she'd sighed and pressed her lips together and said he seemed to be making a habit of getting up and walking out of things.

They had fought then, and Samson said he wished she would stop blaming him for something, an illness, that had happened to him. 'Sometimes I think you might be happier if I'd died,' he said, knowing how cruel a thing it was to say, saying it anyway. Anna looked as if she'd been punched and began to cry. Later he apologized, but the words hung in the air between them, hardening like the unidentifiable spilled things on the street that solidified into horrendous fossils. That night, while they lay in bed, Anna had said, 'Maybe we don't belong together anymore.' Samson had not known what to say and so he reached for her hand in the dark. He didn't tell all of this to Lana. He stopped after the bit about walking out of class.

They rode the elevator up into the stacks. Lana showed him how to find books in the shadowy, obscure districts lit by failing bulbs. Then in a hushed tone she said, 'Good luck,' and turned a corner and was gone, leaving behind a slight electric disturbance in the air. He took down a few books she had recommended and, sinking to the cold floor, began to read. Soon he ceased to notice the slightly sickening smell of old paper.

He went back to the library often, and sometimes he met Lana for lunch after her classes. She was *starving*, she would say, and had to eat something before she *fainted*. They sprinted across Broadway dodging traffic and ducked into a noodle shop, or they bought falafel wrapped in paper and took them to Riverside Park, where they ate watching kayaks skim up the Hudson, imagining a wilderness of Indians. It was only the beginning of September and fall was still a long way off from the green shore of New Jersey, unspoiled and almost idyllic upriver. They discussed the possibility of swimming across, how long it would take and how far the distance, the drama of plunging in the murky water and looking back at Manhattan.

'There was a girl who swam across the Bering Strait,' Lana said. 'Maybe twenty years ago. It was some kind of statement. She wanted to encourage friendship and understanding between America and the Soviet Union. A long-distance swimmer, I forget her name, but the water was freezing and all she wore was a bathing suit.'

'And she made it?'

'She made it. She'd already swum the Channel a few times. I read somewhere that they have to have a special kind of body fat. Spread evenly over the body for insulation.'

'You wouldn't last a minute,' Samson said, gesturing at her railthin frame.

'Hey, I'm tough.' She flexed her biceps, a joke.

'I'm sure.'

'My main problem is that I don't like deep water. The idea of being suspended with miles of darkness, with who knows what, below.'

They watched as a rusted tanker moved downriver toward the ocean.

'I wouldn't exactly volunteer myself.'

'But what an amazing thing, don't you think? A girl swimming alone across the strait that once carried the first human beings to this continent.'

He imagined Lana stroking through open waters toward Siberia.

'Amazing.'

He liked to listen to her talk, her unguarded way of telling him what was on her mind, about a fight she'd had with a friend or a book she'd been reading. It was a freedom that seemed consistent with the way she moved, with her limbs that, if she did not concentrate on restraining them, were rarely still. Everything about her seemed accelerated, and the natural intimacy that had so quickly grown up between them surprised and delighted him. At times he felt convinced that they must have sat like this countless times before, paper lunch bags on their laps and the river below, but Lana insisted they hadn't. He understood the unlikeliness of it too, he being her professor and she his student, and yet it seemed impossible that he hadn't noticed her especially, hadn't looked after her with something like wonder as she gathered up her things after class and piked off, an explosive, heart-stopping thing. At the very least, she must have been the sort of girl who, if he'd met her when he himself was a student, would have been like a sword going clean through him.

She was the first friend he'd made aside from the dog, and somehow he wanted to keep her to himself. He didn't tell Anna about her right away because it seemed like they shared almost everything else – ten years, a marriage, bed, bathroom, records, dishes, furniture, telephone, friends. He wanted something of his own, a small acreage outside their life together that belonged to him alone.

He balled up his lunch bag and threw it into the trash basket.

'If you decided to swim across the Bering Strait in a bathing suit,' he said. She looked at him. 'I'd follow you in a paddle boat and shout encouragement.'

'Thanks. And if you ever decide to walk across the country again, I'll follow you in a car.'

'You'd cheer me on?'

'All the way,' she said.

His Dream Life was simple. He dreamed that he was running through endless doors toward a reservoir under a cosmic sky. On bad nights he dreamed that he was being buried alive. He dreamed of charred trees and hills of white ash, landscapes without people from which he woke, oddly, with a feeling of gladness. His dreams were remarkably unpopulated. Only once did he dream of his mother. The dreams had no plots, and most of them could be described in a line or two in the journal Dr Lavell had asked him to keep. He logged these minimalist scenes every morning and occasionally he brought it to his appointments with Lavell, who looked it over like a schoolteacher checking grammar. He omitted one dream only, of Lana reading naked in the empty library, watched from somewhere above as she turned pages. At times he resented having to submit his every thought to medical observation to be tagged and logged like archaeological fragments.

Halloween came and went, the streets of the Upper West Side crowded with small bands of witches and cartoon characters, girls with broken wings, aluminum foil warriors. Samson put some Mardi Gras beads on Frank and took him out, and a flock of ballerinas rushed up to coo over him, then whirled and curtsied away down the street like dervishes. The weather that until then had held out like an afterthought of summer, suddenly turned, and a freezing rain came down in sheets while the year skipped a season and fell comfortably into winter.

Anna began to give things back to Samson, dropping them in his lap without explanation. Old notebooks, his Swiss Army knife, his class ring. Things that belonged to him that had been there all along, in drawers, on shelves, things he didn't know about and didn't miss.

She handed him his address book in silence. He flipped through it.

'It's depressing, all these people.'

'Then throw it out,' she said, retreating to the bedroom and closing the door behind her.

He wore an old bathrobe and surfed through the television channels, snapping the remote. Anna didn't understand why he didn't want to call anyone, or even try to contact the people he remembered, friends from childhood or his great-uncle Max, who had been almost like a father to him. He felt it would be too difficult to hear their voices. It's not that he didn't think of them sometimes, but what would he say? He didn't want to know what twenty-four years had done to them.

His great-uncle Max would be in his nineties now; Anna had said that he was in an old age home in California. Max who had escaped from Germany and taught him how to curse in Yiddish and throw a good punch, who snuck him books when no one was looking as if they contained pornography. *Good stuff,* he would whisper, closing Samson's fingers around a volume of Kafka. He was not a religious man, but taught Samson to read the Torah in Hebrew so that he would not be ignorant of where he came from. *Listen to the sound of the words,* Max would say, singing a few lines of the Amidah. *The sound tells you everything.* He took Samson to synagogue, and it was while davening among old men who smelled of menthol and wool that Max told him there was no such thing as God. *Then why do they come?* Samson asked. *To remember,* Max replied, and looking around at the group into which he had been initiated with this secret, Samson was overcome with pride. He couldn't bear to think of how few of that congregation of wise men were left alive now.

And the others: friends from his freshman dorm, ex-girlfriends, friends with whom he'd backpacked across Europe, women whose numbers he'd asked for but never called, professors, colleagues, friends' parents, friends of friends, people he occasionally met for a drink, people whose parties he attended once a year. People he swore to call whenever he ran into them, people he never called. All these must have been listed in the book. He probably would have pleased Anna had he asked about each one, studiously copying down their statistics in the margin: profession, height and weight, beauty on a scale from one to ten. But he didn't care to. He was tired of being reminded, of photographs like flash cards, of Anna's surgical disapproval of what she called his resistance. He didn't know how to gently tell her what he'd begun to understand: that the life she was trying to return to him he didn't want.

But in recent weeks it seemed like Anna was beginning to give up too. She acted more stoical, as if something in her had finally broken and turned hard. She tried less and less to cross the distance between them. The bedroom had become her territory and he only went in it to sleep, and sometimes not even then, spending the night on the sofa.

He fell asleep with the address book in his lap, watching TV, and woke up with a start at three A.M. First he noticed that his mouth was dry and then he heard the television happily singing to itself. He got up, switched off the power, and stumbled into the kitchen. Two or three windows of the building across the street glowed blue. He opened the refrigerator and the light fell across the floor. He gulped from a carton of Tropicana and scanned the shelves for something to eat. Everything in the refrigerator now seemed foreign and unappetizing, as if it were the nourishment for another species, stronger, more enduring than humans.

Once, when he was nine or ten, he had written a letter to NASA requesting information about other galaxies. A few weeks later a package had arrived from Florida with a Xeroxed letter signed by John Glenn, a photograph he'd taken of the moon with his over-the-counter Minolta, and a conciliatory silver package of freeze-dried ice cream. Samson took the ice cream to school with him and displayed it prominently on his desk. When someone looked his way he would carefully choose a chalky piece and let it dissolve on his tongue. During recess he told a group of girls that his father was an astronaut and was training for zero gravity at Cape Canaveral. The truth was his father had left when he was three. His mother never explained why, and Samson imagined that he had simply walked out one day, turned the corner, and kept on going. That he had shed his life like a set of old clothes, walking into a public rest room and coming out in a brand-new white suit, with a funny little smile on his face. Dumping a plastic bag in the nearest trash bin and setting off with a jaunt in his step, whistling. Samson had pictured this scene so many times that as the years passed, it became, in his mind, indistinguishable from reality. His mother refused to speak about him. All Samson had known as a boy was that he was alive somewhere. He believed that one day his father would return for him: the doorbell would ring and he would run to open it and find him standing there like Cary Grant in a blinding white suit. It was one of the first thoughts he'd had in the hospital once he'd fully grasped his situation: that his father had shown up at some point during the years he'd forgotten, and now there would be no way of knowing it. He hadn't brought it up with Anna because it did not seem possible that he would have told her about it, any more than he would have advertised his deepest secret in neon lights.

The week before, he and Anna had gone to the Museum of Natural History together. They glided through the dark halls past the glass display cases of yaks and bison, of gray wolves sailing through the blue dusk, hovering in the air above the snow. It was a Monday, and the museum was almost empty except for the small bands of children whose voices now and again reached them like the cries of survivors. They picked their way through the dinosaur bones and butterflies not saying much, and as they were making their way out of the museum they wandered through a little room with a special exhibition of a time capsule contest sponsored by the *New York Times*.

The winning design – two tons of stainless steel, with compartments that folded in on themselves like origami – was scheduled to sit in a courtyard of the museum for the next millennium. In the year 3000, it would be opened and, in the compartments filled with argon gas, suspended in thermal gel, the future would find their fortune: rabbit's foot, hypodermic needle, horseshoe, ready-to-eat meal. Countries had donated objects like relief for a strange, hybrid disaster. Yo-yo, church bulletin, penicillin.

Samson had moved along the walls of the room, reading the small print about lost time capsules, time capsules in converted swimming pools to be opened in the year 8113, buried Gramophones, spaceships sent orbiting into other galaxies with copper-coated records that could play, in the hands of aliens, the first two bars of Beethoven's Cavatina.

He went back into the living room and picked up the address book. He turned the pages looking for his father's name, and when he got to the end without finding it he closed it and tossed it on the table. It was a quaint and childish notion to believe his father would have ever come back to find him. He had left. Whatever the reasons had been, he had gotten up one day and walked out the door, and the life he now had – if he was even alive – was a deliberate decision that did not include Samson.

He fumbled for the telephone and dialed the operator. He asked for Lana's number and it was played to him on a recording. How many people had called for her number before, he wondered, that they should have a recording of it?

The telephone rang five or six times until she picked up, her voice muffled with sleep.

'Hi, sorry to wake you. It's Samson.'

'Hmm? What time is it?'

'I don't know – three-thirty maybe.'

'I'm sleeping.'

'I know, sorry. Do you want to go back to bed or can you talk for a little while? Don't feel like you have to.'

Lana groaned but Samson thought he heard the light switch. 'Okay. How are you?'

'Okay. Do you know there's this guy who's encoding the DNA of cockroaches with the great works of literature?'

'What guy?'

'This guy, this scientist. I read about it at the museum. He's going to inscribe great books onto roach DNA. When it reproduces it will pass the book on and eventually, when there's a nuclear disaster and we're all wiped off the face of the earth, these indestructible roaches will be the carriers of Western civilization.'

'Jesus,' she breathed into the phone. He silently congratulated himself on her interest.

'They figure it will only take fourteen years until every roach in Manhattan is archival. There was this diorama of a couple of dead ones, test roaches who didn't make it.'

Lana was silent on the other end.

'Imagine they could do that to humans,' she finally said. 'Tattoo our DNA with Goethe maybe, or Shakespeare or Proust, so that we would be born with the memory of the madeleine or full of *Hamlet.*'

'Small children taking their first steps saying. "To be or not to be."'

Lana giggled.

'You know what the Spanish for cockroach is?' Samson asked.

'Uh-uh.'

'*La cucaracha*. There's poster on the subway about asthma and sometimes it's in English and sometimes in Spanish. It's of these kids sitting around and each of them says one thing that causes asthma: *El polvo! La polución! Las cucarachas!*'

'I've seen it. How come you're whispering?'

A siren screamed and faded into the distance, the sound of someone else's emergency.

'Because the room is dark. And I don't want to wake Anna.'

'How's it going?'

'Not so well. I guess I've pushed her away and now she's talking to me less and less.'

'What are you going to do?'

'I don't know.'

'What did Dr Lavell say?'

'Lavell? Lavell doesn't dispense advice. He tells me the malpractice for advice-giving is like five times as much as a craniotomy. How do salmon know to swim upstream to spawn and die? That's the sort of thing Lavell and I chew over.'

Lana told him how she was leaving for the film program in Los Angeles in three weeks, right after the term ended. Samson nodded, forgetting that she couldn't see him.

'Hello?'

'Hello.'

'What do you think of that, that I'm going to L.A.?'

'What do I think? I think you're lucky, that's great. You'll probably be a big star.'

'I want to direct.'

'Still.'

Samson told her about an aunt of his who had gone on a date with Jerry Lewis, after he was Dean Martin's kid but before he ended up fat in Vegas with a house tacky as fuzzy dice.

'What do you know about cloning?' he asked, but there was no answer on the other end, only the steady flux of breath. 'Apollo to Houston,' he said, 'Apollo to Houston.' He listened to her breathe for a few minutes then he carefully hung up. *Isn't that something*, Armstrong said to no one in particular as he took that first, lazy step on the moon.

In the far corner of the room the dog moved his feet in his sleep, as if he were treading water.

When he left there wasn't much to take. A few days before, they had stayed up all night talking. The first light had found them with Anna sitting upright in a chair against the wall and Samson standing at the window. They had both said too much, and the room had the stale closeness of a sickroom. It was early December, and when Samson cracked open the window a gust of freezing air came through. Anna shivered. At some point in the night she had told him that there was a part of him that was the same, and she was still in love with him. That at certain moments – mostly when he wasn't aware of her presence – she felt he was back with her as he'd always been.

'But then I say something and you turn around. And I can see there's nothing there. I mean, nothing that belongs to me.'

When he suggested that maybe he should move out, she didn't argue.

'What is it like, I wonder,' she finally said, 'to be you?'

'Like an astronaut,' he said, and in the dim light he thought he saw her vaguely smile.

On the morning he left, she went out with Frank while he packed. When she came back he was sitting on the couch with his bag at his feet.

'Isn't there anything else?' she asked, the dog crouched between them like a small country. Samson looked down at the duffel that contained some clothes, the address book, his CT scans, now smudged with fingerprints. He scanned the living room. A burglar would find nothing here, would pocket only the pewter candlesticks to be thrown away later, found at dawn by the garbage collectors.

'No. I can always come back later. If there's something.' But then his eyes caught on the camera on the shelf. Anna took it down and handed it to him.

'Take it.' He lifted it to his eye and found her through the lens. She stood patiently, like someone whose face is being felt by the blind, but when he pressed the shutter she flinched. 'To remember me by,' she said, and smiled grimly. The dog rolled over as if he were dead.

Lana had already left for the canned sunlight of California, and that night Samson slept alone in her bed. It was a relief to lie with no one next to him, to be staring at the ceiling in a room he didn't have to try to remember. To be so alone, free to retreat further into the emptiness of his mind: it gave him goose bumps. There was also the thrill of sleeping in the bed of another woman.

The pillows smelled of Lana's shampoo, like a tropical drink. She'd left a note on the refrigerator telling him to make himself at home and reminding him to water the plants, which he did as tenderly as if he were feeding baby animals. 'Cheaper than cats,' she'd said when she showed him around the apartment the week before. He'd told Anna that he'd run into one of his old students, and that she was leaving for L.A. and offered him her place. He watched Anna for any sign of recognition of Lana's name, but her face displayed only a withdrawn sadness.

The phone rang, and the machine picked up after a few rings. 'Hi, you've reached Lana,' her voice spooled through the dark apartment. 'I'm in California until May,' and then the flat note of distress, of modern longing.

It was someone named T.J. He wanted her to call him when she got the message.

'She's in Los Angeles,' Samson said, picking up the phone as the boy began to soliloquize about where Lana was at this very moment.

'Oh,' he said flatly. 'Who are you?'

'I'm subletting her place. While she's gone.'

'Oh,' again. 'Well, give her the message.'

Samson listened to the dial tone.

People in the department had started to talk. 'Who cares what they say?' Lana had said before she left, and Samson understood that she enjoyed being the subject of gossip, the alleged younger woman, though the truth was that nothing but conversation had taken place between them. Samson's colleagues, who were willing to accept a brain tumor and amnesia, who sat on the coffee-stained chairs in the faculty room discussing the tragic loss of a brilliant mind, found his burgeoning friendship with a student unsettling. Plus there was the larger problem of what to do about his job.

He avoided going to the department, but ran into other professors at the library, where he spent most of his time. Eventually the chair of the department, Marge Kallman, a Romanticist who wore pants suits and carried shapeless handbags, called him in for a meeting. She sat behind her desk and the light came in from behind, catching like a halo in the spun web of her blow-dried hair. She spoke highly of Samson's work, praising his book on the American tradition whose spine she rubbed as she spoke. She eulogized his teaching skills and his popularity among the students, his ability to *speak their language*. The tone of her voice shifted smoothly when she arrived, inevitably, at his illness and she repeated again how aggrieved at his loss everyone was. Gently she told Samson that they felt they had no choice but to begin the search to hire another Twentieth-Century person to fill his position.

Samson nodded encouragingly. He made it easy for her. He told her they could empty his office, he didn't want anything. He asked only that Anna could keep living in their apartment, which was faculty housing, and that he retain his library privileges. Marge looked relieved, glad to have avoided a scene. Samson complimented her brooch, a gilt peacock with rhinestone tail feathers.

'Would you believe I bought it in Las Vegas?'

'I've been there,' Samson said, standing up.

'Yes,' Marge Kallman said, signing forms.

'The desert,' Samson added.

It was Lavell's favorite part of the story. 'Why Nevada?' he asked, pacing like a detective along the circumference of a crime. He answered himself: 'Because it's perfect.' Because the desert is where you go when you find your brain scorched, blown-out, uninhabited. You go there for camouflage. Like a wild animal, you follow your instinct.

He stopped seeing Lavell. There was nothing left to say to him, as there was nothing to say to Marge Kallman, or even Anna. He lay still in the subterranean dark of a strange apartment. He fumbled for the camera. He opened the back and flipped on the lamp and in an instant the exposed image of Anna was burned out of existence.

He went to the library only to take out and return his books. He brought them home in stacks. He kept a ready supply of cash for the Chinese deliverymen that cycled the wrong way down the avenues the quicker to bring him a midnight pizza. He read widely, without a plan. He had no agenda.

He favored books about astronomy and voyages in space, though he also liked biographies of movie stars or great leaders; without a past of his own, he was fascinated by those of other people. He read *People* magazine and sometimes *Rolling Stone*. He read about the end of the Cold War. He read all of the novels on the curriculum for his Contemporary Writers class, which he found on Lana's shelves. He read about the life of John Glenn, the life of Yuri Gagarin, who traveled through space where only a dog had been. Carried out of the capsule when he floated back to earth, his body wasted by zero gravity.

Anna called him to discuss insurance and bank accounts. Sometimes she called only wanting to hear his voice.

'You okay?' Samson asked.

'Yeah,' Anna said, though she sounded subdued.

'How's work?' he asked.

'Okay. Fine, I guess.' Silence. 'Is anything new? Anything you want to talk about?'

He wracked his mind, thinking of something he might say to rescue them from another failed exchange. 'I'm using the camera. I go on walks and take pictures.'

'Good,' she said. 'That's a good thing to do.'

They arranged their finances. The medical bills had cut into their savings, and Anna's salary from the social services agency wasn't much. Samson took what little he needed, and left her the rest. He wanted her to be okay, and anyway he didn't want the money. He wouldn't have known what to do with it.

She put Frank on, who panted sullenly into the phone.

It was true that when he occasionally went out to wander the city he took the camera. He rolled a new film into the back, advanced. He took pictures of things that interested him, bridges, construction sites, wreckage, though he never developed them. He kept the yellow canisters of film in a plastic shopping bag. Lana's neighbor, an astrologist named Kate whose clients came to see her during their lunch hours or late at night, thought he was a professional. He took a photograph of her with her collection of crystals and did not disabuse her. Once, when he came home late, she heard him unlocking the door and came out in a purple robe smelling of alcohol. She leaned close and pushed herself against him. She put her hand on his groin. He ducked out of her embrace muttering an apology, slipped into the apartment, and listened against the wall, flushed with heat, until he heard her quietly shut her door. When he ran into her the next week, neither of them mentioned it. She told him that Mars and Jupiter were shifting signs while the Sun met Uranus, signaling new opportunities. On New Year's Eve they made daiquiris and watched the ball drop on her little television. Kate lit candles all around the room and swayed to Neil Young's 'Sugar Mountain.' She pulled

Samson off the floor and he moved his hips and flapped his arms to the music. When she placed her wet mouth over his, he didn't object. She pulled his buttocks into her and, tipsy on rum, he happily grinded against her as the crowd filed out of Times Square. The next morning he woke up in her bed with a splitting headache. Kate was still asleep and in the gritty light her flesh looked blue. He dressed and slipped out the door. He swallowed some aspirin and got his coat and camera. It had snowed a few days before, and now the sun was out, reflecting off of everything.

A month later it snowed again. By evening there were three inches on the ground and Samson walked to Central Park where the Great Lawn shimmered in the moonlight, the snow not yet trampled by dogs. He walked under the white trees, snow crunching under his shoes. He came out on the south side of the park and walked down Broadway, toward the Day-Glo of Times Square. The bars were filled with people watching the Super Bowl, the windows fogged with heat. They cheered as he passed.

From ten blocks away he could see the giant screen suspended above Forty-second Street. Neon saturated the air, hemorrhaging a hundred words a minute. The football players jogged soundlessly across the screen, the snow falling past them like ticker tape. Samson stood on the traffic island and watched them huddle and break, men who didn't know their own strength, whose entire existence was dedicated to the laws of the field. He wanted to get down on his knees, to prostrate himself before them. When the game ended he couldn't feel his frozen hands and feet.

When he got back to the apartment the phone rang as he was stripping off his wet clothes. He thought of letting the machine pick up, but at the last second lifted the receiver.

'Hello?'

'Samson?' The call unsettled him; it disturbed his anonymity.

'Yes?'

'You watch the game?'

Anna had given out his number before he asked her not to and sometimes people called. 'Who is this? I'm sorry, maybe Anna didn't tell you.'

'You don't know me. How are you, Samson?'

'Fine.'

'You don't mind me calling so late, do you? I'm on the West Coast, it's earlier here.'

'Well, it's not the best time. I just stepped in. It was snowing outside and I'm freezing. Who did you say you were?'

'I didn't. It's Dr Malcolm, Ray Malcolm. Lavell and I have known each other for years. He told me about your case. Fascinating.'

'Thank you.' Samson leaned his forehead against the window. The snow continued to come down, falling evenly over everything.

'Well, look, Samson. I won't keep you now. I just

wanted to introduce myself. We don't know each other yet, but I have a proposition for you. Something I think you might find interesting. Ever been to California?' His voice sounded crisp and pristine, as if it had just been taken out of a box.

'I was born there.'

'L.A.?'

'No.'

'Well, it would mean you coming out here for a while. Hold on a second, will you, Samson?'

He heard the doctor put down the phone and then the muffled sound of voices.

'Sorry about that. Someone just came to the house, so I better run. I'm eager to speak to you, though. What do you say I call you back in a few days? We'll talk then?'

'Yeah, sure.'

'Glad I got through to you. Stay out of the cold.' Ray Malcolm hung up.

Samson stood by the window watching the flakes of snow, each an original, irreducible fact, fall through the lamplight. He briefly worried that the call had to do with his health, that the doctor had bad news about the tumor somehow regenerating. But the final battery of tests Lavell had performed two months before was supposed to have been conclusive. He pushed the thought out of his mind; if anything had come up, Lavell would have contacted him himself.

He undressed and got into bed, and for a long time he lay awake, imagining that his resting body was broadcast above Times Square. He was so still that those who watched him below did not know he was alive until suddenly he stretched and rolled over in the dark.

PART II

From the air there seems to be a system: recognizable designs, networks on the desert floor. Crosshatches of ridge and fissure. Lines that fan out from the source. The shadow of the airplane slips across basin and range. Frost forms between the plane's double windows, each geometric crystal an argument for the stillborn beauty of pure math. Eventually the cut of a road appears, as deep as a fossil in shale. Unbound by destination, a road simply for the sake of moving, however slowly, through miles of nothing. Through the system. The first grid is the strangest, the geometry of better living etched onto the desert floor: identical houses of a planned community pleated around the nucleus of a swimming pool. One and then another, until the desert is paved under streets and scattered with countless pools like a deck of blue cards.

Samson waited at the Information Desk at LAX for half an hour, watching the arrivals screen as it logged the landing of another incoming plane, another disaster averted. The pale passengers streaming down the ramp full of static cling, a look of relief and determination on their faces. Eventually he wandered over to the newsstand and paged through the glossy magazines – bare midriffs, numerology, diet tips. Periodically he glanced over at the Information Desk to check for Ray Malcolm.

He was reading *Rolling Stone* when he heard his name over the loudspeaker among the ranks of the missing, jet-lagged foreigners, jilted lovers called back at the last instant, lost children calling from courtesy phones: 'Mr Greene, Mr Samson Greene, please report to the Airport Information Desk.' He leaned around the rack and saw a man who matched the description Ray Malcolm had given of himself. It was not yet too late to turn and walk out the sliding doors. The doctor scouted the crowd. Samson turned a few more pages, brought the magazine up to the cashier and paid, then walked toward him like a hunted man surrendering. When he saw Samson a slow smile settled over Ray's face.

'Terrible traffic. I thought maybe you'd given up on me,' he said, reaching out his hand now, the voice crisp as it had sounded on the phone, the hand rough and papery.

'Dr Malcolm.'

'Call me Ray.'

Ray Malcolm gave the impression of agelessness. He had a full head of white hair and tan, leathery skin surprisingly unwrinkled, except around the eyes where it had creased into deep crow's-feet. He was small, even shrunken, yet he moved with a springy elasticity, as if he had the joints of a younger man. He was dressed in fine linen slacks and a button-down shirt, with the collar open and the sleeves rolled up to reveal a chunky silver watch, the kind worn by scuba divers, waterproof at a thousand feet. Samson guessed him to be about sixty-five, though he wouldn't have been shocked if Ray turned out to be fifty or eighty. He was the kind of man people looked at twice, deciding whether or not to stare. What are the criteria for gaping? Samson wondered. Extremes: tremendous beauty or prizewinning ugliness; deformities; violent or noisy behavior. All rash, obvious reasons to gawk. But the great candidates for stares seemed more subtle, those that quietly, diplomatically challenge the authority of the norm. So it was with Ray, who now picked up Samson's bag and glided him along, steering him toward the parking lot with gentle nudges like a Seeing Eye dog. Out on the highway, he maneuvered the white convertible with the same assurance and skill, deep in his bucket seat.

They didn't talk at first. Ray had wired him the money for the flight, but it was understood that there were no obligations. He could still change his mind and step out of the car at the next red light. Ray would be disappointed but he wouldn't try to stop him. It was understood that he had no interest in coercion. Everything was aboveboard with Ray;

105

he wanted volunteerism, he said, people who understood the magnitude of the project. He wanted
believers. People who would drop everything to go
out to the desert.

Samson wasn't sure why he'd come. After Ray
had called the second time, Samson had spoken
to Lavell, who said that he was a brilliant man,
that his work was pushing the boundaries of
science. Samson liked the sound of Ray's voice
and the excited urgency of the phone calls. He
was a doctor, some kind of research, that's all he'd
said – that he wanted Samson's help.

They accelerated past long-necked palm trees
and pastel houses with grilles on the windows.
The roar of the wind made it difficult to speak.
Ray shifted smoothly, a little ring with a cloudy
blue stone on his pinkie. Samson stayed put for
the time being, his thumb hooked on the seat belt
across his chest. One hand on the tattered envelope in his lap with the CT and PET scans Ray
had asked him to bring, the magnetic resonance
images of his brain.

The sun was starting to set and the corroded
orange light reflected off the cars. They turned off
the freeway and began to wind up through the hills,
the car murmuring as Ray nosed it around hairpin
turns, past the lawns like Astroturf, the darkened
windows of mansions, past cedar gates, cars, boats,
motorcycles, flying saucers for all one knew, hiber-
nating under canvas. It was mid-March. The air
was warm and smelled of eucalyptus and Samson

inhaled deeply the scent of his childhood. Eucalyptus and the faint brine of the Pacific. A strange sadness crept into some corner of him. The light was just beginning to turn thin and dusky, the floodlights of a Mexican-tile house coming on too early, a paranoid precaution against the night.

'What a fucking city,' Ray marveled as they rounded a bend and the view cleared so that they could see the glitter of lights coming on in the valley. 'No matter how many times I see it, it always amazes me. Especially coming back from the desert.'

'Were you just there?'

'Came back last night so I'd be here to pick you up. Remind me: your first time in L.A.?'

'I probably came once or twice when I was a kid. I *feel* like I've been here.'

'You watch a lot of movies? Because it unsettles even people who live in L.A.: the nagging sense that they've seen a part of the city before, exactly like this.' Ray turned into the driveway and removed a remote control from the glove compartment. The gates swung open and they started uphill.

Samson loved the movies. He used to save his allowance and his mother would drop him off and pick him up at the theater because the only movies she liked were documentaries or epics, history revived on the silver screen. She would happily endure numbness and cramped legs for the glory of *The Sorrow and the Pity* or *Spartacus*

107

seen straight through. His tastes were more catholic: he would see anything with a plot, with dialogue, with the flicker of twenty-four frames per second.

'It's the movies or déjà vu. The mind taking the same picture twice, a little seizure, a coup by the cameraman, carried away by his own aesthetic,' Ray said, glancing over at him. 'Or maybe you actually *have* been here before. Maybe you have a damn good memory.' A joke. Samson snickered, then straightened up, surprised at himself.

They drove up to a large house, a low-slung glass and stone contraption that skirted across the cliff.

There was no wind now. Ray cut the motor.

'You look tired. I'll show you around and then you can get some sleep. We'll talk in the morning.' He opened the door and got out, lifting Samson's bag easily from the backseat.

The house backed up onto the cliff edge, and the living room ended in a wall of glass over-looking the city. They stood together, looking down at the valley.

'It's beautiful,' Samson said, feeling he could say such a thing to Ray, feeling it was what the doctor wanted, though he meant it all the same. It *was* beautiful, the ambition of it, the freehand interpretation of a city. From such a height, the knowledge of the small, simultaneous faraway was comforting: people dialing the operator, swallowing pills, breaking off romances, signing their names. Twelve million people inhabiting one of the most volatile places on earth, naturally disastrous, prone to flood and fire. Sharing wavelengths. *Ten-four, you're breaking up, come in.*

'Isn't it, though? I remember when I first moved here. It was more than thirty years ago. The house didn't look like this then. I had a wife and children. I used to get up in the middle of the night and stand here, looking out. I felt beneficent. I felt I could help people. Once someone called me, the wrong number. He thought I was a psychiatrist. Sometimes they do that, look you up in the phone book. He was threatening to kill himself and I spoke to him all night. He had a stutter and I listened. He wanted to know was I still there. We spoke for hours and sometimes we were silent, me looking out at the city and him at the street corner where he lived, he wouldn't say where. I thought I could hear the ocean but maybe it was the air conditioner or the wind. When we finally hung up he said he'd changed his mind for the time being. The next few days I read all the obituaries, but he'd never told me his name. Deaths like that don't make the papers anyway.'

'Help them with what?'

'What?'

'What did you think you could help people with?'

'I don't know, really. I'm a doctor. I wanted to help people. I was idealistic. I didn't look at it like a city. I felt I knew them. Intimately.'

'The ones with a certain longing?'

'A vague unhappiness, yes.'

'And you?'

'Me? I woke up at night wondering about the safety of my own children. I would look in and see their little humped forms under the covers. Rising and falling. You have children?'

'No.'

'I didn't think so. Arthur didn't say.'

'What *did* Lavell say? I've been wondering. That you would fly me out here, based on what he told you.'

'He said you were found senseless in the Mojave Desert; you had a craniotomy to remove a juvenile pilocytic astrocytoma; you have no memory except of your childhood, and though you are capable of making new memories, you display little or no desire to remember. Should I go on?'

'Yes.'

'He said you were highly intelligent and that you displayed an interest in the possibilities of science and technology. He told me about a fascinating scenario you described having to do with the future of cloning.'

'That's what you do?'

'Cloning? God, no.' Ray grinned.

Samson looked around the dark living room. The outlines of paintings loomed on the walls. There was nothing extraneous, only a minimal amount of furniture for sitting uncomfortably: the home of an obsessive-compulsive or a genius. It occurred to him suddenly, 'What kind of doctor are you?,' wondering now if he had come all this way for a crackpot, the crazy rich. A Scientologist or a man with a degree purchased on TV.

'Trained as a neurosurgeon, but now I only do research, neuroscience. Not much interaction with them anymore,' Ray said, making a gesture toward the valley.

'Like Lavell.'

Ray smiled. 'Yes. A memory man.'

'Where are they now, your wife and kids?'

'My wife died of cancer more than fifteen years ago. The children are both married. Matthew lives in San Francisco, Jill in London. They have children of their own. They come for Christmas. Can I get you something to drink?' Samson nodded, and Ray went to the kitchen and came back with a glass of orange juice. And did it really matter if he had purchased his degree on cable?

'Feel free to take whatever you want from the kitchen. There's not much; I told Larissa – the housekeeper – to buy some things, but I've been on my own peculiar diet for so many years that I think it threw her. I just found a package of cookies on the counter.'

'What kind of diet?'

'A sort of macrobiotic thing.'

Samson wondered if organic meals spun in the blender were responsible for Ray's ageless appearance. He looked – especially now, in his own house – fortified against disaster. Samson remembered a boy he once knew, a friend of his, who had a brother with no immune system. He had to wear a plastic suit, like a bubble, all the time so that no germs could reach him. They kept him in a hospital in San Francisco and once he went with his friend to see the brother, called Duke. The mother drove them and during the car ride they crouched in the backseat and shot at passing cars with empty water guns. When they got to the hospital Duke was waiting. He had been told they were coming, and he had a huge, bucktooth grin on his face behind the plastic helmet. His mother hugged him through the heavy synthetic fabric. Duke just closed his eyes. Samson couldn't tell if this kid liked it or not, if maybe he was so used to not being touched in the bubble that even the mother's hug was awkward and a little threatening, like the affection of a huge dog. She brought him a few presents and after he ripped them open they all played together. Whenever anyone bumped into him there was the rustle of synthetic material or the strange, inhuman knock of something hitting hard plastic. When it was time to leave, Duke stood in the hallway waving to them with a grin and sad eyes, watching them walk away.

When he looked up, Ray was watching him curiously. A telephone rang somewhere in the house, and when Ray switched on a lamp the bulb made a faint pop and flared. He walked down the hallway, and Samson heard him pick up the receiver and talk quietly. He felt the strangeness of being there in Los Angeles, in Ray's house, on the other end of the phone calls he'd received over the past month. Macrobiotic: eat simple grain-based food and you experience a reversal of health deterioration. He'd read about it in a health magazine. In the macrobiotic view, disease starts as fatigue and ends as cancer or mental illness. Grains, the one universal fact all our ancestors shared. Not all seeds are grains.

Ray came back into the room. 'So what do you say we talk in the morning? Like I said, no strings attached as far as the plane ticket is concerned. If nothing else you can turn it into a sun-and-sea vacation. Fuck, take the convertible. Go to the beach.' The occasional curse that flecked Ray's speech was like the last surviving vice of a reformed man; a vague hint of immorality that made him seem less holy, more human.

'I don't know if I know how to drive.'

'Right, of course. Well, we can call a cab.'

Samson followed Ray up the wide, flat stairs suspended from the ceiling by steel rods. The guest room was at the end of the hall and looked out over the side of the house, onto a swimming pool with dead leaves floating on the surface.

'Here's the bathroom,' Ray was saying. 'There should be towels.' He flipped on the light.

Samson nodded and smiled. He felt a little rush of tenderness for Ray Malcolm and had to suppress the urge to grasp him in a hug.

'Thanks.'

'I'm glad to have you here, Samson. You sleep

well and I'll see you at breakfast. Wake you at eight?'

'Okay.'

'Good then. Good night.' Ray began to shut the door.

'Ray?'

'Yes?'

'I was wondering, that first night you called me? After the football game, remember?'

'Sure.'

'Did you call me from here?'

'I think I did, yes.'

'Someone came over, remember? Was it someone else who lost his memory?'

'No. Actually it was a guy who has a memory that interests me. Something pretty extraordinary.'

'Oh.'

'Get some sleep. Don't worry, we'll talk.'

Samson took a shower and air-dusted himself with the talcum powder he found in the medicine cabinet. He towel-dried his hair – it was longish by now, falling in his eyes so that he often had to wing it back. He felt along his scalp for the scar.

He read *Rolling Stone* cover-to-cover and then turned off the light. He didn't exactly know what he was doing here, in this strange house over-looking Los Angeles. Perhaps he shouldn't have come. But there was something about Ray Malcolm's voice that comforted him, and it seemed he had nothing anymore to lose.

Right now Lana was perhaps driving on the highway, making her way around an exit ramp. Getting on or off, switching directions, listening to the radio and singing to herself. Anna was probably asleep. Frank was breathing in the dark. There was a certain comfort to the idea that all these things were happening at once.

Samson was staring out the window at the half-empty swimming pool when Ray knocked at eight. He had always wanted a pool, and when he was six he'd gotten the idea of digging one in the backyard. *I'm digging a pool*, he told his mother. She looked up from her magazine, her face shaded by a straw hat. *Wonderful*, she'd said. *I'll change into my suit.*

'Take your time,' Ray said.

In daylight the house looked older, shabbier than it had the night before. The white paint was peeling and water-stained on the outside.

'I built it in 1970. It was very modern at the time,' Ray explained, carrying a pot of herbal tea and a bowl of fruit. Samson followed him out onto the slate patio. There was a table and a few lawn chairs, the kind with plastic straps that leave leg welts.

'I hired a well-known architect, mostly forgotten now. The house appeared in magazines, et cetera. My wife had to fight him over everything. He wanted to suspend the children's bedrooms from ropes. They would come down by a system of

116

pulleys. A two-year-old and four-year-old, like Tarzans.'

A lawn mower hummed in the distance.

'I'd bought the property four, five years before and we'd been living in the ranch house that came on it. The house of a television sitcom. The plan was to demolish it and build this as soon as we had the money, so we didn't allow ourselves to get too comfortable. Funny, though, when we moved into the new house, the feeling stayed. We lived here like honeymooners.'

Samson realized what all along the house had reminded him of. Ray had knocked down the house of a television sitcom and built a movie set in its place.

'It's beautiful, it really is. But it doesn't seem very comfortable for a family.'

'True.' Ray leaned back in his chair, a man who had built a house – an empire – and this allowed him the magnanimity to admit his mistakes. 'I ought to sell it, I'm hardly here. But at least when I get back it's waiting. This is where my children grew up. There are memories.'

'Seems like maybe it's a burden to keep.'

Ray bobbed the tea bag around and fished it out of the pot. He looked up at Samson. 'The memories or the house?'

'Both.'

'It's unforgiving. You have to move through it at right angles. But I feel a great deal of warmth for this house. Like a woman you loved who spurned you for years, to whom you feel a certain gratitude because you realize she gave shape to your life.'

Samson looked out at the view. He wondered if there had been another woman, before Anna, someone he had loved who had refused him. If so, her mark had been lost along with everything else. He shielded his eyes against the glare of the sun.

'Your research, it's in the desert?'

'Right. In Nevada.'

'What's there?'

'Nothing – some scrub, squat buildings: brothels, casinos, and military bases. Cheap and no neighbors.'

And now he could almost believe that he really was in a movie, a character as cool and composed as Bogart, shocked by nothing. 'Should I not ask questions? I guess what you do is legal.'

Ray laughed. 'Very.'

'Don't get me wrong, you seem very reputable.' Samson looked away, embarrassed. He had wanted to play Ray's equal, for the doctor to feel that nothing was beyond him. Instead he had come out sounding naïve. 'You seem like a good man, Ray. No neighbors, you were saying.'

'Thank you, yes. We have a lab out there, a pretty substantial facility dedicated to a single project.'

'Your project?'

'You could say. It's something I've been working on for years. But there's a whole team of us working together now. Science like this, at the level we're working at, demands incredible cooperation. Experts pooling their knowledge.' He lifted the mug to his lips and swallowed, holding Samson's gaze. When he spoke again his voice was low. 'We're out there engineering something truly fucking amazing. Getting inside the brain in a way that's never happened before. It's a beautiful thing.'

'And what is it, exactly? The project? I guess that's the twenty-million-dollar question, right?'

'Hundred-million.'

'What?'

Ray smiled. 'It's a hundred-million-dollar question, and yes, you should be asking, and I'm going to tell you. A man doesn't get a call to drop everything and come three thousand miles without getting a good answer why.'

'Good. Okay.' Samson bobbed his head, a little relieved though he wasn't sure why. He felt Ray was on his side, and now he wanted very much to be on Ray's. 'Actually there wasn't much to drop. I wasn't doing anything in New York.'

'Then it's convenient for both of us that I found you when I did. By the way, what I'd really like to do is talk about you. Because I'd say you're now an unusual expert on the subject of memory. What did I say last night about your turning this into a vacation? I'm amending it. You're not off the hook until you talk to me about what it's like inside your head. We'll say you owe me that.'

Samson happily raised his mug to toast, and knocked back the rest of the tea.

'What is this stuff anyway?'

'Thistle. Feel like a walk?'

The air was already warm, a late-winter morning in California where snow is something that happens when you shake a plastic globe, coming down over the Nativity. They passed driveways guarded by cameras, outdoor sculpture, topiary. A man driving a red convertible accelerated past them, his hand out the window to catch the breeze while the car stereo played Stevie Wonder, '*very superstitious.*'

The next day Samson sat alone in the back of a cab, sweating. Heat was coming up off the asphalt, simmering under the sprawled city. They were crawling through midday traffic on the freeway, and he was scanning other cars for pimps and starlets. In his mind he played back the things Ray had told him, one piece at a time. In the monastic tradition the desert is a sacred place of simultaneous being and nothingness, Ray had said. A proving ground in which the sense of individuality is obliterated on the way to achieving a higher state. Samson thought about a pay phone in the middle of nowhere, something against which to measure the desolation. It was in a movie he once saw, a girl in cowboy boots chewing gum and scrounging for quarters to make the only sort of call the phone booth knew, the call of the long-lost and the missing. During which only the wind or stealth bombers breaking the sound barrier between silence and silence.

A woman with fuzzy blond hair in a ponytail wriggled in her seat in the car next to the taxi, singing along to the radio. When she looked over, Samson winked. The girl was embarrassed at first and so was he, but then she smiled and fluttered her fingers that ended in two-inch pink nails. They rolled along at the same pace, glancing happily at each other and waving whenever they were realigned after one lane went faster than the other.

'Get her number,' the taxi driver encouraged him, grinning in the rearview mirror.

'I have a girlfriend,' Samson said, to avoid conversation and keep his eyes on the girl.

'Two girlfriends!' the driver said gleefully, and went back to the job he was now taking very seriously, of staying neck and neck with the girl's car. When they came to the exit and had to turn off, it seemed everyone was a little sad, the girl, the driver, and Samson, who wondered what her name was; he should have at least called across the lanes to ask her name.

They drove up and down the streets at the edge of campus. He had Lana's address on a piece of paper he'd kept in his wallet. He'd tried calling her from Ray's house, but no one had answered. Probably she was in class, and he decided to go over anyway, figuring she might be back by the time he arrived. It was thrilling to know that these were the streets she walked down every day, her bag slung across her shoulder, punching up her hair from underneath so that it looked like she just got out of bed.

'Girlfriend number one?' the driver asked, pulling up to a beige condominium and craning around to look at Samson.

'Huh? Yeah,' Samson said, counting out the crisp bills Ray had given him.

The driver pretended to zipper his lips. 'Good luck!' he sang, then screeched off, taking the secret they shared with him.

Samson knocked on the door of the ground-floor apartment. When no one answered he tried the handle, which was unlocked.

'Hello?' he called, knocking again on the open door.

There was a couch along one wall, basket chairs, a blow-up dinosaur, and a junked television in the corner with wires sticking out of the back. A lone, gravel voice floated in from somewhere, and it took a second before Samson realized it was the radio, the low vibrating hum of distance below the voice's bottom register.

'Lana?'

There was no answer so he followed the sound of the radio to the bedroom. The blinds were drawn and the room was dark except for the glow of a computer screen. Someone was hunched in front of it, his back to Samson.

'Hello?'

The kid turned around and it took him longer than it should have to register another person there, as if he were trying to refocus, to shift from one parallel plane to the other.

'Oh, hi. You looking for Lana? She'll be back – shit, what time is it?' He glanced at his wrist but there was no watch on it. 'Back in, like, an hour.' A look of puzzlement crossed his face, something not necessarily local, solved in an instant as the features returned to slackness. He reached up and lowered the volume on a duct-taped radio, just enough so the words of the broadcast were still audible: *Normal aging of monkeys' brains causes a twenty-eight percent decline of neurons.* He fingered his glasses and ran his hand through the back of his hair, matted down and stuck up, the troubled hair of an insomniac or day-sleeper. 'Did she know you were coming?'

The interesting thing, Ray had said, is that when we are working with the brain, we are dealing with an intelligence far greater than our own.

'I'm a friend of hers from New York. I thought I'd surprise her.'

'Oh,' he nodded. 'Well, I'm just working on this . . . thing.' The boy – he didn't look much older than nineteen or twenty – swiveled the chair around and looked at the screen. He tapped a few keys and waited to see what happened, then turned back, distracted. 'Yeah. You want to wait until she gets back? I'm Wingate, by the way.'

Samson shook the clammy hand and, when he introduced himself, Wingate brightened up and pushed some magazines off of a brown velvet chair that had little bald spots like a sick dog. Samson hadn't heard of any of the magazines, *Nuts and Volts, Midnight Engineer*.

'You have to send away for them. I know the guy who writes most of the stuff in *Volts*.' He flashed a grin. 'So you're Samson. Cool. Lana told me about you.'

The fact that Wingate knew about him was the only assurance Samson had that he'd come to the right place, because aside from some girl's sneakers at the foot of the bed and a bottle of nail polish on the night table, there was nothing to suggest Lana had ever been here. He wondered what Lana had said about him.

Wingate chatted easily, rooting around in his hair as if he'd lost something there. He didn't move to open the blinds or turn on a light, and so they sat in darkness, viscous bubbles floating across the computer screen like a lava lamp. He balled up his flannel shirt and threw it in the corner of the room. The radio piped up: *There are several hurtles before this therapy can be tried on humans*. Occasionally Wingate pricked up his ears, like a wild dog listening for the pack in the wind.

Wingate told him how he'd drifted down from Palo Alto a few months ago, had migrated beyond the range of hackers with silicon dust on their fingers. After he'd graduated from Stanford he'd stayed for a year trying to decide whether to do a Ph.D. He wrote code for his adviser and for an operating system called LINUX, and hung out in the back of the coffeehouse on campus with guys from small Balkan countries doing work in the Robotics Department or Symbolic Systems, figuring out how to model consciousness using game theory and Boolean logic, who saw the world in terms of binary equations, one or zero. These were guys who had spent a decade in the department, Wingate explained, who watched the tall, blond undergraduate girls like wildlife, who drove beat-up cars whose backseats were full of juck even though their work was intangible, virtual. They had a keen and scheming and slightly adolescent sense of humor only understood in their own circles. Maybe they had come from war-torn countries that sent their brightest to American universities, but now they would never return from California. Wingate had come from the suburbs of Chicago but he might as well have come from beyond the Iron Curtain. He knew as soon as he got to Stanford – wandering dazed through the mission-style buildings, hiking in the foothills up to a massive radio telescope – that he had come as far as he would go.

Samson had no idea what Wingate was talking about. He seemed a being returned from the future, already evolved, and Samson felt his stomach drop when it dawned on him this was the company Lana was keeping.

'I grew up near there,' he said, interrupting Wingate's monologue. He wanted to ask Wingate things, like what the hell was LINUX and what were people like from the other side of the Iron Curtain? He wanted to ask him what, exactly, was the nature of his relationship with Lana. At the very least, he wanted to hear the names of the familiar streets of his childhood, to sketch out a map and identify landmarks.

Instead he said, 'I was Lana's professor at Columbia.'

Wingate nodded but seemed unimpressed. He jumped up and twisted the volume on the radio. He leaned in, his hand resting on the box. *And now it's time for Laotian Community Radio. Remember: keep your mind open and your radio tuned to the left.*

'Damn. I thought it was going to be something else.'

They listened to the first few minutes of a man talking in heavily accented English about flooding along the Mekong and then Wingate switched off the power. The gooey bubbles slid across the computer screen, doing a convincing imitation of weight and mass.

'What happened to your radio?'

Wingate picked up the battered box and opened the battery hatch as if the answer were hidden there. 'It's just an old transistor I unpacked and put back together again. I wanted to see if I could pick up this pirate station out of Pasadena.' The

kind of kid, Samson thought, who takes everything apart to see how it's wired. Who starts out
by leaving pennies to be flattened on the railroad
tracks and ends up controlling push-button
bombs.

'This guy beams his signal to a hundred-and-
eighty-foot antenna planted on the roof of his
house, and then it gets picked up, amplified, and
rebroadcast over FM. On a vacant frequency, right
under the nose of the FCC. They busted him and
he just packed up and moved his transmitter down
the street.'

'What does he say on the air? It seems a lot of
effort to go to.'

Wingate shrugged. 'He's an anarchist. A guy who
will go that far to make a point. There are plenty
of people doing it; you can order transmitter kits
easy off the Web. There's a kid in Florida sending
out advice fourteen hours a day on how to blow
things up. He's a freak but mostly you've got
people who want to chip away at corporate
control, anticapitalists who want to shake up the
media conglomerates from beneath. People who
live for open systems.'

In the desert the hippies camp out at the hot
springs, Ray had said. They splash around nude
while the high-voltage wires audibly crackle overhead, driving power across the valley. While the
military empties rounds of M-16s in the dirt. In
the desert there's the military and the anarchists
like a perfect equation, like scales of judgment.

The rest are there biding their time: the Confederate Mexican Army hiding out like Ché in Bolivia, waiting to take back California by guerrilla tactics, the Japanese American arm of Yakuza packing paint guns for flash drills, skinheads staging mock rallies in the shadow of the Panamints. Loners waiting out the apocalypse.

Wingate turned around and began punching the keys on his computer, searching for something on the Web, a site he wanted to show Samson, while Samson imagined a delicate network of light and glass, shimmering and transparent, crossing and spinning out, trying to become infinite. Once, when he was a kid, he had taken a ball of string and taped it to the walls length by length, turning the tiny vestibule between rooms into a human trap that his mother had blithely walked into.

He stared at the back of Wingate's matted hair and for an instant his mind froze and he felt he could not remember how he'd arrived in the dark bedroom, or who Wingate was, or how he'd come to know him. Loudly, as if he himself were trying to transmit his voice through vacuum tubes, Samson explained that he knew next to nothing about computers. The most he could do was find call numbers on library terminals. He hadn't even turned on the computer he'd found in his office at Columbia. It was a question of he couldn't find the switch.

Wingate blinked. There was something charming about how, once he was on a roll talking, another person's interjections seemed to bewilder him. As if conversation were not a native skill but something he had awkwardly learned to imitate, like an ape in captivity taught to sign and give hugs but that remained ambivalent.

'What's the last year you remember?' he asked.

'Nineteen seventy-six.'

'Damn.' Wingate whistled appreciatively. 'So if I were to say, I don't know, Iran-contra? Mean anything?'

'No.'

'Break dancing?'

'No.'

'Moon walk?'

'Sure, I watched it on TV.'

'No, like this—' Wingate stood up and glided backward across the floor.

Samson raised his eyebrows. 'What is that?'

Wingate paused, his face grave. 'I hate to break it to you, man. Fucking Elvis is dead.'

When Lana got back she screamed and tackled him, hooked her arm behind his back and grinned as if for a photo. Samson felt old and pitiful, like a lecherous uncle sweeping through town in a Cadillac to take his favorite niece to Sizzler. A bolt of misery streaked through his mood, and he wished he could find a loophole out of the moment. He stifled an odd, unaccountable urge to shriek, 'Hi! How are you? Hi! How are you?' like the Asian Lionel Richie ferreting around the halls of Lavell's hospital.

He followed Lana to the kitchen, where she found a six-pack of beer in a cabinet. She seemed even taller and more prone to accidents, yet less fragile, more beautiful.

'You live here?'

She rattled the ice tray over the sink. 'I met him basically the first week I got here. It meant I didn't have to bother looking for a place.'

Samson lowered his voice. 'You're at school and he stays home fiddling in the dark? Bombs and so forth.'

'Hah-hah. He's a genius, if you must know.'

'Is that what they call it? What kind of name is Wingate anyway?'

'Hey,' she said, 'I'm really glad to see you.' She handed him a beer and a glass of ice. In the light he noticed she had a silver ring through her eyebrow.

'They missed your ear again.'

'You're a regular comedian. Everyone calls him Winn.'

'Who's everyone?' He trailed her through the living room and down the hall, holding the bottle in front of him like a lantern.

They ate dinner at a plastic picnic table outside the India Sweets and Spices Mart on Venice Boulevard, steamy tubs of tikka masala and lamb korma and little dishes of chutney and lime pickle. Samson couldn't remember tasting Indian food before, and he sampled it in small forkfuls. Lana and Winn shoveled it in their mouths, dribbling rice and panting from the spicy heat, washing the stringy chunks of meat down with beer. Winn licked his fingers and talked with his mouth full, excitedly describing to Samson the hum and click of servers breaking up data, routers sending it out at the speed of light in signals amplified from station to station at the bottom of the sea. He was brilliant and magnetic: put him on a soapbox and he would draw a crowd. Samson could not help feeling disappointed that some nearness he'd wanted from Lana seemed impossible now.

While they ate dessert Samson told them about Ray Malcolm. He spoke quickly, focusing on a spot somewhere over their shoulders, at a lottery billboard across the street with an electronic number trailed by zeroes. When he started to tell them about Ray's research, Winn froze, his coconut pastry stalled in midair.

There was a moment of silence when he finished and then Winn leaned across the table. He spoke in a hoarse whisper, as if people around them were listening, but there was only the shopkeeper and his wife, who dug around in the gunnysacks of beans and nuts and dried tamarind, shuffling up and down the aisle in squashed house slippers.

'Let me get this straight: A man calls you out of the blue, in the middle of the night. He asks you to take a plane across the country and when he picks you up he tells you he more or less works for the government. He wants you to go out to a research compound strategically placed in the middle of nowhere in the Mojave. He tells you that he wants to play with your mind. And you say you think that sounds fine? Are you nuts?' A blue vein in his temple stood out, blood his body was deprived of, pumped up to feed the oversize brain.

'He doesn't work for the government.' A hundred million dollars, Ray had said coolly, as easy as flipping a penny into the fountain. Some from the government in the form of a federal defense grant, the rest from private investors: the price of a pair of Hollywood movies. 'And he doesn't want to play with my mind. He wants to study it.' There was a way Ray had of talking about his case, how unusual, how *quite remarkable* it was, that made Samson swell a little with pride over his flawed medical record, his damaged brain, over the whole bloody history of a condition that also happened to destroy his life, not to mention Anna's, but which he had survived, intact and almost – as Ray didn't quite say but seemed to imply – gifted.

'Winn, chill a second, will you?' Lana turned to Samson. 'This is someone whose life is basically driven by a deep suspicion of all forms of authority. Of – how do you put it, Winn? Of any centralizing force. Which explains why he's some-times' – she looked at Winn – 'slightly paranoid.'

Winn was about to protest but her expression stopped him. Not one of severity but of love, the kind of tender look from an unusually beautiful woman who should not love you but does, that can reduce a man to silence. The evening light fell across her hair, greasy blond at the roots. The sun was going down somewhere in the city, or just beyond the city, at the desert's edge where grids of vacant streets with blank signs lay waiting for the metropolis.

'Okay,' she said, and the story began for the third time, changing slightly again: 'This guy, this Dr Malcolm, calls you up. He asks you to come to L.A. He offers you a fair amount of money . . .'

Before they got in the car Samson took a photograph of the two of them. They stood together with the lottery billboard behind them, Wingate's arm around Lana's waist. Just as he pressed the shutter a semi rammed past, obscuring the trail of zeroes, a streak of uncertainty moving behind them.

On the way back they pulled off the road to watch a small crowd gathered in front of a mall: cars parked sideways, doors flung open, people swaying on tiptoes gently held back by security guards. The group was struggling in numbers, with just barely enough bodies to qualify as a crowd, but a long way from being a full-blown mass whose voices might mesh into a single electric roar, powered by adrenaline, capable of trampling people alive. Everyone – the crowd, the security guards, and the former star who eventually rolled up in a limousine van – seemed to be going through the motions, having pledged to protect at all costs the illusion of fame, without which the city would be swallowed by a brutal wave of sadness and banality. The aging rock star got out of the car. He clasped his hands in the air and shook his fists. He gyrated a few times, and people shouted encouragement and playfully dodged with the security guards, who let a few of them get through to touch the hem of his coat.

'Jesus, he looks pathetic,' Lana said.

'Who is it?'

'Billy Joel.'

'You're kidding. Ouch,' Samson said.

Winn shook his head. 'I can't even watch this,' he said. 'We used to sing 'Piano Man' in my seventh-grade chorus. I kind of idolized the guy.'

'You *idolized* Billy Joel?' Lana's eyes widened in mock horror.

'The truth comes out.'

'For a couple of weeks. Come on, tell me 'Captain Jack' is not a good song.'

Lana raised her eyebrows and turned back to the spectacle of a last few, listless humps.

The whole event lasted two minutes and then Billy Joel disappeared into the mega record store and the slack, dutiful crowd dispersed, leaving only the revolving lights that continued to search faithfully for Billy Joel in places they would never find him: the windows of neighboring buildings, under cars, in empty sections of the sky. 'Come on, 'She's Got a Way'?' Winn continued as they walked back to the car. 'Great song, admit it.' He stepped in front of Lana, serenading her with a few lines. Something about the whole thing had saddened Samson, the many years that had passed, the charade of pretending to keep alive what had long faded into history.

When they got back to the apartment Winn went off to work on the computer and Samson and Lana sat out on the steps. The sun had gone down; the sky was indigo. A couple was having an argument on the second floor of the house next door, the woman hollering *shut up shut up shut up* every time the man tried to speak. After a few minutes she came out carrying a small television set with the cord trailing behind her. She put it in the backseat of her car and drove off. When the motor died away down the street the man came to the window wearing no shirt. He looked down and waved.

'They fight all the time. She leaves with one or two appliances or some clothes, but she always comes back the next day or the day after.' Lana lit a cigarette and kicked off her flip-flops. She had strong, boyish feet, feet so striking and expressive that it seemed as if the whole of her personality were centered there, migrating up the long legs and coursing through her body that hummed like an instrument.

'So are you in love with him? Winn?'

Lana shrugged. 'Maybe.'

'He seems like he's good to you.'

Samson was glad to be alone with her. Since she'd left New York and he'd stopped seeing Lavell, there had been no one he could really talk to. There was something frank and unfinished about Lana that put him at ease. She knew, at least from afar, what he had once been like, but seemed undisturbed by the suddenness of the change, perhaps because she herself was always changing. She seemed to move through the world in a casual, haphazard way, absorbing whatever she happened upon; sometimes she reminded Samson of the sleepwalking characters in cartoons who blindly totter along the edge of cliffs but never fall. He knew she liked him but he couldn't say why, and now he wondered whether she became so quickly intimate with everyone she stumbled across.

'How are things with Anna?' she asked.

'Better since I left the apartment. I always felt guilty there. I only realized it later, but looking at all those photographs and lying in our old bed, I kept feeling I'd somehow betrayed her. After I moved out, I think she began to accept things, to stop hoping so much.'

'I'm glad for her. It must have been awful.'

'She came over to your apartment to say goodbye before I left for L.A. At one point she was standing by the window, just thinking. Like she'd forgotten I was there. And for a minute it seemed clear to me the reason why I'd fallen in love with her.'

'Sure, the minute she no longer belongs to you.'

'She just seemed so much herself.'

Lana groaned and blew out a cloud of smoke. 'Men. You want a woman just when she doesn't want you.'

'Thank you, from your vast experience of human relationships.'

'Hey, you sound like my old professor. The one cool professor in the department.'

'Do I?'

She ashed her cigarette and smiled faintly.

'Anyway,' he continued, 'that's not it. It was like I saw her the way she might have looked the first time we met. Before *we* happened. And I felt like I understood something, that's all.'

A sound of audience laughter came from the couple's apartment, perhaps a spare TV the man dragged out on nights like this when his wife made off with a dangling electrical cord into the night. Samson took the cigarette out of Lana's hand and sucked on it. The smoke burned his lungs and he coughed.

'Anna told me I used to be a very sexy smoker.'

'Are you serious? Because you used to tell us it was a disgusting habit whenever you caught us smoking before class. Which reminds me, I thought of something the other day. Something you told us last year in Contemporary Writers.'

'What's that?'

'I think we were reading, I can't remember what now, but it was about memory. You told us about an angel in the Talmud or something, the Angel of Forgetfulness, whose job it is to make sure that when souls change bodies they first pass through the sea of forgetfulness. How sometimes the Angel of Forgetfulness himself forgets, and then fragments of another life stay with us, and sometimes those are our dreams.'

'I said that?'

'It was a good class,' Lana said, mashing the cigarette into the step. 'The kind you leave in a daze, a little in love with your professor.' She smiled and looked up at the apartment filled with the noise of recorded laughter, her face blurred in the shadows like a photograph in black and white.

When Samson got back to Ray's the house was dark and there was a note saying he'd gone to bed. Samson was supposed to tell him in the morning what he'd decided. As casually as he'd acted in front of Lana and Winn, he was nervous about the decision. It was true that he could use the money. He himself didn't have many expenses aside from the rent he was still paying for Lana's apartment, but he felt a responsibility to Anna, to be sure she was taken care of at least for the foreseeable future. And yet having struggled these past few months in New York to cut himself loose, he wasn't sure how he felt about joining up with anyone now, especially a whole team camped out in the desert. Still, the project as Ray described it seemed a monumental thing, a team of doctors working alone in the emptiness of the desert. And there was something about Ray's voice, as mesmerizing and intimate as a midnight disc jockey inviting his listeners to stay with him through the night. There seemed to be greatness in Ray, and it flattered Samson that the doctor had singled him out and asked him to take part in the effort.

He was scared, but he wanted to tell Ray now that he would go, that he was ready to leave at any moment. He had done what he needed to in L.A.; there was nothing here for him. When he said good-bye, Lana had leaned against him and brushed his lips. He had wanted a sign that he was somehow special to her; that he was not just another person who blithely wandered into her life and fell under her sway. But it was only a sweet, vague apology and it awakened a longing, a sharp scrape across his chest, which he found unbearable.

Only Ray was asleep now. It was part of his regimen: macrobiotic meals, eight hours a night. Diving to a thousand feet. Possibly one of the few men who tested the limits of such watches, bringing the proof – a delicate bloom of coral – back from the Caribbean.

He thought about the conversation he'd had with Ray the night before. They had been sitting on the patio after dinner, discussing what it meant to lose the memory of so much experience and still have, as Samson had, a sophisticated sense of the world. There were the memories of his childhood, of course, Ray had pointed out, leaning back in his chair, his eyes patiently trained on Samson. But there was also a memory that was, he'd said, 'a wisdom not our own.' A memory inherited from evolution, something like intuition that gives people the sense of union with which they enter the world. The lights had been on in the valley below, sputtering through the vaguely rustling trees: sodium streetlamps, approaching headlights, glowing beacons atop towers to warn low-flying planes. Ray's view of the city *noir*, and something about the vista, the perspective, seemed to inspire him.

'There's a lot we don't know, Samson. About the brain and the nature of consciousness. People squirm when the subject of spirituality comes up, and I don't blame them – the meeting of science and spirituality has produced some pretty flimsy thinking.' The ice cubes melting in his water glass had slipped and clinked together. Ray glanced down, then fixed his gaze back on Samson. 'Though we shouldn't forget that the fucking Bhagavad-Gita helped build the bomb.' A fleeting smile had crossed his lips before his face settled back into its relaxed lines. He'd cleared his plate to the side, as if to make space for what he was about to say.

'Look. What if we just defined the spiritual aspect of human nature as the need to belong – be it at some cosmological, biological, or social level. What people call spiritual experiences usually involve a sudden feeling of being supernaturally connected

140

in some way, right? White light, a communion with God, a moment in which you suddenly comprehend the whole fucking universe. Whatever it is. But who knows about God or no God? And at the end of the day, who really knows anything about the workings of this thing we're in, called the universe for lack of a better word? No one. To me, that's a very lonely idea.'

He had watched Samson's face, registering the reaction to each word, the way a great performer constantly reads his audience, testing its weather.

'What we *do* know is that we are all in this together. So what if it were possible to ease the terror of it by experiencing one another's consciousness? In a very controlled way, like sharing a memory.'

He had paused, letting Samson absorb the information.

'See, science is about sharing. The reason we want to quantify is so we can communicate and share more clearly. The more carefully I can define something, the better I'm able to share it. So if a guy tells me, "I've just seen the light," and I don't know what he's talking about, then I can't share that. But if he gets me to have the same experience, that begins to be science.'

Samson had felt that he was starting to understand, that the picture was coming into focus. 'So this whole project, finding a way to transfer memories, has to do with a hope that those sorts of moments can be shared?'

'Yes, but it's more than that. The reason I became a scientist – I was a doctor, remember, but from the beginning I was moving toward pure science – was because I wanted to ease the yearning. My own to begin with, but it was clear to me I wasn't the only one. People – physicists, whatever – will tell you we're all tuned into the universe, to something greater than ourselves. What I say is, why can't we try to share, at the deepest possible level, that distant connection? What I'm saying is, *why can't we get inside each other's heads?* From time to time, to get out of ourselves and into someone else. Simple idea, but the ramifications are extraordinary. The possibility for *true* empathy – imagine how it would affect human relations. It's enough to keep you awake at night.' Ray grinned. His teeth were perfect. 'Or to send you out to the desert.'

They had sat in silence as Ray watched him. Samson averted his gaze and looked out at the view. He tried to keep his mind from racing, to allow the immensity of all Ray was proposing to sink in. He imagined having Anna's memories of himself transferred into his mind: to feel what it was to be *her* remembering *him*. To experience what it was to remember himself.

'We're not so unalike, you and I,' Ray had finally said. Samson straightened up in his chair and met the doctor's eyes. 'Are we, Samson?'

He fumbled in the dark for the telephone on the hall table. As it rang on the other end, he remembered that it was three hours later in New York and that Anna was probably asleep. He liked the idea of waking her, the intimacy of a late-night intrusion, her voice soft and unprotected. But when it continued to ring and no one picked up he began to wonder what she was doing out so late, or even if she was sleeping elsewhere. The thought agitated him, and he tried to remember if during the past weeks she had mentioned anyone, a man who might have begun to slip effortlessly into her life in the space he'd left behind. He hung up and dialed again, but no one answered. He was about to try a third time when a door opened and Ray came out wearing a pair of pale blue pajamas.

'You all right?'

'Yes. Sorry if I woke you.'

'Not at all, I'm a light sleeper. A slight breeze and I'm up.'

Samson looked down at the phone in his hands and replaced it in the cradle. 'I was just calling . . . I thought maybe Anna – my wife – was home. We're separated now. She asked me to call when I got here.'

'Did you get through?'

'No one answered. I'm just a little worried—' Samson glanced down at his watch in an attempt to appear convincing. 'It's late there.'

Ray nodded. A few seconds passed and then he said, 'Give her time. Give yourself time. It's a tragic thing to lose someone, whatever the circumstances.

But it's amazing how resilient people are. Sure, it's hard to believe now, but one day you'll both wake up and realize it's all right. You'll open your eyes, and maybe the light will strike you in a certain way, and you'll sit up and think to yourself, *okay.*'

'It's harder for her.'

'Maybe so. But you shouldn't underestimate the stress you're under. Even if you're the one who decided to leave, it doesn't mean you're not allowed to feel sad. Anyone would. Sad and confused, I'm sure.'

He was grateful for Ray's generosity, for the sage calm that could only have been the solid remainder of so much experience.

'Well, I'm glad you're up,' Samson said. 'I wanted to tell you that I've thought it over and I've decided to do it.'

Ray grinned and balled his fists in the air. 'Terrific! That's fucking great news, Samson. You don't know how pleased you've made me. You'll see – what we're doing out there is just *extraordinary.*' His gaze was brilliant, piercing. Finally he glanced down at the phone. 'What do you say we try calling her in the morning, huh?'

Samson nodded.

'Just terrific,' Ray repeated, then turned and retreated to his room, calling good night behind him.

Samson stood by the bedroom window looking down at the dark swimming pool. The longing he felt was a sense of missing that had not occurred to him yet, though he could not say exactly whom or what he longed for, whether it was his wife or Lana or something else entirely, something much larger that he couldn't name. A long time passed before he lay down on the bed and closed his eyes. In his mind he walked like an ascetic across the scorched emptiness. He resolved to go further, to give up more. He drew a blank and clutched his knees to his chest and in the morning he woke like that.

Once they were outside the city limits Ray shifted into fifth gear and did eighty miles an hour, chewing on pumpkin seeds from his pockets and spitting the shells out the window. He called out the names of the tortured vegetation along the road, greasewood, sage, the first stunted Joshua trees with crooked arms that once pointed believers through the desert.

They stopped at a stand with wind chimes that sold cacti and other succulents. A college-aged kid with a red baseball cap told tourists who bought the baby potted plants, *water it once a month*, knowing the souvenir succulent would be dead in the cup holder no more than a few days into their trip, baked and dehydrated.

The plant stand was next to an Arco, and Ray filled up with gas while Samson called Anna from a pay phone. He caught her just as she was leaving for the park. A friend, an amateur ornithologist, was taking her to see the red-tailed hawks that nested in a window ledge above Fifth Avenue. There was a row of hard-core enthusiasts with telescopes who did round-the-clock surveillance.

'Were you with him last night?'

'What do you mean?'

'I called and no one answered. I thought maybe—'

'I was probably asleep. I'm a sound sleeper, and the phone is in the living room, remember? I didn't hear it.'

'Oh. But I would understand if there's someone else . . .'

She didn't reply, and he was unsure of the meaning of her silence.

'How is it?' she asked. He pictured her in the kitchen, wrapping the extra cord around her wrist.

'Fine. We just left L.A. I'm calling you from' – he glanced at a road sign – 'Lancaster. I'm basically already standing in the Mojave.'

'The Mojave? I thought Dr Malcolm was in L.A.'

Ray smiled from the car and waved.

'He was. I can't talk for long, Annie. Ray's waiting.' He paused, confused. 'Where did I get that? Did I ever call you that?'

Silence. 'No.'

'You don't like it.'

'No, I do. It's what my brother used to call me.' Samson couldn't remember a brother, a man who shared her eyes or mouth. That Anna had never mentioned her brother made Samson jealous, as if he were an old lover whose photograph she'd kept.

'I'll call you something else,' he said quickly. 'What I was going to say is that his research team

147

works out of a ranch in the desert. There's a lab there, facilities. About three hours from L.A.' Built in the 1940s as a spa, Ray had said, a failed attempt by a tycoon to attract the rich for the curative effects of the semiarid climate. Mineral baths from the salts of dry lake beds. Open spaces, rugged mountains, wildflowers. Abandoned for years before they found the daughter who owned the deed, a schoolteacher in San Jose. The laboratory now named after the failed spa, Clearwater.

Samson watched something translucent, a scorpion, scuttle across the packed earth.

'It's way out in the desert. The nearest town is military.'

He waited for Anna to speak. In the last month, while he was still in New York, she had seemed to be trying to distance herself, not to become estranged but to give up the desire she'd felt, like a constant pressure, since he'd disappeared. For months after the operation she had nightmares, things she wouldn't vocalize. Dreams inside of dreams, she said, so that she didn't know if she was waking or asleep. She seemed to be struggling against it now, against being dragged back into all she felt for him, against the desire to save him.

'What exactly is the nature of the research anyway?' she finally asked. 'You think it will help you remember?'

She had channeled it back into her work. She spent late nights at the center; she took in paranoid schizophrenics and psychotics and served them juice in Dixie cups. She trained the staff. *Never get between them and the door.*

'No, it's not really like that. Mostly he wants to study my mind.'

'I better run, I'm already late. Is there a telephone number?' she asked.

'I'll call when I get there.' He paused while a truck pulled out onto the highway. 'Anna, this guy – Ray. He's advancing our knowledge of the mind, talking about things we never thought were possible. There's something . . . I don't know . . . *noble* about it.'

'I'm sure. Dr Lavell said he's brilliant, right? If you're interested in what he's doing and can be a part of it, that's great.' When she'd picked up the phone the crisp nearness of her voice had surprised him, but now she sounded vague and distant. 'Just take care of yourself, okay?'

The scorpion came back and scurried off in the opposite direction, tail arched. A recorded operator broke through the line, warning that he had a minute left and the call would soon be terminated.

'My card is running out—' He had wanted to tell her about what he'd felt last night. Not about Lana, but about the feeling, which had quickly moved on from the slender, frenetic girl to become pure desire, spreading out like a blot of ink on paper.

'Samson?'

'Yes?'

'If you want to know, you used to call me

Annabelle,' she said quickly before they hung up. 'You added things to the end. Annabear. Silly things like that.'

When Samson got back in the passenger seat Ray handed him a granola bar and a lotto ticket.

'Scratch out those little squares. If you get three the same you win.' Samson scratched at the silver wax with his fingernail.

'Pay phone romance?' Ray asked, looking over his shoulder.

'My wife.' There were two pairs but the fifth was a dud.

'Ahhh,' Ray said, 'no luck.'

There was a movie, Samson thought, a black comedy, where Ray would be cast as God. Beneficent. All-knowing.

Without memories to cloud it, the mind perceives with absolute clarity. Each observation stands out in stark relief. In the beginning, when there's not yet a smudge, the slate still blank, there is only the present moment: each vital detail, shocked color, the fall of light. Like film stills. The mind relentlessly open to the world, deeply impressed, even hurt by it; not yet gauzed by memory.

Samson explained this to Ray. They turned off the highway onto a two-lane blacktop stained with motor oil. A cinder cone rose up, prehistoric, in the distance. He explained how sometimes one or another of his hands suddenly fell numb. Cut off from his heart. He could say such things to Ray, a doctor with knowledge and compassion who wanted to help. A man who had dedicated his life to science, who understood the discipline of renunciation. Giving it up all at once or bit by bit. The religiousness of it. The blood only getting as far as his elbows but not reaching his hands. He told Ray about his own project, having woken up to emptiness, the thrill of giving up more, to renounce home and wife, a whole city, to give up and give up until there was nothing left at all.

And then? Ray asked.

There were dirt roads with wheel ruts that turned off toward the mountains. One valley over, there were still track marks from General Patton's tanks. On the moon – he read this in a book – a footstep will last intact for two million years. No wind. There were fossils on the desert floor, the impressions of Pleistocene fish preserved rib by tiny rib. The absence more beautiful than the vanished fish.

And then? Once you've given up everything, Ray asked again, excitedly tapping the wheel, pushing ninety now, *don't you have to set down the first mark?*

It was a conversation they had over and over until Ray finally exploded a bomb in his head. At that moment, though, they were hurtling into nowhere, and though Samson didn't yet know what Ray really meant, he somehow felt understood.

Soon it was only the flat earth on all sides. *The*

desert is a hunger artist, he remembered Ray saying; *it renounces everything*. Later he was never sure that Ray had ever really said it; sometimes it was like Ray was right inside his head.

'Hey, you want a picture of me?' Donald was wearing a pilled flannel bathrobe and had his arms crossed tightly over his gut as if he was about to flash. 'How come you don't want a picture? You saying I'm not good-looking?'

'You want me to take a picture?'

'I'm saying.'

Samson lifted his camera and focused. 'Tell me when,' Donald said, planting his feet like a batter taking his stance.

'Okay: one, two—'

Donald pulled open the bathrobe and grinned. He was wearing a pair of white boxer shorts printed all over with red lipstick marks. There were elastic sock marks around his shins, the legs thin and ropy beneath the bulky girth around his middle, as if the body parts belonged to different lives.

'Heh.' If Donald laughed too hard it triggered a coughing fit in his lungs. It was a risk each time and mostly he just made a shallow, wheezy grunt in the back of his throat. 'That's gonna be a prize. Show me when you get it back.'

Samson breathed on the lens and wiped it with a special cloth, removing stray dust particles. He fussed and polished and sprayed it with compressed air, listening to Donald hum in the bathroom. Steam rising as Donald tested the temperature of the water, fogging the mirrors. He hadn't taken the picture but it wouldn't have mattered since he never developed the film anyway. He felt that there was an asceticism, a lawfulness about it: composing images that remained invisible as long as they were kept from the light.

They were living in the old bathhouse now converted into pleasant rooms, himself and Donald Selwyn, who owned property outside Las Vegas. For the moment the land was still nothing, a wasteland of desert.

'The way I figure,' said Donald, eternal lounge lizard, positioning his face in front of the air conditioner, 'it's gonna be worth millions. We're talking the fastest-growing city in the country. Eventually it's gotta reach me.'

He had a mat of hair on his chest and arms, enough for a sweater. He coughed, a deep, phlegmy hack. He was in his sixties and in poor health, and Samson refrained from mentioning the obvious flaw in Donald's plan, the unlikelihood of his living to enjoy the windfall.

Meals were served in the dining hall, with glass doors that opened to a landscaped garden of cactus, Indian paintbrush, and ocotillo. A maid came to their rooms every day to change the towels, make the bed, and fold the end of the toilet roll into a neat V. The old wooden signs had been repainted and the buildings were still referred to by their original names – the Bathhouse, the Sauna – like sinister euphemisms, as if the spa were fronting for an illegal operation. There was minimal security, only a lazy guard swatting flies in a booth: the only thing marking the entrance aside from a small sign and an unceremonious cow grate. Anyone who accidentally happened upon the place would guess it was a discreet health resort, well hidden, the sort with poor signage and an elite clientele.

The research team – neuroscientists, neuro-psychologists, computer scientists, engineers, and lab technicians – worked in a thirty-thousand-square-foot laboratory kept slightly warmer than a meat locker, powered by a huge generator. These were people who had left their universities and state-of-the-art hospitals and come out to the desert, following the stream of speculators who had come for silver, gold, and tungsten, for casinos and cattle, for prospective spas. People who believed in the power of science the way others before them had believed in the wrath of God.

They lived in bungalows with backyards that butted up against the mountains. On the week-ends, to alleviate the occupational hazard of compulsively picturing their own brains at work, they grilled steak and ate coleslaw, watched their children play in the sprinklers, iridescent rainbows forming above their sopping heads. *If* there were children: many of them had come alone, leaving husbands and wives and significant others who had careers of their own, city dwellers who thought of the desert as something you drive through to get to other cities. It was an intimate group and when they socialized they tried to avoid the subject of memory. They had SUVs they took into the rugged mountains, scree crunching under the wheels that occasionally went flat, at which point the men rolled up their sleeves while the women lined their thumb and finger up with the scale in the map's legend and measured how many miles to the nearest service station.

Donald could do impersonations. He scuffed his feet around on the floor, got down in a stance, and said, 'Who am I?' He took on the whole body, not just the face and voice. He grabbed an invisible microphone, swiveled and dipped. He lugged a lame leg around, crouched and flicked an air cigar.

The nearest town was called Hillcrest, one of those single-purpose towns, sprung up in the middle of nowhere with a suspicious water source. Ray told Samson that Clearwater's food and other supplies were trucked in weekly from Los Angeles: bottles of Perrier, fresh baguettes, coffee, freeze-packed salmon. People from the lab went into the town out of boredom, to poke around the Wal-Mart and the Christian Fellowship charity shop. This was a town that came to a grinding halt for the playing of taps. People stalled at the crosswalk saluting the sun going down in a nuclear sky. *Day is done, gone the sun.* Post-Cold War, the town was advertising itself as an oasis for retirement: high-desert elevation, three hundred and fifty days of sunshine a year, no smog, thirty-five churches, community events, gateway to unlimited recreation sites. Snugly fit into the crook of the navy's single largest landholding, seventeen hundred square miles of missile testing ground. *All is well, safely rest, God is nigh—*

He was there but he could leave at any moment.

Donald was an Input, one of a group of paid volunteers who had been elected to donate a specific memory that had been chosen and agreed upon by both themselves and Clearwater Labs, the neural patterns, the firing synapses, axon-to-dendrite, distilled into billions of shards of data and stored in gigabytes. The Input leaving in a hired car with a generous check.

Donald hacked and looked around for a place to spit.

'What I'm saying is you take the fastest-growing city in America, and eventually it's gonna hit a certain target. If I bought ten miles closer I woulda had to pay more per acre, but there woulda been less time to wait. In the end I was willing to wait the extra ten miles. Bigger payback.' He rubbed two fingers together. 'More moola, if you catch my drift.'

Donald could do Jack Nicholson, Wayne Newton, Marlon Brando. In the shower he could do Elvis. 'This one's easy,' he told Samson, then stripped down, turned on the water, and began to bellow. They were not so entertaining for their likeness (it took Samson a long time to identify them, and often he couldn't, a shortcoming that Donald attributed to his memory *problem*) as for the live power they lent to Donald's otherwise placid face. 'You lookin' at me?' Donald said, pulling an invisible gun out of the stretched-out waistband of his pants.

It was five P.M. and Donald was bored, having already scouted the Clearwater pool for any young blood. There was a smattering of teenage daughters with stringy hair who were bused out to schools with Indian names on the weekdays, girls so desperate for something to happen that they might have condescended to talk to Donald. He kept interrupting Samson's reading, which consisted of the new issue of *Time* – he had mostly gotten bored of *People*. Donald was trying to convince him to split a taxi to Vegas. He insisted they could get there in time for a show.

'Whad'ya want, magic? You want girls? You name it. Whad'ya want, live animals?'

Samson turned the page.

'We go for the night and we're back by lunch.

158

They won't even know we're gone. Whada they care? We signed our papers.'

Samson had signed a nondisclosure agreement Ray had given him when he got to Los Angeles, and a form giving the Clearwater Labs permission to study his brain, but that was all.

'Lemme guess: you've never been to Vegas. See, we gotta spread the word. Educate people about the good life, the low cost of living. Not the things they heard of, the poker and the strippers, but the eighteen-hole golf courses and good schools, the goddamn indoor ice rink. We're talking a city that has wired the trees with *ultrasonic systems* so no birds will land and shit on innocent people. Remember, you heard it from me: the city is gonna grow to something unbelievable. The biggest city on earth. Putting the whole goddamn China issue to rest. It's a question,' Donald said from where he was lying spread-eagle on the bed, 'of simonizing the masses.'

'Galvanizing,' Samson said, turning the page of his magazine.

'What?'

'*Galvanizing* the masses.'

'Sure, Sammy, whatever you say.'

There was something in Donald's voice that made Samson look up from the page he was reading. When their gaze met he noticed Donald's eyes for the first time, watery and pale blue, in a certain light almost colorless. Their eyes locked and Donald blinked. They were the hungry eyes of a dog that missed nothing, eyes that had gone so light as to avoid the question entirely of whether they were under the power of some darkness.

'I'm gonna call you Sammy, you mind?' The name, like all nicknames, a small plea for the familiar. 'Whad'ya say to that plan, Sammy, we call a taxi and in an hour we're in Vegas.'

'I don't think so. I think I'll just read tonight.'

'Sure, Sammy, okay.'

There wasn't much to do in Clearwater. There was a rec room for the kids and sometimes the lab technicians played a few rounds of mindless Ping-Pong that quickly turned competitive. There was a VCR and a big-screen TV and a small library of movies. A satellite dish beamed in a selection of four hundred channels, half of them in Spanish. The porn channels, Donald reported, had been blocked off.

'Can I ask you something, Sammy?' Donald piped up after a few minutes.

'Yes.'

'What happened to your—' He tapped his head.

'I had a tumor. It was benign but it damaged my memory. There are about twenty-four years I don't remember.' Even as he said it, it seemed like something that had happened to someone else, to one of the celebrities in the magazines he read who seemed to be forever surviving tragedies – leaps out of windows, high-impact car crashes – the experience of which they claimed to channel back into their art.

160

'Jeez.' Donald sucked the air and sat up, swinging his varicose-veined legs over the side of the bed. 'Nothing came back?'

'Not really. When they found me – actually it wasn't far from here – I didn't know my own name. But after the tumor was removed the memories from my childhood returned. I remember up to when I was twelve.' It was a story he'd told countless times, now whittled down to a few phrases; a story that, like all true stories, lost something with each telling.

'I'm trying to think,' Donald said.

Outside the light had turned the color of fired bricks, filing in through the window slats. If there were a cloud in the sky the sunset would be beautiful; that was the basic rule, Ray had said, the light needing something to reflect off of.

'You had a family?'

'My wife.'

'You had no idea?'

'I didn't remember her.'

'And now?'

'We're friends.'

Donald rubbed the area of his chest above the heart, making a scratching noise in the hair. 'You loved her before, I'm guessing?'

'Yes, I'm sure I did. She's very lovely: I think it wasn't perfect, but from what I understand we loved each other.'

'It's like you're talking about someone else, Sammy. Like you're a goddamn third party, you don't mind my saying. Makes me think how lonely for her. One day you're making love to her and the next thing, *wham*, she's a total stranger.'

'It *was* worse for her in a way. But it's been almost eleven months since I woke up and saw her face and there's a way in which I love her now.'

'If you loved her once you can love her again.'

'It's not that easy.'

'It never is.'

Donald stood up and started to dress, laying his clothes out on the bed as if packing for a cruise.

'And you? Married?'

Donald held up three fingers. 'Three times. The first time I was too young and the last time too old. A twenty-five-year-old; it lasted four months.'

'And in between—'

Donald buttoned up a blue Hawaiian shirt, then stuck his hand under the collar and rubbed his chest. It seemed to be what he did when something moved or unsettled him. 'It's a long story. Whad'ya say I tell you on the way.'

'I'm not going.'

Donald pulled his socks up and shrugged. 'Suit yourself.'

He swept the coins off the night table and pocketed them, picked up a key chain with enough keys for a small fleet of cars, for an entire retirement community of luxury homes with the desert beginning in the backyard.

'Why all the keys?'

Donald held them up and jiggled them, watching how the light hit the metal. He smiled, threw them in the air, and caught them.

'Over the years, a man acquires.'

He ran a comb through his wet, iron-gray hair. Just to look at him, there was something distinguished in his face.

'Okay, last chance . . .'

Samson shook his head. 'Have fun though.'

Donald strode across the room and opened the door. The light flooded across the floor.

'Don't say I never told you, Sammy. The biggest city. A regular Shanghai.'

The day after he'd arrived, Ray had given him a tour of the lab. He'd introduced him to whomever they passed, head scientists, technicians, engineers. 'This is Samson Greene. We're going to be studying him for Output,' Ray had said, and men and women in white coats had stopped what they were doing and risen to greet him. Ray knew them all by name. He looked over their shoulders at their work, answered questions, made jokes, solved problems. He moved lightly, all spring and bounce, as if under the governance of a different gravity. Samson followed him down the hallways, through hushed, ever-cool rooms. They passed a wall of glass behind which a technician wearing white cotton gloves sat among a chaotic mass of electrical wire and metal boxes, scrolling through numbers on a screen.

'What's that?' Samson asked.

'Looks like something a crackpot built in his basement, right?'

'Sort of.'

'It's a supercomputer. The thing links thousands of microprocessors on a lightning-fast network. Each processor has about five gigs of RAM running on a 4GHz memory bus. The CPUs clock at just over three gigahertz, so the whole cluster can handle around ten teraOPS when it's load-optimized. You probably don't know what any of that means, but it'd blow your mind if you did. Astonishing power. Costs a fucking fortune just to keep it cool.'

Ray tapped lightly on the glass, but the technician didn't look up. 'He can't hear me. The man is beyond language. Working in a different sphere.' Ray tapped one more time and then, as if on cue, the technician's screen faded to black and a three-dimensional brain appeared revolving through space, so vivid it was more real than real itself, glowing signals of activity pulsing across its lobes, a mind going through the motions of thinking detached from all consequence, without blood or breath or beating heart to guide it. It made Samson weak in the knees. He watched it spin in its own orbit, the awesome spectacle of a brain *remembering*, and everything Ray had described to him high above Los Angeles condensed into fact and he understood, in an electric shock of comprehension, that he had come to the desert to hail in the future. His breath fogged the glass.

'It's freezing in here,' he said, feeling goose bumps rise on his arms.

'Goddamn polar,' said Ray.

He went into the lab every day for them to study his brain. They put him in a chamber with Ping-Pong ball halves taped over his eyes, slathered conducting cream onto his scalp, and fit a helmet over his head. They closed the five-hundred-pound steel door and he sat alone in the dark, thinking. He listened to the instructions that came through the speakers. There was a certain thrill in being the subject of such intimate attention: to know that on the other side of the steel walls a team of scientists was tuned in, tracing the currents of his mind, the migrations of his thoughts across the hemispheres of his brain. Sometimes they came in to fix a loose electrode. They put their hands on his head like a benediction.

Other days he inhaled something radioactive, then lay in the bowels of a machine that took pictures of the gamma radiation of positrons colliding with electrons as the substance moved through his cerebrum. Later they showed him the images, but though he studied them closely, he could find no sign of the empty field that he had returned to again and again for refuge since he had woken into his life. Once, coming out of the cool, dark lab into the heat of the desert sun, he'd briefly wondered if the emptiness he'd been so staunchly guarding was, not the absence of memory, but actually a memory itself: a recollection of the blazing white potential that had existed before he was born. The emptiness an infant possesses in the very first moments, when consciousness begins like the answer to a question never asked.

When he wasn't needed in the lab, he hiked in the hills behind the laboratory with a field guide, identifying plants and animal tracks, finding rocks scored by glaciers, each day going a little farther and marking his trail with stones. He didn't know what had brought him to the desert the first time – or if it even *had* been the first time when the police picked him up, a man without a past walking half-dead in the noonday sun. Very likely he had arrived by accident, but if so, when the last stand of houses fell away and he found himself in such an expanse of emptiness, it must have relieved him to drift in a landscape that did not aggravate his mind but surpassed it in oblivion. He might have gone weak with gratitude to at last meet the scorched face of his own mind. Or maybe along with all memory his ego itself had been obliterated, so that he could no longer distinguish between himself and the world, and, reaching the desert, it was as if he passed clean into it. Maybe the look on his face the police officers had taken for blank was the ecstasy of absolute freedom, of becoming only weather. And then, just before he had dissolved into nothing, they had pulled him back by a thread, and he had woken again in the locked box of his mind, conscious of a clock on the wall that read 3:30.

At night he sometimes visited Ray in his office. He would find the doctor staring at the computer, lost in thought. At all other times Ray was keenly aware, a man who'd always sensed he was more intelligent than the rest, who'd learned to direct what was happening around him almost imperceptibly. It pleased Samson to find him so unguarded; it made him feel closer to him. Once when he'd come in Ray had been silent for a long time, so long that Samson began to wonder whether he'd noticed him enter.

'Ray?'

The doctor turned. 'Samson. Sorry, I'll just finish up this e-mail. Letter to a colleague of mine in San Diego,' Ray said, fingers rattling across the keys. 'Odd guy. Knows everything about the hippocampus. The world expert on the hippocampus. Knows more about a ridge located on the lateral ventricles of the brain than he does about his own kids.' He leaned back and hit a key with a pianist's flourish. 'There. Finished.' He motioned to the chair on the other side of his desk. 'Sit down, Samson. I'm glad you came by. I was thinking about something this afternoon and you came to mind.'

'Thinking about what?'

'The old thoughts. The whole subject of loneliness.'

167

'What, you think I'm lonely?'

'Are you?'

Samson shrugged. Some jazz was playing low from Ray's stereo, and it reminded him of Anna as he had come across her once, humming and swaying barefoot to a plaintive saxophone coming from the radio. He studied a paperweight on Ray's desk, a starfish suspended in glass. 'I suppose you don't get very lonely,' he said, 'what with so many people around you all the time, with the whole team working together.'

'Me? I've been lonely my whole life. For as long as I can remember, since I was a child. Sometimes being around other people makes it worse.'

'Really? Because it always seems . . .' Ray looked at him, waiting. 'Anyway, what about your wife? Didn't you say you were married?'

'When you're young, you think it's going to be solved by love. But it never is. Being close – as close as you can get – to another person only makes clear the impassable distance between you.'

Samson hefted the paperweight and paused to think of how his great-uncle Max used to take him to the pool at the local Y, how he would tread water and float on his back while Max did leg lifts in the water, talking to him about love. He spoke to Samson as if he were an old crony, one of the liver-spotted survivors in to do a few asthmatic laps, to exert a last burst of prowess, a man withered by exposure to the elements. He had been barely twelve. *Love*, Max would say, his gnarled toes breaking the surface, *love is the goal of the species. Not shtuping. Shtuping you can do anytime. It's love that's not so easy to find,* lowering the left foot as the right floated up in a regiment of European bathhouse calisthenics.

He put the paperweight down and looked at Ray. 'I don't know. If being in love only made people more lonely, why would everyone want it so much?'

'Because of the illusion. You fall in love, it's intoxicating, and for a little while you feel like you've actually become one with the other person. Merged souls, and so on. You think you'll never be lonely again. Only it doesn't last and soon you realize you can only get so close, and you end up brutally disappointed, more alone than ever, because the illusion – the hope you'd held on to all those years – has been shattered.'

Ray stood up and walked to the window, and Samson marveled again at the starched clothes, the linen sleeves neatly cuffed at the elbows, the pants with razor creases, a man untouched by weather.

'But see, the incredible thing about people is that we forget,' Ray continued. 'Time passes and somehow the hope creeps back and sooner or later someone else comes along and we think *this is the one*. And the whole thing starts all over again. We go through our lives like that, and either we just accept the lesser relationship – it may not be total understanding, but it's pretty good – or we keep trying for that perfect union, trying and failing, leaving behind us a trail of broken hearts, our own included. In the end, we die as alone as we were born, having struggled to understand others, to make ourselves understood, but having failed in what we once imagined was possible.'

'People really want that, what did you say, merging souls? Total union?'

'Yes. Or at least they think they do. Mostly what they want, I think, is to feel *known*.'

'But don't you think that being alone is somehow' – Samson struggled for the right word – 'I don't know, *good?*' He thought of Anna dancing in her underwear, her T-shirt falling just at her hips. Anna looking out the window, on her face an expression he'd never seen, the trace of some part of her that remained unattainable. 'That to love someone is one thing, but if it means giving up the part of you that's alone and free—'

'That's just it!' Ray shouted. 'How to be alone, to remain free, but not feel longing, not to feel imprisoned in oneself. *That*' – he stabbed the air with his index finger – 'is what interests me.'

Ray hurried over and pulled his chair next to Samson's. He leaned in, his face so close that Samson felt the need to draw his head back to preserve the few inches that served as an unspoken barrier, a small margin of difference uncrossed except for intimacy. As much as he liked Ray, as much as he wanted to be personal with him, the sudden closeness set him on edge.

'You're such an unusual case,' Ray continued. If he noticed Samson's discomfort, he didn't let on. 'Not just what happened to you, not just your condition, but your *response* to having lost your memory. You chose freedom. Instinctively you chose it. Just left it all behind and headed out into a new life.'

'I had a tumor—'

'Okay, sure, but afterward. You didn't want it back. You just turned it all away. No ties binding you to anyone. It must have been – it must *be* – exhilarating. And now you're dealing with the consequences. The loneliness. I know. From the beginning I could see it. That first day, when I picked you up at the airport, I could see it in your face.'

Samson raised his fingers to his face, as if he could feel what secrets he had given away, things Ray had read in his expressions that he didn't even know himself.

Ray talked and he listened. The arid heat that dulled Samson's own thoughts seemed to concentrate Ray's into perfect, terse structures, purified of all excess. It was at once captivating and unnerving, the ease and grace with which he spoke, as if he had rehearsed it before, and yet there was nothing unspontaneous about it. If anything, Ray seemed gifted at being able to seize the moment. He spoke of human solitude, about the intrinsic loneliness of a sophisticated mind, one that is capable of reason and poetry but which grasps at straws when it comes to understanding

171

another, a mind aware of the impossibility of absolute understanding. The difficulty of having a mind that understands that it will always be misunderstood.

'The misery of other people is only an abstraction,' Ray insisted, 'something that can be sympathized with only by drawing from one's own experiences. But as it stands, true empathy remains impossible. And so long as it is, people will continue to suffer the pressure of their seemingly singular existence.'

'And mistreat each other, won't they?'

Ray nodded. 'Horrendously.'

The low jazz played on, and outside, the desert was Ray's stage. When Samson finally left, stumbling back to the Bathhouse in the pitch-dark, he felt a little thrill in the pit of his stomach, a rising of goose bumps on his skin that was not only because of the fierceness of the stars and the chill in the air. Despite everything Ray had said, he felt the doctor understood him, and that he in turn had witnessed something like another man's mind laid bare.

Samson ran the hot water in the bathtub. The nights were still cold once the sun set, and he lowered himself an inch at a time into scalding water, each new level of submersion happening before he was ready, the water a hot itch, a small punishment to clear the way for comfort. The water dissolved the day's sweat and dust. Silver bubbles like mercury formed on his skin, the skin taking on a green hue under the water, making it look rubbery and inhuman. Droplets of sweat beaded on his forehead. His whole body in, he squeezed his eyes shut and slipped his head under, and in the hot, muffled silence he would hear his waterlogged pulse. He stayed like that, holding his breath for as long as he could, and when his head broke the surface he blinked and gasped. He leaned forward and rubbed the steam on the mirror, and slowly his face began to take shape.

It was a fine face, nothing unusual, only a little rugged from the sun; a face that no one would look away from in displeasure. He hadn't shaved for a few days – he still found the habit awkward – but despite the shadow of growth it was still the face of a man who wouldn't be averse to helping an old lady cross the street. Who, feeling her bulky handbag against his hip, might imagine making off with it only to discomfort himself with his proximity to the barbarians. A face not puffed out by drugs or heavy drinking, the healthy face of a thirty-seven-year-old (a birthday come and gone) who ate generously from the five food groups and exercised regularly, evidence being membership to the West Side Racquet Club and the profusion of grayish gym socks and nylon shorts with the built-in underwear perforated for air circulation that he had found in his bottom dresser drawer. There seemed to be a belief that one's face reflected certain qualities of one's inner life. He tried to come to terms with this now, to claim the face as his own. Since he first saw it in the hospital mirror, his face had been like someone who was following him, attempting an impression of himself.

A fine face. If not that of a hero, then of a man who had the potential for passing the endurance tests and the grueling training needed before blastoff and moon walk. Though now the moon was nothing, he'd learned, provincial, and it was Mars that constantly made the news. Just recently he'd read in *Time* magazine that the Global Surveyor orbiting Mars had sighted gullies ending in fanlike deltas, suggesting a relatively recent water flow on the planet; water that had been on or near the surface only thousands, or even hundreds, of years ago, billions of years later than previous estimates. The news had been leaked to the press, and experts had talked on the condition they not be named. Nothing gushing or springing, they said, no rivers or hot springs, for goodness' sake, just the possibility of liquid water. And where there is water there could be life, they said, speaking from their homes, their words later quoted under images of the red surface marked with tiny furrows, flow marks, traces.

He had left New York barely a week ago, and already the city was receding, becoming another life that did not necessarily relate to what came before or after it. It was the thing he found most difficult to grasp: the sense of a continuum, where the world was not something that happened in shards, moments of illumination in the darkness of consciousness. Because it was not, despite what he'd said to Donald, that the twenty-four years between the last glimpse of childhood and waking under the hospital clock had been obliterated. On the contrary, they *existed:* empty, submerged in silence, filled with nothing but the distant thump of a pulse. There, there was only time – not as the waking-alive knew it, with a before and now and after, but time as endurance: *here, here, here.*

The water had gone cool and the fog retreated to the far corners of the mirror, left in patches like wisps of cloud after inclement weather. He stood up and dripped, the water only reaching his calves, wading water, water the level of a baby pool or a mildly threatening flood.

Donald's small suitcase was on the floor by his bed, decorated with colored decals from a host of American and Canadian cities. Samson hadn't seen the suitcase earlier and it almost brought tears to his eyes now, the unswerving optimism of the stickers, the pride and extroverted friendliness of the gesture. He half wished he had gone with Donald to Las Vegas and spent the night drinking tropical cocktails under a plastic palm tree, listening to him proudly recount his adventures in each city. If the stories were made up, if Donald had only bought the decals all at once, in a souvenir pack at a local gift shop, it hardly mattered. What mattered was listening to him. Somehow the stickers – reflective or transparent, illustrated with landmarks from Salt Lake City, Portland, Anchorage, Port Edwards, Phoenix – made him feel more compassionate toward Donald. It was as if he had come to Clearwater on a holiday. He thought about Donald's eyes: careful eyes that took in more than they expressed, eyes incongruous with the impersonations and the real estate. It occurred to him that he hadn't asked Donald what memory he was donating to science; what powerful and unforgettable image, what stream of neural firings to be used as the lab saw fit. He didn't even know how much Donald knew about the whole Clearwater project; neither one of them had mentioned it. From what Ray had told Samson, they were currently recording one of Donald's memories on a massive computer. The

176

team had already created the technology to read and record the brain's activity during the process of remembering, break the information down, then produce a map of its entire chemical and electromagnetic activity while experiencing the memory. What they were still working on was how to trigger another brain to perform the same functions – how to actually transfer a memory. Ray had asked Samson not to discuss what he'd been told; for all he knew, Donald knew nothing except that a memory of his was being recorded for the future.

He walked outside and waited for his eyes to adjust to the dark. If there was no moon, as there was not tonight, the stars went berserk, billions of them shuddering against the black. Sooner or later, in the corner of his eye, he would see a meteor streak past, hitting the atmosphere and burning up. A few months before, a meteor had lit up over the Yukon and pieces of black rock came down over Canada. A man, an ordinary layman, picked them up out of the snow, carbonaceous chondrite that he slipped in plastic kitchen Baggies and froze until the proper authorities could send someone to fetch them. Little hunks of the universe preserved next to deer meat in his freezer, until the snow melted and the UPS man could get through.

He found the path that passed the laboratory before it began to ascend into the hills, winding past the dark outlines of rock formation. At the top were a busted couch and a few chairs, most likely dragged up there by some kids who used it as a hangout when the place was still abandoned. He took out a pocket flashlight and directed the weak beam on the star chart he'd bought in town: a plastic disk with a rotating cardboard center notched with the hours and months and a map of the constellations.

He thought of the moment, during the last week of summer before the seventh grade, when he was lying on his back in the grass next to Jollie Lambird, moving his fingers toward her hand as she said, *Taurus, Pegasus, Cassiopeia,* knowing he could keep reaching as long as the list went on. When his fingers touched hers she whispered, *What sign are you?* His heart was pounding.

I don't know.

When were you born?

I'm trying to think, he wanted to say, give me time, and finally it came to him, *January 29.*

Aquarius.

Water Bearer, eleventh sign of the zodiac, the stars taking the shape of a man pouring water into a jar.

He shone the flashlight at the star chart and tried to find some connection between the flimsy rotating disk and the massive, breathing field of stars. It took a minute before the scattered lights focused into distinct groups, shapes that the ancients had seen as animals, hunters, and dippers. He sat down on the busted couch. A bat flew by, almost grazing his head. He thought about everything Ray had said to him over the past week. He could see the laboratory below and heard the distant hum of the generator. He thought about how he had arrived in such a strange and compelling place, all the unlikely events that had led up to this.

Then his thoughts returned to Jollie Lambird, to that night when he was twelve and nothing yet had happened.

What about you? What sign? He had her hand then, her cool fingers folded into his, and he moved his thumb gently across hers. He didn't care if he never spoke to anyone else in the world, as long as she was there, whispering, *Andromeda, Polaris.*

Leo.

He inched toward her until their sides were touching, arm to arm, leg to bare leg. *Sam?* she whispered. *Do you think* – This was Jollie Lambird, whom he had been in love with since the second grade, and he was ready to answer any question she might have for him. But he didn't hear the rest of it because just then he kissed her, a kiss that may have lasted for hours while porch lights shuddered and went out across the neighborhood. While stars themselves lit up or went out, stars that had not yet been given names by which to remember them. It was the last week of summer before the seventh grade, and afterward he walked her back to her house. He kissed her again, shyly and gently, now with the thrill of knowing that he had a small claim on her affections. He ran the rest of the way home, leaping over toys left lying in yards, over rosebushes and garden chairs, running through countless dark yards, his heart pounding in his chest, each step an exercise of joy, and that, really, was the very last he remembered, running through the dark before the world stopped, and in the empty silence all he could hear was the sound of his pulse.

onald came back the next day at noon. There was only one access road to Clearwater, a long dirt road lined with cottonwood trees, and Samson could see the trail of dust the taxi kicked up before it shuddered to a stop in front of the Bathhouse. He waited outside the door and watched Donald struggle out of the car, his shirt untucked, reaching for his wallet.

He shuffled past Samson without a word and flopped facedown on the bed.

'So?'

'Who am I?' he said into the pillow.

'How was Vegas?'

'I didn't go.'

'You didn't go to Vegas?'

'I'm telling you I didn't go.'

'Then where did you stay last night?'

He rolled over and grinned. 'Wouldn't ya like to know.'

'I would.'

'Give me a minute, will you, Sammy? I'm luxuriating.'

★　★　★

He had gone to see a friend of his called Lucky. That was the name she went by; it was a stage name first and then it was her name. He had meant to go to Vegas but then the taxi passed right by Lucky's place; he'd had no idea it was so close. She'd been happy to see him because the only people who visited her these days were truckers and military personnel.

'So what, you caught up on old times?'

'I guess you could call it that.'

'What do you mean, you guess?'

'Whad'ya mean, what do I mean? We. Caught. Up. On. Old. Times,' Donald said, thrusting his hips for punctuation.

'Donald.'

'Yeah?'

'*You went to a whore?*'

'No, Sammy. I went to see Lucky the human vacuum cleaner.' He pulled himself up from the bed. 'Of course I went to a whore.'

There was silence and then they both started to laugh, Samson rolling around on the bed, and Donald coughing and choking, leaning over as if he were going to hack his lungs up. They quieted down and then Donald gave a few dry, scraping wheezes and the whole thing started again.

When he'd finally gotten ahold of himself, Samson said, 'That cough sounds awful.'

'Toucha cancer. Nothing to get worked up about.'

'Really? God, how many packs a day did you used to smoke?'

Donald looked up at him and coughed some more. Finally he straightened up, his eyes tearing, a funny grin on his face.

'Would ya believe, I never smoked a day in my life.'

'You're a liar.'

'I kid you not. My old man smoked. What do I want with brown plaque on the teeth and a nicotine stench?' It was true: Donald was a remarkably hygienic man, taking a half hour each morning and night to complete his toilet of flossing, shining, scrubbing, spitting.

'The whole time I was in the army, not a goddamn puff.'

'I didn't know you were in the army.'

'Name one thing you know about me besides I got a mean cough, a whore named Lucky, and some prime property, whad'ya call it—' He paused for the right word, looking to Samson for help. 'Sounds like masturbating. The thing they do with babies born too early.'

'Incubating?'

'Right, some prime property *incubating* outside Vegas.'

'What do you know about *me* except that I lost my memory and I have a wife?'

'My point exactly. You could be a mass murderer. A regular Charles Manson. Who, one of those lab nerds tells me, used to hang around not far from here when he was waiting for helter-skelter.' Donald wiggled his fingers in the air and made popping eyes.

'I'm scared,' Samson said listlessly, propping up his pillows. 'So what did you do in the army?'

'I don't even know. It's been like a hundred years. I was maybe nineteen and I had a girl in California who I was crazy for.' He paused, thinking. 'You believe I don't even remember her name?'

Samson raised his eyebrows.

'I'm serious, that's terrible. Lemme think a minute and it'll come back to me. It was some movie-star kind of name. Very sexy. Anyway, I used to write this girl letters like you wouldn't believe and when I got some time off I went back to see her. I was nuts for her, so the first chance I get I hitchhike all the way to San Francisco, and when I get there I find her sister and the sister won't tell me where she is. So obviously I get a little hot under the collar.'

'That's understandable.'

'I would say so, having just come all that way, bouncing around and snorting diesel in the back of a pickup. So next thing I know, this guy walks out of the back room – the sisters were sharing a place – and he tells me Ruby – that's her name, Ruby Davis, for cryin' out loud, I'm not Alzheimer's yet. So he says Ruby's gone and she doesn't want to see me ever again. *Scram*, he says. I remember it like it was yesterday, the pathetic brown plants on the windowsill. And then I smash him across the jaw. Something comes over me and I smash him. Everybody's stunned for a minute and then I just walk out the door and turn the corner and that's the end of it. Except it isn't because to this day I still wonder what the hell I did that made her turn off me. We were gonna get married.'

'So what happened?'

'What happened is nothing. I came back here—'

'You were stationed near here?'

'Yeah. I came back here and when I had half a chance I got acquainted with some girls along the lines of Lucky.' Donald grunted so as not to upset his lungs again. 'I was green behind the ears. Boy did we have fun. I guess it was for the best in the end, what happened with Ruby. I might have spent my whole life unawares of certain' – he searched for the phrase – 'pleasures of the flesh.'

He struggled against the urge to call Anna. He wanted to hear her voice, to test out how it sounded in the hollow space of the desert, to perform his own experiments on the nature of absence. But something in him didn't want to give in to it, didn't want to admit to whatever else it was that made him want to call her. In the end he picked up the phone and dialed anyway. She wasn't home. It was nine o'clock at night in New York, too late for her to be at work and too early

185

for her to be asleep, which meant she was somewhere out in the glowing city.

Donald was needed in the laboratory about four hours each day. He sat in a room by himself, attached by electrodes to the supercomputer, the system they nicknamed the Catcher after the dream catchers the Indians wove out of string and feathers to catch nightmares in their webs, allowing only the good dreams to find their way through to the dreamer. Donald sat, dosed with sodium pentothal to increase the vividness of his mental images, and tried to concentrate on remembering the thing he had agreed to remember, while Ray observed him through mirrored glass and the engineers and scientists watched the data stream across their screens. One memory, a few moments that happened more than forty years ago, broken down into billions of binaries, one or zero. Often his mind wandered, and much of the cerebral white noise they recorded had to be discarded. He came back drained and exhausted, woozy from the drugs, limping for comic effect to hide the fact that he was shaken. After he'd showered and lain under the air conditioner long enough to recover a little, he strutted around grabbing invisible lapels and announced, in a high-pitched, mock English accent, his speech slightly slurred, that he had been chosen for the electro-magneticism of his neural patterns.

''Ello, old chap,' he said, passing the mirror. 'Just 'eard I was elected for my magnetic neurons.'

Billions of binaries, one or zero: simple as that. Like a game of Twenty Questions, an endless series of deductions performed to break down the world into its smallest parts. *Are you Samson Greene, one or zero? Is this your wife, one or zero? Do you love her? One or zero. We repeat the question: Do you love her, one or zero? The subject appears to be having difficulty answering. Is this a difficult question, one or zero?* Until the world is reduced to math and all the equations equal zero, and in the tremendous silence of that final moment they ask in a trembling voice, the only ones left: *Does the world exist? One or zero.* And the answer comes back, though there is no one left anymore to hear it, the digits on the clock rolling back to start again with nothing.

Donald slept the rest of the afternoon, his breath steady while his eyes fluttered across the images of his dreams. Samson watched a yellow column of dust whirl across the valley. He sat on the windowsill and watched it until it dissolved in the wind.

He wanted to ask Donald about the memory they had selected to record and transfer. The one part of Donald that would continue after he died, that might live as long as it took for Vegas to reach him. He had told Samson how he'd gone into the hospital about his lungs, and one of the doctors who saw him, a friend of Ray's who knew what he was looking for, called Ray up and said he had someone. From what Samson had gathered from

Ray, in the last year ten or fifteen people had been through Clearwater to donate a memory. The sort of Inputs Ray looked for were ordinary people who had witnessed radical things, people who had suddenly found themselves part of something greater than themselves.

But Samson didn't ask, and Donald never discussed the memory. Instead Donald made jokes about it, insisting that they were recording for posterity the moment of the biggest known orgasm of the twentieth century, experienced by a woman while under the touch of one Donald Selwyn, or that he was really the long-lost Elvis, that he was cutting a solo album of the silence in his head.

From time to time, Samson sensed an incandescent excitement pulse through the team, something they might have felt passing like a storm, disturbing their steady calculations. At such times, they seemed to move carefully around each other, as if it was shock weather, as if they might transfer electrical currents if they touched. He overheard them talking about it, a day in the future when, if everything went as planned, the journalists would be waiting at the gate. He imagined it, people scribbling notes, snapping photos of anyone who entered or left, scrambling over each other to point their enormous microphones in the direction of any noise. Recording the coyotes for atmosphere, talking on satellite phones to their superiors who sat in air-conditioned offices with two walls of glass. There had already been a few leaks to the press,

Ray said, false alarms that had brought vans with revolving antennas and a small band of Christian protesters or a traveling doomsday group. Word had gotten out, there were rumors in the scientific community, and someday in the future, whenever it happened, they would come in crowds and send back their stories in digital, while the anchors on the big networks hosted live panels of experts debating the philosophical and ethical consequences of their work, of memory transfer, or M.T., the complex process to which they had dedicated years of their lives already entombed in the colloquial as a set of initials. Samson imagined a press conference where Ray would answer questions in front of a makeshift backdrop with the blue and white Clearwater logo behind him, comfortable in front of the cameras, bantering with the journalists like a presidential candidate, a spokesman for the future, his watch glinting in the sun, age undetermined.

The press would be there to guide the public through it, allowing the news to settle over them in waves, helping them get accustomed to the idea, to absorb it into their daily routines of making the coffee, picking up the dry cleaning, getting the kids off to school. For the first week they would be able to turn on the television at any hour and it would be there, like a foreign-language immersion program. In the ensuing weeks, the media would continue to saturate them with special reports and expert panels, but each day with less frenzy. They would slowly wean the public off the special hour-long programs as the whole thing began to seem as run-of-the-mill as a heart transfer, even if it would be years before the technology was cheap and efficient enough to be made available to the public. Perhaps Ray would take the Nobel. Hollywood would already be at work on the movie, the final hurtle of total consumer absorption. The journalists, by then, would have long since packed up and left the desert, leaving behind empty cans and plastic forks and film canisters and crumpled napkins that caught in the tumbleweed and blew in the wind.

He called Anna again from a phone in one of the offices, and this time she answered. Her friend, the amateur ornithologist who was also, as it turned out, an architect, had taken her to an open rehearsal of a dance performance, and she told Samson how the choreographer had stood around in the spotlight talking into a microphone headset about the inspiration for the pieces, while the dancers limbered up and hung from their waists and lay around karate-chopping their thigh muscles onstage. It was late and the office was empty and silent except for the hum of the copier. He wanted to keep her on the line and when he ran out of things to ask her – about the weather and if she was sleeping well and how was Frank – he told her that he missed her. It surprised him, the words coming out without him first forming them in his head, words pressed up from his gut where he felt a gnawing desire to feel her skin and inhale her breath and feel the length of her body against his. She was silent on the other end, the great, vast, pin-dropping silence that only fiber optics can achieve, and he wondered if she was going to cry. But when she finally spoke her voice was clear and steady. She said it was nice to hear, but she wasn't sure if it was something they should talk about just now.

'But do you miss me?' he quietly insisted, drawing lines and arrows on a yellow legal pad by the phone.

'Samson,' she pleaded, her voice going breathy and failing at the end.

'I just want to know. If you don't, it's fine. I understand.'

'Please, Samson. Would it be enough to say that sometimes I still wake up crying?'

Immediately he felt mean and foolish for having pushed her.

'I'm sorry.'

'It's not a question of sorry. It happened and now we need to move on.'

'Sometimes I think—' he said, but didn't finish, because what he really wanted to do was turn off the overhead fluorescent light that was not a continuous, reliable light, but a light that his great-uncle Max once told him was made up of thousands of pulses per second, a sort of strobe light that was actually plunging him, every fraction of a second, into darkness. He wanted to shut it off and sit in the dark once and for all, to cup his hand over the phone and say, *Tell me, was I the sort of person who took your elbow when cars passed on the street, touched your cheek while you talked, combed your wet hair, stopped by the side of the road in the country to point out certain constellations, standing behind you so that you had the advantage of leaning and looking up?* – and so on with a list that would keep her talking through the night. But he didn't ask because he didn't know if he wanted the answers. It was better, he felt, had felt from the beginning, not to know. He only wanted to pose the questions, as if just caring enough to ask might give absolution.

'I have to go,' she said quietly. There was a long silence, a silence that they both breathed into until finally she said, 'Frank misses you,' and hung up. Frank, who possibly looked up when he heard his name, wondering why now, of all times, he had been summoned.

That week a letter also came from Lana, long and rambling, written in neat script on loose leaf torn out of a notebook. She was staying on in L.A. for the summer, had gotten a job working for a director, actually working at his house where he did all his editing, a house at the end of a long dirt road, built around an open courtyard, with tropical plants imported from Polynesia. Things were going okay with Winn, she wrote, although she had a crush on one of the guys she worked with, a sound engineer who played her samples of thunder and door slams and the shatter of plate-glass windows. He had recorded her picking up the phone, and whenever his computer ran into trouble there was the sound of a telephone ring and then her voice saying 'Hello?' It was a little confusing, she wrote, *I mean my feelings for him*, since she was pretty sure she loved Winn. *But how are you and what's going on with the research? Are you coming back to L.A.?* And at the end of the letter, just above the little heart she drew followed by her name, she scribbled *Call me*. He couldn't remember seeing her handwriting before, but the sight of the girlish letters caused a brief wrenching feeling in his stomach. Though he tried to understand his feelings for her, Samson couldn't say exactly what Lana meant to him; he only knew that she seemed to awaken in him something that must have been, for some time, asleep.

There were times when Samson himself felt the simmer of excitement: to be part of such an effort, at the frontier of science, moving among the people who would not only be remembered by history but whose work might alter the very nature of remembering and history. The days passed and he waited because he believed he was needed. Only much later, when it was already too late, would the terror of it occur to him: a future where memories could be hijacked, where the last, deepest region of privacy could be invaded and broadcast. Where memories could be loaded unwittingly into the mind of a man who has forgotten everything. Who else would make such a perfect host? Twenty-four years gone in an instant, creating a vacuum. It was this emptiness that Samson had first described to Lavell that had so interested Ray, keeping him up late after Lavell called him that October evening. It was the first time Ray had heard a loss of memory described like that, a tundra, a distance that could be crossed. But if Ray ever wrestled with the demons that waited at the end of his work, he never spoke of it. He only described the beauty of sharing, and his enthusiasm was intoxicating.

And then? Ray asked. They were driving in the car with the top down. *Once you've given up everything, do you dare to set down the first mark?*

Samson didn't answer. He leaned his head on the back of the seat and closed his eyes and felt the wind and the sun moving across his face.

They had been walking three or four hours before they realized they were lost. Donald was thirsty and Samson was telling him about the possible discovery of water on Mars, reservoirs of liquid water hidden under the frozen surface. Donald perked up and started in about a property scheme on Mars, something he'd seen on the Web, a niece or a nephew had shown him, a company selling acreage. Martian Consulate, it was called, the only legal Martian property registry in existence on earth, $29.95 per square mile, he marveled, plus $3.25 shipping and handling. Donald sat down on a rock and kicked at the dust.

'An investment. Not for us, but our children.'

'You have kids?'

'I'm saying symbolic-like,' Donald said. 'Jesus, I'm goddamn parched. What I wouldn't do for a glass of water, and I'm ready for dinner. Palmolive, take me away.'

Samson shielded his eyes from the sun; he had a cheap pair of aviator sunglasses he'd bought at the Hillcrest drugstore, but the light was still harsh, flattening everything out and dulling the colors of the landscape, giving everything a uniform glare. Even the jagged rocks appeared flat and listless, rocks that had once been under the sea but now couldn't be squeezed for a drop of water. He turned in a circle, trying to figure out the direction from which they'd come. They had been following a path but it had broken off at a certain point and they'd kept going, scraping their ankles on the scrub. Donald pulled his legs up, sitting Indian-style on the rock. He put his hands in the air, pinching his thumbs and fore-fingers together, and closed his eyes.

'I'm going to have an out of body experience right now. One, two, three, om, and I'm out of my body and psychically transferred to a chaise longue by the pool. Drinking a spiked grapefruit juice.'

Donald was panting quietly and his face was damp and flushed. Samson began to wonder whether it had been a good idea to bring him along after all. He should have considered the fact that Donald was in poor shape. On top of that, he had been so busy talking that he'd forgotten to mark the path with stones and arrows. But Donald had been adamant about coming along, insisting that he wanted to see a rattlesnake because he couldn't spend a month in the desert and come back without a brush with a poisonous snake.

'Didn't work,' Donald announced. 'I'm still here. Let's take the shortcut back to the complex.

The compound. The Clearwater Spa,' he said, enunciating each syllable as if he were recording a tape for English as a second language.

'Hold on. I'm just trying to figure out—'

Donald flashed him a look. 'Don't even tell me.'

Samson turned in a circle, and the more he turned the more the landscape blended, merging into a single sweep of range. He stopped and looked up at the sky, checking the position of the sun. It was maybe four o'clock, the heat still oppressive with at least three hours to go until sunset, the hour when the Hillcrest population would come to a screeching halt, hands over their hearts that fluttered for the well-stocked arsenal of America.

'I hate to say . . .'

'I'm having palpitations.'

'Let's just be calm about this. We can't have gotten that far.'

They walked in single file with Samson at the lead and Donald puffing behind him. He wasn't exactly sure where he was going, but he didn't want to upset Donald any more than necessary. He thought wistfully of Frank, who would have peed periodically along the way and gotten them back in no time.

Samson talked aimlessly in a cheerful voice, telling Donald everything he'd learned about Mars in an effort to divert him from his thirst and sore muscles with the prospect of extra-planetary real estate. He told him about the Polar

Lander that had been programmed to slam into Mars at four hundred miles an hour, surviving damaged but intact enough that it could crawl around for a few days on the surface, checking for water vapor and recording Martian sounds and dragging its busted ligature around like a cripple. How the story ended with the Lander exploding in space due to poor calculations by NASA, where everyone then cried for days, especially the program manager, who knew the craft intimately, who thought of it as his own, having spent a year moving around it in paper booties, face mask, and gloves to keep his germs from getting on it and infecting Mars.

'Fuck Mars,' Donald suddenly piped up from the rear. 'If you want water just go to goddamn Vegas. You've never seen so much water in your life. You've got cascades, pools, fountains. You've got flowing and dripping. Water raining from hothouse plants making dew on plastic grottoes. A whole freakin' ocean in front of Treasure Island, flaunting water like it's flipping the bird at the desert.' Donald stopped and religiously gave the finger in each direction, as if it were some kind of Native American ritual.

'The Israelites, can you believe,' Donald said, stumbling on a bush and hobbling like a gimp whenever Samson turned to look, because this was something he did – like reaching under his collar and rubbing his chest – when he was unnerved. 'In the desert forty days and forty nights. What

198

would you say, Sammy, if we went out into the desert, got lost, and came back prophets? I mean what did Jesus do besides camp in the desert a couple of months? Without the proper equipment back in the day, without tents and I don't know what kind of gear, it was your basic miracle.' Donald stopped to catch his breath. 'You a believer, Sammy? Myself, I'm half-Jewish so I'm torn about the Jesus issue.'

'Uh-uh, can't say that I am. My mother was Jewish and my father was who knows what. I got presents on Hanukkah.'

'What do you know, together we make a whole Jew. You never knew your pop?'

'No.'

'Not that it's my business, but that must have been tough. Growing up and all.'

'It was okay.'

They walked a few minutes more in silence, with only the dry rasp of the blackbrush and sage and creosote underfoot, grudging plants that could be harnessed for medicinal purposes, plants whose resins left fragrant traces on their fingers. There was an occasional nervous rustle in the scrub, lizards and small fry darting off to safety while carrion birds hung motionless in the sky.

'Hey.'

Samson turned around and looked at Donald, who had taken his shirt off and tucked it into the band of his shorts. Beneath the carpet of hair, his skin was pale.

'You should put that shirt on. You'll get burnt.'

'So I've been thinking,' Donald said, ignoring the advice. 'I don't want to get misty-eyed or anything, especially considering our present circumstances, it being important to keep a positive attitude and so on. But I've been thinking that in case I don't make it to cash in on the property, someone should be around to claim the profit. So what would you say to my adopting you, Sammy? No father-son crap, just for pure legal purposes.'

'Wow, I'm flattered, Donald. But isn't there someone else you'd rather—'

'Shut up and come to Papa,' he said, throwing open his arms and closing his eyes.

An hour or two passed and eventually the light began to condense and the shadows crept out from under things and lengthened, leaning away as if they didn't want to let go of the day. Samson's head was beginning to throb and, when he tried to swallow, his tongue stuck to the roof of his mouth. The heat confused him and he began to panic, realizing that he might have taken Donald miles in the wrong direction. The view was unconsoling, each jagged hill as barren as the next and too steep to climb to get any perspective. Donald was struggling for breath and his face had turned scarlet. Samson thought about leaving him and trying to make it back himself, then leading an emergency team to Donald. But the thought of Donald slowly dehydrating alone, talking to himself while the buzzards hung motionless nearby, was too much to bear. He imagined them dying together, side by side, and was not unaware of the irony of having been found near here last May, as if he had received a vision and was walking toward his death.

'Sammy, I don't feel so good.'

If they had to go, let them go beautifully. In a flash flood, the water coming not to save them but to carry them away, lifting their bodies and floating them out through the canyons. Otherwise, they would be preyed upon by scavengers and maggots, or – if they were lucky – baked clean by the heat, cauterized by sun and wind, preserved in shriveled forms with every drop of liquid evaporated. Ray said there were hundreds of old corpses found every year in the desert, mostly dumped homicides. A hand attached to nothing, found palm-up by the road.

'Let's stop for a while and rest. No use running ourselves to the ground. They'll realize when we're not at dinner that something's happened and they'll send people after us.' *If* they lasted as long as it took to be found, rangers from the Park Service spreading out and dividing the map into a grid, searchlights on their heads, burrowing through the night like miners.

There was a moon that night, heavy and orange at first, turning paler as it rose. The air was cold and Donald cursed himself for not being a smoker after all, because then he would have carried matches and they could have made a fire, for warmth and smoke signals. He sat in the dirt, leaning against a rock and talking quickly. He licked his lips, flicking his tongue across the white, parched mouth, his eyes jerking around nervously. There was a sound in the scrub and he jumped.

'What the heck?'

'Jackrabbit, I think.'

'Scared me half to death. I think that stuff they're giving me at the lab is starting to get to me. Like I'm seeing things. You think there are bobcats?'

'No,' Samson lied.

'How do you know? Could be watching us right now with their beady yellow eyes.'

'The field guide didn't say.'

'A friend of a friend got mauled by a bobcat. Wife could hardly identify him.'

'You're making that up.'

'I'm not gonna make it, Sammy. Tell the lawyers I said the property is yours. I'll write it in the dirt here with a stick.'

'You're going to make it. I'm telling you they'll find us by tomorrow, maybe even tonight. And then you'll be back at Clearwater, and soon enough you'll be home. You know, I don't even know where you live.'

'I ask myself.' There was a faint slur in his words.

'So where do you?'

'They know me at a couple of places in Vegas. I come and they give me a room for free. Mostly I stay with my sister and her kids in Phoenix, but I don't like to outstay my welcome. I have a van but it broke down last month. I sleep in the back when I'm on the road. Let me ask you a question, Sammy, because I feel like pontifying if you don't mind.'

'Pontificating.'

'Like I said.' Donald's tongue fluttered across his lips. 'Because let's just accept the fact that these might be our last, you know, together. And what I want to know is, what makes you happy, Sammy? Tell your old pop now, because I *gen-u-inely* want to know.'

Somewhere the flap of wings, a desert owl or a raven or some other bird the amateur ornithologist would know by name, followed by a trail of facts and statistics. Very possibly cooing in her ear, *his wife's* ear, with the authentic spotted-owl noise.

'I'd have to think. It's not something that, you know, on the spur of the moment. To compose a list.'

'All right, I'll go first. A beautiful pair of tits, simple. Let's actually talk about this. Seeing Vegas lit up at night, coming down from Hoover Dam. I'll warm you up. It doesn't have to be big. I mean the small pleasures, the late show of the Folies-Bergère. The sound of my wife's – Helen's – voice.

203

C'mon, your old pop's last wish.' Donald was making an effort, but his voice was thin and tired.

'You're being dramatic, but okay.' Samson gathered some pebbles and aimed at a rusty can. 'Let me think.' A few moments passed with only the pathetic sound of the rocks hitting the metal, while Samson meditated on the subject. He thought of the first few days after the operation, when everything he'd looked at had startled and moved him. He thought of New York, of Frank and Anna, of the endless walks he'd taken trying to absorb the city and circumstances of his new life. He thought of his childhood.

'What, your Alzheimer's kicking in?' Donald slapped his forehead. 'That you can't think of what makes you happy? Because it's beginning to depress me.'

'Okay, okay. There's Jollie Lambird, for a start.'

'Jollie what? Is this person, place, or thing?'

'Girl.'

'Now we're talking.'

'Mostly it's things from my childhood. Fishing with my great-uncle Max. Playing baseball with a couple of friends out in the field near my house. The summers. I was a happy kid, for the most part. Which one was Helen?'

'The second.'

'The long story?'

'That's the one.' Donald was breathing heavily.

'We have time, why don't you tell it?'

'Lemme catch my breath, Sammy. Tell me about

Jollie. Sounds like a French girl. I like the French. Very free people. The women go topless.'

'This is when I was in the seventh grade, a girl who was twelve. Her chest probably as flat as mine.'

'Sounds precious,' Donald said. 'Next.'

'It's always tits with you.'

'It's tits with every guy! Stop any guy on the street and he'll tell you it's tits. Tits tits tits! And sometimes ass. And always pussy. That you don't know this disturbs me. You're like a kid, Sammy. Somebody's gotta teach you a thing or two. If we get outta here alive, first thing is I'm getting you a whore. The best whore in the whole goddamn state of Nevada. Because it's embarrassing. If you were my own kid – which technically you are because I said so – I'd be embarrassed.' Donald shook his head. 'Repeat after me: Tits, pussy, ass! Tits, pussy – ass! Titspussya—'

'Shut up,' Samson said, struggling not to laugh. He pelted the can with a stone, sending it skittering across the ground.

'Fine. Don't say I didn't try to teach you.'

Samson waited for him to go on, but Donald only closed his eyes and lay still in an exhausted slump.

'There are other things too,' Samson offered. 'If you still want to know, there was a beach near where I grew up – my mother and I used to go there. That would be one.'

They sat in silence.

'Don't think I don't appreciate,' Donald said, 'all those memories, gone.' He coughed and didn't move to cover his mouth. 'That you can't remember, it's tragic. If I could, the memories I would give you. I had enough good times for two people. More than two. What do I need them for now?'

Samson looked at his face, but his eyes were still closed and his expression gave away nothing.

'Donald?'

'Yeah.'

'Can I ask you? The stuff they're working on at Clearwater, how much do you know? Did Ray explain it to you?'

'I got a decent idea.' Donald stretched out on the ground. 'But what do I know about science? I go in and I do a job, I don't ask too many questions. You on the other hand, you ask questions.'

'*You* just asked *me* . . .' Samson said, but Donald was already asleep, breathing with some difficulty, making epiglottal sounds.

The moon lit up the dead wood of yuccas that wouldn't rot, worn smooth like bones. A couple of coyotes howled, and Samson tried to think of them as dogs, related many times removed from Frank, who was sleeping with his head on his paws at the foot of Anna's bed. Donald was sleeping with his arms around the rock he'd leaned against and claimed as his own, the way the shipwrecked cling to a shred of timber. An old man with terrible lungs in the autumn of his life, a dark, sad season that might be sped up drastically unless something, some intervention, happened soon.

He watched the old man sleep and felt the vast loneliness of the world, the loneliness passed from person to person like a beach ball at a rock concert, kept aloft at all costs, and this was his moment to shoulder it. Or maybe it was his own personal loneliness, a solitary, errant longing no one else could ever know, and the knowledge of this stoked the already existing loneliness, made it widen and blur at the edges until it included everything. The mountains and the stunted trees and the blazing, palpable stars and the coyotes and the power lines and the over-powering smell of sage. He knew that somewhere close there were trails: footpaths left by the Paiutes or Shoshones, forty-niners' wagon trails, threads the field mice had worn down in the grass on their way to bitter water. Tracks which, if he could find them, would lead him through the mountains and out of the state into a greener country. But he was too tired to look any more.

It was being a small part of a great effort, performing a role that couldn't be filled by anyone else, that drew him into the project. It was Ray's belief in the greater good, the larger picture. It was his unstinting acceptance of Samson, of who he was, not *then* but *now*.

He lay on his back and listened to Donald

breathe and thought about his childhood and soon he was thinking about his mother. It was a loss that was almost too painful to consider, and he could only do it now, in the vaulted silence and stillness of the desert. It was as if he had been sleeping while she died, or worse, laughing his head off at a party. It had always been the two of them; it was as if he had closed his eyes and then, when he opened them, he was old and she was gone. As if she had taught him everything she could and this was the final lesson, the one that all the others had prepared him for. To touch and feel each thing in the world, to know it by sight and by name, and then to know it with your eyes closed so that when something is gone, it can be recognized by the shape of its absence. So that you can continue to possess the lost, because absence is the only constant thing. Because you can get free of everything except the space where things have been.

He was lying on the floor of the southern Mojave Desert remembering his mother, and now tears were running down his face, his face that, though he had not known it, had given all of his loneliness away. Curled on the desert floor under the unjust stars, silently weeping for all he had forgotten and could not change, he let himself remember the only things he could. He was remembering and there was a chance that in New York, where the streetlamps would have already begun to fade against the gritty light,

Anna was lying between the white sheets of their bed remembering him. There was a chance that in some cosmic equation a burden was added to your load each time you made for someone's memory.

A mass of rock loomed up about a mile away, or maybe ten miles; it was difficult to judge the distances. And beyond that there were other rocks, buttes and flanks and sheer sandstone faces with secret lithologies, mountain ranges being born or dying, temporarily landlocked, unable to break off and drift into oceanic obscurity like parts of California.

His mother must have liked Anna, with her grace and giddy laugh, if you could make her laugh; the daughter she never had. It still surprised him when Anna knew things about his mother; things she had observed herself, but also details she couldn't possibly have known and which he must have told her. How you could tell if his mother had been in a room because of the lingering scent of expensive perfume, the one luxury she said she would have even if she were destitute. How her politics were radical, and she liked to argue about them with anyone willing. How she took up causes and fought tooth and nail, organizing marches and night meetings from which she came back exhausted but elated, her eyes sparkling and a halo of stray frizz around her face giving her a mad look. How, before she went out on a date, she would poke her finger into a few stubby lipstick tubes and paint her lips, the combination of shades always producing the same bright red that left streaks on her teeth. How she was merciless in board games and made a show of beating his friends at chess, and appeared not to be watching the road when she was driving – checking her makeup in the mirror, searching under the seat for a token. How she rarely mentioned his father, though once or twice he found her on the floor reading a packet of old letters. That when she cried, tears would stream down her face and she would open her mouth but no sound would come out, as if she were surprised and unclear as to whose emotions had possessed her. That Anna knew these things about his mother made him feel bound, even indebted, to her.

He shivered in the cold and thought about curling up next to Donald to conserve body heat. But the old man's spindly legs were sprawled as if he had been knocked down running, like a victim of lava preserved instantly in the stonework, a delicate and lasting thing, and Samson left him as he was. He was too cold to fall asleep, and he thought of the bonfire his great-uncle Max had made one Fourth of July on the beach, how he and his cousin had played a game of staying inside the circle of heat until they practically glowed and their eyes stung, and then turned and plunged themselves in the ocean. He fantasized about taking all the facts he knew of his life up until the age of twelve and, using a complex formula, mapping out his life exactly as it would later happen, multiplying out into the inevitable future. The whole life spread out like a model city. In the fantasy he could take his twelve-year-old self by hand – waking him up, the hand clammy with sleep – and walk him outside to see it, like a view from above: the small, faraway rest of his life. He wondered whether the boy would approve of it all: whether a respectful silence would come over him while he stood in awe, or whether he would in fact turn his head and look away in disappointment or disgust or even shame. Tears gathering in the corners of his eyes which he would angrily push away with a fist.

He woke a few hours later at dawn to the light breaking over the valley and the sound of a car passing in the distance. Donald was curled into a ball in the dust. Samson sat up and listened, then jogged in the direction of the noise. In a couple of minutes he found the blacktop. There was a speed limit sign sprayed with bullet holes. He stepped onto the road, walked to the middle, and stood on the faded broken yellow line, looking both ways down the length of paved gray to where the tarmac dipped and vanished in the haze. He stood there for a couple of hours until the sun was diffuse and white in the sky, and eventually he saw a car move slowly out of the distance. He watched it approach for a long time, like a movie with no plot, and when he could see the figure hunched behind the wheel he waved his arms.

He ran back through the scrub to where Donald was sleeping with his face in the dust, and gently nudged him awake. The old man rolled over, and when the sun hit his face he lay still for a minute, and then he said, 'Who am I?' and opened one eye.

They would come to him and he would put his hands on their heads. He would feel their skulls through the tips of his fingers and then he would flatten his palms around the crown and call on the powers to heal them. When he was young, Ray told Samson, that's how he wanted it to happen. That was before he spent nights in the anatomy lab, slumped in a chair with a headache from the formaldehyde, in the freezing basement of the medical school. There were students who hadn't had time to dissect an arm or hand and so cut off the stump and took it back to their dorms wrapped in newspaper. Young apprentices lugging body parts through the night. The next day the sanitation men would find a slashed heart in a Dumpster and call the police department. But Ray had made friends with the night guard – he brought him a sandwich and coffee around midnight – and he let him in to work in the lab until his shift was over at dawn.

The first time Ray had opened a skull, sawing along the cranial suture line, he had gone weak in the knees. He had cut the brain loose from the spinal cord and held it in his hands. The gray matter was not gray at all but a dull brown. At five in the morning he stumbled back to his car and drove home. The woman who later became his wife was sleeping in his bed, her face buried in the pillows and her feet crossed on top of each other like a child's. He watched her sleep and struggled to see her as she was, but what he saw instead were her muscles and bones. He saw right through the skin to where her femur connected to her tibia by way of the ligaments, to the hairy web of nerves and the delicate forest of her lungs, to the abstract heart pumping blood through her arteries. It terrified him how easily these systems could fail her. He sat down on the bed and laid his hands on her head, the palms over her crown of shiny black hair. She turned and looked at him, and for a moment she seemed not to recognize his face.

Ray and Samson were walking together after dinner; it was part of Ray's regimen, a leisurely walk after meals. Not far, just down to the entrance gate and back, with the mountains bruised by the dying light and the first bats wheeling out. There were moments when, listening to Ray, Samson felt he understood how people took up with cults, deciding to give up everything to follow one charismatic leader, sleeping in vans, selling literature on street corners, and dancing with bells. Chanting and keeping a picture of the leader in their pockets, a balding man with tinted glasses, arm raised in absolution ever hovering above their heads, a man who spoke to their masses through a microphone held close to his lips, using the reverb to increase the drama. How they went to work for this man, bringing back money from selling crafts they had made with their teeth and toes, complicated things made out of raffia. There were times, when Ray was on a roll, that he seemed touched by a certain light, and Samson could almost understand how people with families, two-door garages, and good jobs might turn it all over to the leader and follow him down to a tropical forest to set up a town with a bland, ominous name. He had read about this; such things actually happened.

A week had passed since Samson and Donald had gotten lost in the desert and been rescued by Ray. Ray had gone out to find them, trawling the road until he saw Samson's thin figure step out onto the blacktop. Donald had been silent as they drove back to the lab, clutching a plastic bottle of water in his lap that he swigged from every few minutes, wincing like it was whiskey. His face was streaked with dirt, and he had the subdued and chastened look of a person who has just had a brush with death. He stayed on at Clearwater a few days more to finish up whatever they needed from him at the lab, looking haggard and obviously in pain whenever he coughed. When he finally left on a clear blue Friday at the very end of April, Donald assured Samson that he would know everything was fine as long as Samson didn't hear from any lawyers. If he happened to suddenly kick the bucket, Samson would know right away because he'd have to come and claim the land deed. Samson told him he was talking nonsense but Donald just crushed him to his chest in an embrace surprisingly strong for his weakened state.

'Atta boy. Do me a favor, Sammy, I'm just thinking. Make sure my sister doesn't bury me in one of those rock garden cemeteries filled with geriatrics. Now that I'm on the subject, I'm thinking cremation. Very natural-like, ashes scattered to the four winds. You think you can arrange that?'

'You're being morbid,' Samson said into Donald's Hawaiian shirt.

'You're my next of kin, Sammy. Who else if not you?'

Donald released him from the bear hug and dragged the little, happy suitcase down the path and stuffed it into the taxi, then saluted Samson and bowed in four directions. Samson stood on the steps of the Bathhouse feeling miserable, holding Donald's dog-eared business card with an address in Phoenix and a voice mail number on it, watching the taxi bounce down the dusty road and turn out onto the blacktop.

Begin again with nothing, or almost nothing, and still one must begin. And what Samson felt for

216

the first time since he had woken in the hospital was the desire to finish what he had started. It's not that Ray had lulled him into acquiescence; there were reasons he agreed to volunteer for the final part of the experiment. For one thing, Ray's request flattered him and made him feel slightly extraordinary: a small part of history, going where no man had gone before. And he knew, with the same sad regret that perhaps accompanies a child's first forgetting, that new memories – memories of all that had happened since he awoke in the hospital – had already begun to encroach on the emptiness in his mind: he was losing it by day, by acre. But in the end, he agreed mostly because he'd already decided not to turn back: to carry their conversations through to the end.

They were still years from being able to actually transfer a whole memory from one brain to another, but Ray explained that even at this early date they could transfer something primitive. Maybe it would only be static fragments or the vertiginous sense of remembering a memory that belonged to someone else. When Ray finally asked him outright if he would volunteer to accept the first transfer, however poor or incomplete, they both knew the question was already redundant.

You'll do it? Ray asked, the whole desert leaning in to accept the inevitable reply. *Yes,* Samson answered, *yes.*

At one point or another it simply became the obvious end to his time in the desert. It would mark the end of a year that he might look back on as a hinge, a pivot between two lives. Or not: maybe enough time would pass that eventually he would look back on his life, all of it, as a series of events both logical and continuous.

That May morning he woke early to the sound of rain plinking against the roof, and within minutes it was coming down like a landslide. He stumbled out of bed and opened the door. Outside, the light was metallic, and flashes of lightning cracked across the sky strobing the desert. The thunder hit the mountains and came rolling back as an echo. The rain came down faster than the ground could absorb it, and gullies formed, swiftly carrying the water to reservoirs deep below the surface. Samson thought of the kids who had been diving in some underground pools a hundred miles north and never surfaced, the girlfriend of one crying as the rescuers dove deeper and deeper but never found the bottom. Then the rain stopped as quickly as it had begun. The sun came out and the puddles reflected the sky like mercury, and for a moment the shocked desert stood still.

An hour later Samson was lying in the dark fully wired. The drugs they had given him had begun to seep into his bloodstream, though he couldn't tell if his thoughts were getting more vivid or growing vague. From time to time Ray's voice came through the headset telling him they were almost ready, asking how he was feeling, chatting about the weather outside. The voice sounded more distant each time, as if it had to travel an ever-greater distance to reach him, and the words lost their meanings before Samson stopped hearing them altogether. It felt like his mind was loosening its hold on him, letting him go, and some part of him objected to this, a minor part that wanted to cry out in protest against such abandonment. But the rest of him felt warm and drowsy, content to give in as his mind receded. It was like dreaming awake: the desert, a road, a car moving through so much space.

And then, out of the jumble of images: Anna's face. Pale and luminescent, with the little scar above the lip, a lip that rose a little higher on the right side when she spoke, that had been perpetually chapped all winter. A face he had chosen out of so many others to look upon, to stare at for years. To watch in work or sleep, in sickness and in health, though nothing could come of such a vigil but care and wonder. Tremendous joy washed over him. If he could have, if he had still been able to find his limbs and move them, he would have gotten down on his knees. It was a moment of startling clarity, and then his mind fell into a confusion that did not end until the explosion blasted everything away.

PART III

He woke to the light, sunlight so flat and bright it had to be fake, so at odds was it with the Weather Channel talking nonstop about rain. A few seconds passed before he remembered where he was. When he did, a wave of desperation broke over him. The TV screen hovered on the current temperature in the Las Vegas area, and then the meteorologist came on, pointing to squalls and jet streams, palpitating Florida and the Leeward Islands on the satellite image behind him. Samson held his head in his hand and squeezed his eyes. He got up, drew the blinds, and staggered to the bathroom. His face looked gray in the mirror, the eyes glassy and ringed with dark circles. He noted this deterioration of his looks with a faint relief, if only because it was some proof that he hadn't imagined everything.

He'd been staying in a motel in Las Vegas for two or three days waiting for the phone to ring, keeping the Weather Channel on at all hours because the steadiness of the information comforted him. If he turned it off he was immediately seized with panic, forced to fight for air and pace the room pleading aloud to calm himself. He was flooded with a loneliness that was spectacular, unbearable.

Half an hour passed during which he stared blankly at the TV. Eventually he fell back into a fitful, violent sleep, the weather reports absorbed into his unconscious so that his dreams were filled with wind and rain. *Prepare to get wet*, the meteorologist warned, *we're talking about an inch of rain or more*, though the storm was nowhere near Las Vegas, where the average yearly rainfall was a scant four inches. It was elsewhere, in hurricane country where the houses were built on stilts. What the Weather Channel delivered was a steady clairvoyance and this: the news of other people's disasters.

When he'd arrived in Las Vegas he'd gone into all the hotels Donald had mentioned – the Sands, the Flamingo, Caesars Palace – but no one there had ever heard of Donald Selwyn, not even the tight-lipped managers who came out of their back offices to relieve the staff when Samson remained insistent. After that he started leaving messages on Donald's voice mail, waiting for the three rings followed by a sound like a wind machine, as if he had recorded his outgoing message while clinging to a cliff during a storm. 'This is Donald,' it said as severe head winds blew through the background, 'you know what to do.' He pleaded with Donald to call him back, calling again and again until the recorded words began to haunt him, as if Donald were secretly trying to communicate something under dangerous conditions. *You know what to do,* and then the dull beep that Samson listened to a dozen times until finally he started shrieking about the bomb going off in his head.

It was there in the center of his mind, the memory Ray had transferred; there was no way to get around it. The images were uncannily familiar, as if he had experienced them himself, though he knew he hadn't, and this made them more frightening still. He could recall the heat beating down in the desert, and the sweat pooling on his skin under the fatigues. He felt the boredom and the dull apprehension of waiting, breathing in the dust and trying to move as little as possible. He could see the tanned faces of the other boys, their profiles flickering in the sun. And then the reluctant rising before dawn, the coolness of the floor and the longing to get back into bed, though he was already shuffling along in a line of bodies toward the showers. The metallic taste of the desert in his mouth. Stepping under the flow of water, his heart began to beat faster, blood coursing through his veins. No breakfast, not even a tin cup of coffee, though there were plenty of cigarettes to go around, their tips glowing in the back of the trucks. He saw and felt it all as if the memory were his own, but it wasn't, *damn it,* and this is what drove him insane, more insane, even, than the blast whose force and heat seemed almost *engineered* to drive to madness anyone it didn't kill.

When he'd woken after the transfer Ray had been standing above him. Ray had asked him questions and he had tried to answer, and, groggy from the drugs, it had not at first occurred to him to be angry or even frightened, only stunned. He tried to communicate the vividness. He spoke in half-sentences, stuttering and grasping for words. Ray asked and he struggled to answer, but there was no way to describe it. He was having trouble speaking, and they recorded on a digital camera how he grabbed the doctor's wrist, eyes wide, and said, *Who?* Someone had brought him back to the Bathhouse and, exhausted, he had fallen asleep, but the next day when he'd woken it was still there, bright and ready in his mind, the sound of countdown and the shattering explosion. It was there as he washed his face and dressed, and though he tried to push it aside and think of other things he could not.

He had gone to find Ray because he was ready to talk – he had questions of his own now – but when he got to the lab the receptionist told him the doctor was gone, he had left and wouldn't be back for a couple of days. Samson had looked at her, bewildered, and she'd had to repeat herself, articulating each word so that he could not mistake what she'd said. When the confusion receded, he felt the first stab of agitation, beginning in his stomach and rising until it was full-blown, an angry heat burning in his face. He went back to his room and tried to think – it was just a memory, that was all, to be forgotten with the rest. Except not only could he not forget it, it had also unsettled other memories, being five or six and seeing pictures of a leveled Hiroshima on TV, images that haunted his sleep so that he woke up screaming and his mother had to come and quiet him, pressing a wet cloth to his forehead. In the days that followed he asked her incessantly about the bomb, and though she tried to calm him, in her usual way she began to talk politics, about the arms race and the idiots in Washington and the threat of nuclear war. Later he timed how long it took to run from his room to her bed, a four-poster high enough off the ground that they could both hide under it. *Something smells in here*, she'd kept saying a few days later, but it was weeks before she found the sandwiches he'd hidden there, green with mold.

And now it occurred to him, *who the hell was Ray anyway? You think you know someone and then you end up with a bomb in your head.*

He ripped through his wallet for the telephone number of Ray's house in L.A. Not finding it, he ransacked his bag, dumping the contents on the floor. Probably Ray was already looking for the next Output: he had no use for Samson now, it had worked, that was all he needed to know, there were others to prepare the way for. He couldn't find the piece of paper with Ray's number anywhere, and he held his head and tried to think straight, the blood pounding in his temples. He was enraged with himself for listening to Ray, for not pulling the phone out of the wall that first night he'd called him in New York.

He closed his eyes and sat very still. He would not go to the lab to demand Ray's number. He would draw the blinds, lie on the bed, and try to calm himself. *There must be some explanation*, he thought. Soon Ray would come back – he *had* to come back – and with his soothing voice and his eloquence he would make everything all right.

But three days passed without any sign of Ray, and when Samson finally saw the lights on in his office, he'd run out in the dark and practically busted down the door. Buzzed with adrenaline, he'd walked up to the desk and swept the papers Ray was working on to the floor, along with the glass paperweight that shattered into pieces. Ray, the ageless doctor whose very macrobiotic existence preached a holistic good, the man born to be a leader among men, didn't even blink. He didn't protest or act shocked. He was as imperturbable as Gandhi, at ease among lunatics because he knew that he could summon his strength if need be, his mind-over-body enlightenment, and kill in an instant – a humane thrust of the hand to crack the solar plexus.

They had remained frozen, locked in a gaze until finally Samson, trembling, turned and walked to the window, looking out at the valley. It had been dark outside, but he could still make out the line of mountains past which there was another lone valley, then another jagged range, and so on in waves of violent desolation. He felt betrayed, and there was no one anymore that he could turn to. His mind had been violated in a way that no one else's ever had. The loneliness was savage.

He spun around and glared at Ray.

'Where have you been?' he demanded.

'Let's just try to be calm here.'

'*Calm?*' He wished to plead ardently, to beg for sympathy. 'You hijack my mind and load an atomic bomb into it, and then you disappear without a word and you expect me to be calm?'

'A personal matter came up. My son, Matthew, was sick and I had to make an emergency trip to San Francisco. I'm sorry I didn't get a chance to talk to you before I left. It was the middle of the night and you were asleep. And no one *hijacked* anyone's mind.'

There was so much he needed to say, he hardly knew where to begin. 'It's like I've returned from the dead only to find that everything I knew is gone. That I'm alone and you – the one person I thought understood me, who I could trust . . . I thought you *understood*—' He felt his face redden with frustration at his inability to articulate what was happening to him, to explain the damage Ray had done.

'I do understand. It's the reason I'm here, the reason *we're* here.'

'Understand!' Samson nearly spat. 'After what you said about getting out of our own heads? All that nonsense about sharing?'

Ray shook his head, his look stern and disapproving.

'This is a crucial moment in the research. It's vital that you stay calm,' he implored.

Samson's frustration surged against Ray's refusal to understand, to even acknowledge, how he felt. It was as if he'd been bound and gagged inside his own head.

Ray continued, oblivious. 'There are always moments in experiments, important experiments, where things could go—'

A flash of anger rose up in Samson, and he swung his arm back and brought it down across Ray's face. He felt his fist make contact. Then it was like watching the aftermath in slow motion: Ray's head thrown back (how *old* he seemed then, though the blood that spurted from his nose was bright with life), his body crumpling against the wall, moving a hand across his face as he shrunk from Samson, from something he had not made allowance for in all of his calculations, the possibility of his subject having, what – a mind of his own? Perhaps Ray was a normal man after all, as mistaken as anyone, capable of going terribly wrong where he believed he was serving a greater good. The blood was trickling out from between Ray's fingers now, his eyes searching for what would be delivered next by one who'd just discovered a power over him. Samson regarded Ray with wonder, amazed at his own strength, at how unguarded, how suddenly human Ray seemed. He looked from his fist to Ray's face, aware that something had happened: not the punch but something far more decisive, after which there was no going back. Ray had miscalculated – they both knew that – but only Samson realized just how much. No, Ray was not a bad man. He was something perhaps more difficult to accept: an average man, no better or worse than any.

'Sharing? Getting out of our own heads?' Samson could hear himself speak but he didn't know if his words were reaching Ray. 'I'd say this is the most alone I've ever been.'

'As you *remember* being,' Ray corrected him as he wiped his bloody hand on his shirt and felt to see where the nose had broken. The blue stone on his ring briefly caught the light. 'Maybe it was the wrong memory,' Ray conceded. 'Maybe I should have chosen something less dramatic—'

'Maybe you shouldn't have chosen at all!'

'Damn it, Samson, you *volunteered*, you were fully aware.' Ray spoke through his teeth. The coolness of his tone surprised Samson. 'Don't try to turn this on me, as if I somehow failed you. There was nothing I didn't tell you except whose memory you were receiving and what it was. It would have produced images in your mind. It would have confused the purity of the transfer.'

'Did you think about how it would feel? A nightmare inside your head that belongs to someone else? Did you stop to imagine?'

'It was a test, not a war. I didn't give you torture

231

or killing fields, right? Let's just keep this in perspective.' The blood was dripping onto Ray's shirt in red blotches. 'All you received was the memory of a *test* that took place forty-four years ago. A moment in history. A powerful one, yes, but we needed a strong memory. Something specific and intense that would be impossible to confuse with any memories of your own. And when you and Donald got lost in the desert, when I found you that day on the side of the road, I saw it in your faces, the bond you already shared. It was an ideal situation for the first transfer.'

Samson glared at him in silence, waiting for Ray to say something, anything, to salvage their own bond, the reason he had come out to Clearwater in the first place.

'Come on,' Ray snapped. 'You were the perfect candidate and we both knew it. The nature of your condition – this immense receptivity you have to new memories – made it practically inevitable.' He paused, and shook his head. 'I'm disappointed, I have to say. You seem to have forgotten every-thing we discussed. Taking risks, advancing science. Where no man has gone before, didn't we say?'

'There's a reason for that.'

Ray threw up his hands. 'There's a reason we haven't sent men to Mars. But one day there won't be. God damn it, you're on the frontier of science, Samson. I thought we understood each other. An amazing thing has happened. Yes, we still have a ways to go. But we're even further ahead than anyone thought. That so much of the memory came through, it's monumental. Plenty of people would have fought to be in your place, to go down in history. It's ridiculous to be throwing a fit.'

It would have been better to be angry, to have continued to pummel Ray, knocked over chairs, put his fist through the plate-glass window – to have felt anything but the exhaustion and sadness he felt now. He wished he had never come out to the desert, that he had let the phone just ring that snowy night at the end of January. Everything but the loneliness had gone out of him.

'Like I've always said, you're a fascinating mind, Samson. To lose so much memory and not want it back. Not a fucking thing. It's powerful. A man not blinded by a lifetime of memories, who can appreciate the power of a single one. When Lavell told me you'd been found out here in the desert, it almost seemed like fate. I mean, can you answer me this: I've always wondered, where the hell were you going?'

Samson stared at him in stony silence. 'You had no right,' he said at last, and turned to go. 'You should have let me be.'

'So that you'd be where now? Alone, wandering the streets of New York like some lunatic? You came because you wanted to. You were waiting for that call.'

Samson looked back. Their eyes locked.

'Go to hell.'

Ray flinched, and Samson turned and walked out the door.

Outside, the night was endless, the blackness so complete that nothing did not belong to it. And then the answer came to him: *I was going home.*

He went back to his room and packed his few belongings. The silence was like an immense pressure, like the sound of wind beneath a bird's great wings. He eased open the screen door and started down the dirt road toward the tarmac, his bag slung over his shoulder. He felt Ray was watching from somewhere and he resented it, the idea that Ray might know where he was going even before he did. He'd walked four or five miles east before a car came along, a couple with dirty hair and a skinny dog in the backseat. The sun was just starting to come up. Samson had barely gotten in before the man stepped on the gas again. They were on their way to a conference in Phoenix, two hippies from Oregon who managed a fish farm with wild spawn ponds for a brood stock of bluegill, crappie, and other species Samson had never heard of. The woman kept twisting around in her seat to look at him. They must have been going eighty miles per hour, but the desert was so vast and uniform that if Samson focused on a spot in the distance it seemed as if the car stood still.

The man offered him a cigarette with one hand and rummaged under his seat for a cassette with the other while the woman grabbed the wheel and steered. It was a bootleg recording of a band with the murmur of a crowd in the background. Samson accepted the cigarette and lit it off the glowing coil from the dash. The woman wagged her head in approval, tapping her knees to the music. 'It's live,' she said, wrenching around as the dog skittered onto the floor. They dropped him off in Vegas at the Four Palms Motel, where they'd once stayed, waving and tearing off through the vacant parking lot.

When he woke again the TV screen was black and it was dark outside. He got up to turn the Weather Channel on, but nothing happened. He jiggled the button and banged the set, but it refused to come to life. He grabbed the phone off the night table and dialed the reception desk, in a small shack across a field of poorly lit parking lots.

'Hello?' a woman said, her answer quick and eager, as if she hadn't received a phone call in months. The person who'd checked Samson in, a tiny Mexican with deep hollow eyes, had looked terrified, as if Samson had come in threatening to spray the shack with a semiautomatic if the man didn't give him a room right away.

'Is this reception?'

'Yes it is.'

'My television is broken.'

'What happened?'

'I don't know. Something happened and now it's broken.'

'You turned it on?'

'You're asking me if I turned it on?'

He struggled against the urge to shout, to rage into the phone in order to communicate the magnitude of his pain. He wanted so little really – just the sound of the television to help him through the night, the promise of rain elsewhere, and even this small thing he was to be denied. He felt devastated, unfairly wronged, and perhaps the woman heard this in his voice because when she spoke again her own voice was softer.

'I have to ask. You'd be surprised. Some people think the television is supposed to be on when they come into the room, and when it's not they call up complaining it's broken.'

He wondered if he had actually reached the reception shack or if he had accidentally dialed some distant place. Was he truly to believe this, that there were people out there, a regular clientele, convinced that a television remained on unless it was broken?

'Look,' he implored. '*Please*. I'm asking you very nicely, can you fix my television? Be reasonable, *be*—' He kneaded his forehead in exasperation. 'You can't possibly understand how much it would mean to me.'

'Sir?' Her voice was faint. It promised nothing. Probably she was used to psychopaths and murderers. This was Las Vegas, after all. She must have been trained to handle suicides on a daily basis. A woman who knew her chalk outlines, who could recite a hundred ways a body could land sprawled across the floor. A broken television was not a cause for alarm, not for her. There were others who needed her, people calling at this very moment whom she could save simply by answering the phone as she had, acting surprised and pretending they were the only ones. Lost and lonely people to whom she ministered Vegas motel rooms like blessings, people she could help to survive one more night. 'I'll see if I can get someone to take a look at it as soon as possible,' she said. It was the best she could do and because it was not enough, because he could not bear the silence in his room, he stood up and walked out into the night.

He had a memory of Las Vegas, seen through the window of the taxi on the way to the airport when Anna had come to take him home. The lights had stunned him, a city that existed against all odds – against the sheer force of reality – broadcasting a message in the affirmative: *YES! YES! YES!* A year had passed since he'd woken up in a foreign life, in a city that no one could explain why he'd come to. And now, walking numbly down the Strip, it was not the neon but other people that he couldn't account for, knitted in pairs or tight groups, people who looked happy, positively beaming and holding hands, a man squeezing a woman's ass, and she laughing and squeezing his, people who had the liberty to touch each other, who had things to talk about, secret expressions only they understood, who remembered, for God's sake, the first time they met each other.

He walked into a casino and wandered past the tables, edging himself into a crowd gathered around a game of craps. Maybe it's as easy as that, he thought to himself, just wedge yourself between this fat guy and that lady in a gold dress and you're in, part of it, everyone vibrating in the glory of the high roller riding a lucky streak, keeping an edge against the house. And for a little while it was fine, the terror left him. But then the man started to lose and the mood changed, and soon Samson became unwedged and was wandering again in the maze of slot machines and felt tables. He watched as a heavy man, his shirt stained with sweat, let his body go limp while the bouncers dragged him across the floor. The man lost his shoe and it lay there until a cocktail waitress picked it up and carried it away on a tray of empty glasses. A man who was maybe years in debt, who had put up for collateral things he later found he couldn't live without.

There were no clocks in the casino; no windows; nothing at all to suggest that time had any bearing on the place. No mirrors, no self-examination. On the way over he had stopped at a liquor store to buy some whiskey. It fit the new image he wished to form of himself: a force to contend with, a powerful man who would not be taken advantage of. He pointed to the only brand he recognized, Jack Daniel's. A sign on the wall said I.D. was required, so he took his license out of his wallet and showed it to the clerk. The man laughed and gave him a strange look. 'Don't worry, man. I believe you.' Samson stared at the floor as the man counted out his change.

There was a bank of pay phones against the wall, and he walked over to a booth and took the bottle out of the paper bag. Then he dropped a quarter in the phone, and dialed the number of the motel. He unscrewed the cap and took a drink.

'Hello?' It was the saint in reception again, working the phone like a professional. Samson winced as the alcohol burned a trail to his stomach. 'Can I help you?' she asked.

'I'm calling to find out if my television has been fixed.'

'What room number?'

How many people had reported a broken television in the time since he'd called, Samson wondered, that she should already have forgotten him?

'Twelve forty-seven. Don't you remember? I called earlier tonight.' He heard the click of her fingers moving across the keyboard.

'Um, yes . . .' He took another sip of whiskey as she searched the files. Perhaps she was less experienced than he'd thought. Not a saint at all, but a trainee. 'It looks like the repairman was sent over there an hour ago. It should be working now.'

'What time is it?'

'It's ten-fourteen,' she answered, and then, as an afterthought, added 'at night,' in case she was talking to one of the ones who'd lost his mind.

But he hadn't lost his mind. To the contrary, he'd lost everything *but*. His memory, his wife, his job, his friends, twenty-four years of his life – but not his mind. That was all that had been left and he'd retreated into it because there was nowhere else. He took another drink and tucked the Jack Daniel's inside his tan windbreaker. He leaned against the smudged brass rail of the balcony and surveyed the casino floor: dealers dealing, clearing, swiping, doling, shuffling, as gamblers wiped their glasses, rearranged their balls, piled their chips into pillars as lights flashed around them, a bingo player asleep with her mouth open in a chair, a woman holding her handbag under a slot machine that was regurgitating the quarters she'd fed it, and what kind of victory, Samson wondered, was that? No, there was nothing left but his mind. The rest had all been lost or spent, and now he was surveying the damage, drinking down the Jack Daniel's and surveying the ruins of it all.

The alcohol began to blur his unhappiness. He went looking for a cigarette. He passed three boys who couldn't have been more than fifteen or sixteen, dressed up in suits and fedoras like adolescent Mafia.

They were talking in grave voices, probably about the next step of their plan, having managed to sneak into the casino. One of them cupped a cigarette in his palm and hung back as the other two headed off toward the card tables. Samson approached him. The kid looked up suspiciously, bracing himself.

'Hey,' Samson nodded, clutching his chest where the bottle was safely nestled. The kid nodded back, leaning stiffly against the wall. 'Got an extra cigarette?'

The kid liked this. He straightened up and reached into his breast pocket, moving aside his wallet to get to the pack. Probably the three of them were hoping to pool their dough – years of saved milk money, of earnings from summers of lifeguarding at the municipal pool, bar mitzvah money or whatever the Christian equivalent was, baptism or taking-of-the-sacrament money, tips saved from the parents who instructed them to watch their kids in the baby pool – to add together all those sweaty, crumpled, well-counted bills for one hot night with a whore.

The kid opened the pack, shook one out, and passed it to Samson. He flicked open a silver Zippo blazoned with a dragon. Samson leaned in with the cigarette between his lips and the kid made a show of shielding the flame, a symbolic act of brotherhood entirely unnecessary, as the casino was almost airless. Samson took out the Jack Daniel's that he'd been clutching to his chest like a wounded baby rabbit. He took a quick pull, jabbing the bottle between his lips and throwing his head back for emphasis, then passed it to the kid. The kid didn't even wipe the rim, just tilted his head back and drank, as if he didn't want to break the bond between them with a hint of distrust. He had a sharp, beaklike nose too large for his face, surprisingly pale skin, and a sprinkle of acne along the jaw: a face whose finest hour was yet to come.

'Samson Greene.' Samson extended his hand and the kid shook it.

'Luke,' he muttered softly, offering nothing more, still of the age where last names were reserved for a fraternity of peers – tossed around on the playing field and in dark basements, softly hooted by the smoking wall behind the school. *Luke*, the kid said as if it were a defeat, an obligatory admission that Samson was his senior. He reminded Samson of the son of a minister, a boy into which a respectful manner had been drilled until it was a reflex. They leaned up against the wall, shuttling the bottle back and forth. A tour group of geriatrics spread through the aisles of the slot machines like a plague of rodents. The casino began to blur. After the last few hellish days alone in the motel, Samson was glad to have company. He felt a surge of gratitude toward Luke as he handed over the last of the whiskey.

'Nice suit.'

'Thanks,' Luke said. 'I never wear it. I got it . . . I don't remember why I had to get it. My cousin's wedding maybe. I haven't worn it since.'

He had a slight, almost imperceptible accent. No, not the son of a minister but of a *missionary*, Samson decided, his native English pruned like a hothouse flower, kept protected from the invasive and vulgar argot used in the streets of the squalid backwater nation where he'd lived as a child.

Samson noticed Luke looking at his clothes. He could tell the kid didn't know what to make of them: the tan windbreaker streaked with dirt, the wrinkled pants that slumped around his waist. The absurd blue sneakers faded with dust. Luke took it all in and looked up at Samson. A very respectful kid, not quick to pass judgment, a kid raised to love his neighbor, testing out a little debauchery as innocently as he had once learned his catechism. His early years spent in Thailand or Burma maybe, where the missionary father had converted thousands while the boy stared out of the windows of a big house or played alone in the gated yard hunting snakes.

'Where did they go, the other two?'

'Those guys?' Luke shrugged. 'Play some roulette, I guess. Blackjack maybe, I don't know. You gambling?'

A kid not unlike the sort of kid he must have been at fifteen, sixteen. A kid who accepted Samson as Frank had: casually, without questions. He put his arm around him and Luke grinned, eyes slanted at the floor. Samson would have liked to lend him advice and wisdom. To be, for a while, the older brother he himself never had.

He was feeling superbly drunk. So he had lost everything! He was a freeman, released from his life to the living hereafter. He could do anything, go to Burma and proselytize, join a brotherhood of monks on a mountaintop in Asia. Buy a bottle of whiskey, gamble away everything he owned.

'Hey,' he said. 'What do you say we find the bar?'

'Cool,' Luke said.

'Where the hell is the bar in this place?' he asked, sloppily steering the kid across the casino floor.

Some hours later, Samson was sitting in front of a television turned to the Weather Channel in Luke's hotel room on the thirty-fourth floor. The room had cost nothing because the father of one of the boys – not Luke, naturally, but one of the others – was a regular at the casino, a heavy gambler for whom the red carpet was rolled out every time he came to town. Luke was sitting across from Samson, his legs thrown over the arm of a chair, the fedora mashed down on the back of his head. Samson was explaining again, with the blurred and extravagant logic of the very drunk, how he'd ended up in Vegas.

'You're saying totally annihilated? Is that what you're saying?' Luke asked.

'That's what I'm trying to tell you. I woke up and there was nothing. I couldn't remember – at first I couldn't even remember my own name.'

'You couldn't remember your name was Samson.'

'Right.'

'And then some doctor, the Ray guy, calls you.'

'No, no, no.' Samson tried to stand up, to pace, to clarify for Luke and himself the chronology of events that had led to this current situation, this exorbitant drunkenness on the thirty-fourth floor of a Las Vegas hotel called, what was it?

'The Mirage,' Luke offered.

'The Mirage.' But he couldn't seem to make his legs work, and fell back into the chair. 'With the son of a missionary,' he added.

'A what?'

'A *missionary*,' Samson repeated loudly, rummaging with a finger in the pack of cigarettes to see if there were any left.

'Who's a missionary?'

Samson leaned his head back and sighed.

'Your father.'

'He is not.'

Samson looked over at Luke and tried to focus. The kid had taken off his jacket and shirt and was sitting in a white undershirt with the fedora still clamped on his head, like a photograph of an old jazz musician except with no instrument. They always had the instrument in the photos, a battered horn that seemed to have absorbed all the light, casting the room in darkness.

'Then what was he doing in Burma?'

'In *what*?' Luke screeched, laughing as if Samson had just delivered the punch line of a joke.

'*Burma.*'

Luke straightened up, sensing the need for a solemn reply.

'He's an attorney. In L.A. He's never been to Burma.'

Samson tried to absorb this information calmly. Luke fingered the brim of his hat, his eyes on Samson, waiting. Fine, so his father was an attorney. There was no reason to let this steer them off the track they'd been on, straightening out just how it was that Samson had ended up where he had.

'At least you have a dad,' he said quietly. 'So what he's never been to Burma.'

Luke hesitated, trying to follow.

'I don't even remember my dad,' Samson explained. 'He left when I was three.'

'My old man is a total asshole,' Luke said, his face darkening.

'What do you mean?'

Luke shrugged. 'I mean he's an asshole.'

'Does he know you're here?'

'Are you kidding?' Luke snorted. 'He'd flip out. He thinks I'm in San Diego at a science fair.'

Samson stopped to think about this, struggling through the alcohol haze to see the kid for who he really was, though it had been a nice story, a pleasant thing to imagine the kid riding his Chinese-made bicycle through the rooms, believing his father was doing the work of God.

Luke picked at his shoelaces in silence.

'You know what?' Samson said at last.

'Yeah?'

'I'm going to tell you something.'

'What?'

'I want you to remember it, because nobody else is going to tell you.' He paused, looking the kid hard in the eye. 'People are no good, Luke. Take it from me, they'll just let you down.'

Luke nodded. 'Yeah, I guess.'

'It's true. But you know what? Fuck 'em. We don't need them.'

Luke glanced up and Samson flashed him a smile.

'Yeah,' Luke agreed, grinning.

'Fuck 'em,' Samson said, pleased with the sound of it.

'Fuck 'em,' Luke echoed.

Samson nodded, allowing this to sink in. The Weather Channel gave a tropical update. 'Now.' He rubbed his eyes. 'Where the hell was I?'

'In the hospital.'

Yes, Luke was there to stick it out with him, to see the story through to the end. His father was an asshole, so what – one day the kid would grow up and leave it all behind.

'Right. And I remember nothing. And there's this woman by my bed, a beautiful woman.' Let it be like a fairy tale then, a dark and handsome story, simple enough that the kid could one day tell it to his own children.

'Your wife.'

'My wife,' Samson said, settling back in to tell it.

'Your life,' Luke added.

'My wife, my life,' Samson said, feeling generous. 'Anna.'

With Samson orating and Luke clarifying, the master and his assisting scribe, they laid out the events of the past year. It was the first time Samson had told the whole story. Lavell, Donald, Lana, Ray, even Anna – each knew only parts of it, and besides, they had their own biases. Luke, however, was a fair and impartial witness. And so, with cantorial vibrato, drunk on whiskey and truth, attempting again and again to mount the chair to speak from a podium of air, Samson had it out. For nothing, any longer, could be used against him. He had suffered, and for this he would be granted amnesty. Luke would see to that. When it was time – when Samson had built his towering case and climbed atop it to gaze down at the pitiful world, when he had stood for a while in the just silence with the wind at his back before slowly beginning the descent, when his feet quietly, belatedly touched the earth – the kid would be there waiting. Samson would kneel before him, and Luke would lay his hands on Samson's head and bless him. And then, finally, Samson would be free.

It was four in the morning by the time they had gotten through it all. The room was littered with crumpled sheets of hotel stationery and the tiny bottles of booze they'd found in the minifridge. One of Samson's sneakers was dangling from the light fixture where he had tossed it to emphasize a point. They'd covered all the facts three or four times over. There had been moments of exhaustion and many deep troughs of silence, but these had only fueled greater, more florid streaks of language. Luke, with his constant interjections and insatiable, almost fanatical need for clarification, was as inexhaustible as Samson. 'Total annihilation!' he'd shouted whenever they'd arrived at a cul-de-sac in the story.

When they finally emerged on the other side of the confusion, Luke announced that he had a plan.

'The tumor,' he declared.

Samson realized it was meant to be a crucial revelation but it was too terse, too general for him to grasp the kid's meaning.

'Go on.'

'The pilo—'

'Pilocytic astrocytoma.'

'Removed, on the fourteenth of May, in the year 2000, at the University Medical Center of . . .' Here the kid raised his eyebrows and spread his hands palm-up. 'Where?'

'We know this, Las Vegas.'

'Exactly. Las Vegas.' Luke dug around for his shirt and jacket. 'Let's go.'

'Go where?'

'To the medical center!' Luke howled, frustrated with Samson's slowness to catch on.

'And why would we do that?'

'To get the tumor back!'

Samson was not quite so robustly drunk as he

had been earlier, and a slight, almost metallic hint of sobriety made him hesitate before speaking. But after a moment he concluded that he had no recourse but to cooperate with Luke. For one thing, he had already led him too far down the road of excess to turn back now, with all of the disappointment and feelings of betrayal that that would certainly incur in him. He didn't want to shatter the magnificent, glassy shine of the kid's belief, his utter conviction, in the inevitability of *coming to understand*. To raise one's hand in the prime of one's life and admit that one understands nothing, or worse, to understand and still remain powerless, was a bitter and bleak thing, and more than he could bear to shove the kid's nose in. Not now, at the height of their revelries.

But his unwillingness to let Luke down was not the only reason he'd willingly participate in whatever harebrained scheme the kid had concocted. Maybe it was an effect of the alcohol. Or a dawning sentimentalism that gave him a taste for grand gestures. But whatever the reason, going to claim the tumor, *his* tumor, from its clinical storage in the hospital made *sense* to Samson. Luke was right: it was what needed to be done. He would go and take it back because it stood for all he'd lost, because it *belonged* to him.

He wouldn't simply allow things to happen to him anymore. He was alive, and for the first time since he'd woken out of the slumber of his past life, he felt it. It was not that he was painfully aware of each moment, as he had been upon waking from the operation. It seemed to him now that it was probably only the dying who saw the world with such precise and formal clarity as that, knowing it was already lost to them. No, this was something different, as if at some point in the hazy bacchanal of the night he had been handed back his life. A moment of reprieve, his heart bursting with a high-spirited hope, hammering its percussion in his chest.

It was past four A.M. by the time they hailed a taxi from the line waiting in front of the hotel. In a distant precinct of his mind Samson registered that Luke was drunker than he'd thought. The kid's behavior had become more exuberant, downright flashy since they'd come downstairs. Samson made no real effort to calm him except to try and stay his hand as he peeled dollars off the bulging roll in his pocket, giving the damp, crinkled bills to passing strangers as if they were worthless as rupees.

'Save it. We might need it later,' Samson whispered.

'Right,' Luke agreed, retrieving a five he had just tucked into a cocktail waitress's belt.

The taxi deposited them in the parking lot of the emergency room. There was a man going through the automatic doors clutching his chest, but otherwise nothing suggested any crisis. The handful of people sitting in rows of vinyl seats and gazing up at the mounted televisions looked so profoundly bored they might have been taken for stunt doubles waiting to stand in for the bereaved. It was an unsettling change after the casino, and Luke and Samson stood bewildered in the glare of the fluorescent lights. Luke straightened his hat. It occurred to Samson that this is where he must have been brought after the police picked him up in the desert. He wondered whether, locked in oblivion, he had not felt relief to have his fate taken out of his own hands. Whether he had not lain down quite willingly in the gurney, closing his eyes and surrendering without protest all claims to cogency, no longer caring to understand at all.

A stern-looking triage nurse approached wearing the sort of plastic clogs that can easily be washed clean of blood. He wondered whether he should tell her about the memory that had been swabbed onto his mind like bacteria onto a petri dish.

'Have you checked in?'

Samson stared at her, unresponsive.

'Hello? I asked if you checked in yet?' she repeated, enunciating each syllable as if speaking to a foreigner or idiot. An image crossed Samson's mind of her administering electric shocks.

'We've come to the wrong place,' he said, grabbing Luke and pulling him back through the automatic doors.

Outside, Luke rubbed his arm and shot a look at Samson.

'We'd never get past her,' Samson explained.

They shuffled around the perimeter of the hospital until they found the main entrance. Luke had calmed down but Samson didn't trust it; chances were it was only the eye of the storm. On the taxi ride over, Luke had talked a blue streak, unfurling plans of attack that had, even in his own still potent high, struck Samson as far-fetched if not absurd. Still, he was aware that the unspoken pact he'd had with Luke almost from the beginning depended on a conspiracy of mutual indulgence, of humoring each other, and so he made no effort to check Luke's enthusiasm. Sure, they might pose as visiting doctors from Finland, he agreed, or knock out a couple of jani-tors and take their uniforms.

In the lobby was a small exhibition on skin grafts. Luke was immediately drawn to the display case. The charts, photos, and medical diagrams struck Samson as cruelly assembled to nauseate the layman, but Luke was fascinated. Samson went to get directions to the pathology lab, leaving the kid with his face pressed up against the case, a moist cloud of breath forming on the glass.

Yet when he returned a few minutes later, Luke had disappeared. There was no sign of him except for the black fedora lying on the floor. Samson snatched it up and, figuring that Luke couldn't have gotten too far, started down the hall. Not knowing what else to do with the hat, he put it on. It was too small, and finally he gave up trying to work it down and just let it ride high on his head, in the awkward yet rakish manner of the Orthodox Jews he'd watched swarming in frenzied, tropical activity through the diamond district of midtown Manhattan (they appeared to be concealing something large – *a chicken!* he thought freakishly – underneath). This sudden memory surprised him, and hurrying down the hall in pursuit of Luke, he felt a pang of longing for the irregular light of New York, brightness and sudden shade. But he abandoned the thought almost as soon as it came to him. Since leaving Clearwater he'd been desperately trying to avoid all thoughts not directly related to the present moment, aware that the quick deductions of memory would eventually send him crashing headlong into the one memory he wanted, more than anything, to avoid: a thousand men on the floor of the desert, blinking in dawn's light.

He scurried down the hall, hat perched atop his head, ducking around gurneys and the occasional patient in a wheelchair wearing the cotton gown that was the uniform of the ill, shapeless enough to fit the whole range of bodily humanity. Soon the long corridor gave way to other long, equally sterile stretches of corridor and Samson became disorientated. The sour chemical smell in the air, so archly inhuman, and the vile light that cast everything in a flat and sickly hue were enough to lend the place a tense, unnerving quality; it hardly needed the retarded child who suddenly appeared out of the wings, swiveling his head in some eternal effort to uncross his eyes, or the drooling old man with blue-veined legs who still looked somehow hopeful, as if misery were not his fate after all. These characters weighing in with the terminally suffering managed to tip the scales from merely unsettling to full-fledged nightmare. They were putting a serious damper on any happiness being drunk had afforded Samson.

Luke was nowhere to be found but Samson decided to go on with the plan anyway – a plan in the loosest sense, meaning gaining possession of the tumor in any way possible, since they'd never settled on a strategy. There was a chance, admittedly slim, that Luke was now making his own way to the pathology lab on the seventh floor. Or that his movable fascination had discovered something new to attach itself to, something that would safely hold his attention until Samson had carried out the operation himself.

He found the elevator and got in, a huge industrial car lined in metal. Shoving his hands in his jacket pockets, he discovered the last miniature bottle of liquor looted from the hotel, a booster shot of gin. He emptied it down his throat. An orderly got on at the third floor, pushing a patient in a gurney with the same detachment as the Chinese peddlers with their carts that Samson had seen in *National Geographic*. The patient was attached to an IV and looked gravely ill. Samson averted his eyes from her face, relieved when the doors slid open on the seventh floor.

He hurried down the hall toward the sign for the pathology lab. When he got there a young nurse was sitting behind the desk, a palefaced woman who looked like she could use a transfusion herself. He cavalierly struck up a conversation with her, as if she were a barmaid and not a medical professional with a direct phone line to Security. As they talked, a sense of calm confidence descended over him, a composure that stayed with him as, closing his fingers around her wrist, he declared that he needed to get into the lab. Somewhere in him was the new knowledge that he was capable of violent anger. The nurse pulled away and her eyes darted around in search of help, but if anyone else was on duty they were nowhere to be seen. He said nothing about being a visiting doctor from Finland; in fact he offered no explanation at all, just thrust and parried his way through the exchange with such overpowering force and stench of alcohol that the frightened woman, clearly believing she had a madman on her hands, surrendered and let him through.

It was like the well-organized scene of a horrendous and bloody accident. The counters were splattered with brownish stains, and everywhere were numbered jars and buckets filled with yellow-red clots: human clots, bits of flesh, fatty and bloody bits. *Irregular growths*. The smell of formalin hung heavily in the air, and there was a faint hum like a washing machine. Samson's stomach lurched and for a moment his determination faltered.

The nurse followed him in. She seemed to pick up on his hesitation, and took it as an opportunity to try to regain control. She would quickly show him around, she told him, but then he would have to leave. He watched as she snapped on a pair of latex gloves and felt around in a bucket of colored liquid, her eyes cast upward at the ceiling, until she came up with a rubbery, misshapen thing she claimed was a breast. *Gross tissue*, she called it, the technical term for not yet drawn and quartered, pickled and stained, and slapped, to the thickness of a single cell, onto a slide.

Samson's queasiness retreated, replaced by engrossing fascination. Drunk, as if in a dream, he demanded that they make their way through the specimens. The nurse floundered and he hissed a few threatening terms until she hurried back to the counter and held aloft a gallbladder stone pinched between tweezers. She haltingly described the process whereby the gross tissue was reduced to a mere shadow of itself on a slide, like a fingerprint, a calligraphic blot, to be examined under a powerful lens for signs of carcinoma. She opened the closet doors to reveal row upon row of little drawers filled with numbered slides, endless rounds of human misery and reprieve: malignant, benign, malignant, benign.

'Nurse,' he began, adding an edge of special pleading to his voice.

She turned to him, this pale woman in a starched white coat, and said, 'I'm not a nurse.'

He looked at her.

'Then what are you?'

'A lab technician,' she said, and all at once he decided to do away with all civilities and cut to the point. In a loud and commanding voice he demanded back the gross tissue that a year ago had been cut away from his brain.

She backed up against the counter. 'We don't keep it that long,' she whispered.

'What do you mean you don't keep it? Why don't you keep it?'

'The tissue disintegrates. We throw it away after a few weeks. We keep a small piece in paraffin. And the slides, those we keep. Those we keep, basically, forever.'

Samson struggled with the idea of his tumor disposed with the rest of the hospital's bloody trash, bone chips and butchery, used syringes and cruddy bandages. There had been some sober part of him that had known all along that it would be so. But there were the slides – he vaguely remembered them now – and he would have to content himself with those. The technician began to edge toward the door but Samson stepped forward to block her.

'I want my slides.' Until now it had been mostly fun and games. She had complied with his wish to be shown the spectacle of human pulp, trying to avoid an incident. Most likely she, like the woman at the motel reception desk, had had routine experience with lunatics. 'Give me my slides,' he repeated.

She had wet, black pupils, the eyes of a small woodsy animal. Her teeth were large. When her mouth was at ease the front teeth strayed rabbit-like below the upper lip.

'I can't,' she said, the lip quivering.

'But you can,' he assured her, placing his hand on the wall by her head and leaning in to blast his eighty-proof breath in her face. 'They belong to me.'

She pulled back and cringed, her eyelids fluttering. She glanced skittishly over his shoulder at the computer.

'That's it,' he encouraged. 'Let's look it up.'

He pulled her by the elbow and they shuffled across the room. She tapped a key and the battered terminal came to life.

'What's your name?'

He told her. She still had her latex gloves on. His name appeared on the screen. Lot number 66589037. Juvenile pilocytic astrocytoma. Left temporal lobe.

'That's me. Come on.' He led her by the wrist to the closets plastered with orange biohazard stickers. Methodically, almost lazily, she opened the metal drawers and shuffled through the slides. She must have hoped someone would come in and deliver her from the ordeal. Samson bore down on her and she crumpled. She picked out the right slides and handed them over.

There were six of them. He lifted them to the light. Each had three identical half-moons with a small dot beneath. Eighteen shavings, stained fuchsia, one cell thick, of the lump with which all of this began, removed a year ago from his brain. He might as well have captured the Rosetta stone, he was so moved by the secrets the slivered tissue contained. He would have liked to examine them under the microscope right then, but knew it would be pushing his luck. He pocketed the slides and lifted the trembling technician to her feet. He looked deep into her black, woodland eyes. 'Brava,' he whispered, and then he turned and hurried out the door, switching off the lights on his way out, plunging the lab, the technician, and all the gross tissue into darkness.

A minute later he was waiting in front of the elevator when Luke came tearing around a corner, flapping one arm and clutching a plastic model of a brain with the other. He skidded to a stop in front of Samson, looking sheepish. Samson clapped a hand over Luke's mouth and when the elevator doors slid open they stumbled in.

It was light out when they left the hospital. Luke fell asleep in the taxi, holding his knees like a baby, the plastic brain with removable hemispheres lolling on the seat beside him. Luke's hair was damp with sweat, and his face looked sickly. Outside the window, the marquees were shabby in the daylight. Some letters were burned-out, letters that would eventually end up scrambled in a dump like an abandoned game of Scrabble. Samson fingered the slides in his pocket, anxiously turning to look out the back window where he half expected to see the police in pursuit.

When they arrived at the Mirage he gently shook Luke awake. The kid looked at him long and hard as if he were a stranger, and then he stumbled out of the taxi, making it clear he didn't want to be followed. Samson watched him disappear through the brass-rimmed doors, clutching the brain. A flash of his reflection in the glass, and then he was gone. Samson felt a pang of something, perhaps regret. He could already see the ugly scene at the hospital for what it had been: a pathetic, last-ditch effort to regain control of his life. He turned to the taxi driver.

'The Four Palms.'

'The what?' The driver had the nostrils of a bull.

'The Four Palms,' he repeated, his voice strange to his own ears.

Back in his motel room, the message light on the phone was still unlit. The television was working again, the meteorologist saying, *Just find a friend and move to higher ground*, as if he were delivering the gospel. Smiling and saying, *Now, let's take you into Wednesday*, marching through days of the week, across the map of America, and into the bright future.

Samson passed out on the bed. When he woke his head was throbbing. He felt sick to his stomach. Going over the events of the night before, he tried to straighten out what exactly had happened. He found his tan windbreaker crumpled on the floor and reached into the pocket. The slides were there. He held them up to the light. He brought them close to his face and looked through each half-moon with the drifting star. *How did this happen?* he wondered. It was the simplest thought, the most basic, and he thought it again, pacing now. *How did this happen, all this?* He realized that all he knew about Luke was that his father was a lawyer who had never been to Burma, that the guy was an asshole to the kid, who didn't yet know the ways in which this would shape his life. Samson didn't even know Luke's last name. But that was just the beginning of all he didn't know. That was only brushing the surface of his vast ignorance.

He monitored the forecasts, minute-by-minute updates that made it impossible to trust even the bluest sky when the weather team, armed with photographic proof, predicted rain. Most weather mattered so little, really. It was a subject that came up only when there was nothing left to say, and this made it hard to believe that the steady flow of information was not encoded with a more profound message. Hunched on the unmade bed,

Samson considered the possibility that the meteorologists were actually disseminating classified information in code. *Moisture coming in from the south*, the weatherman said. But who was trying to reach whom? Or maybe these were not signals between people after all, but something much greater, a sign emanating from a cosmic source, a power of goodness whose chosen envoy was a satellite coasting soundlessly above in its vigil over the planet. The message, if one could make it out, being only this: *ALLISWELLALLISWELLALLISWELL*.

When the phone rang he froze. For an instant he wondered if it was Ray. When he had gone to withdraw cash from his bank account the day before, he'd discovered that Ray had deposited the promised sum of money. It made Samson feel cheap, as if he'd been bought. It also increased his paranoia that his movements were being tracked. But in a flash he understood that it couldn't possibly be Ray calling. The doctor was no longer interested in him. Ray wanted believers, and Samson had deserted.

It could only be Donald. He lunged across the room, nearly knocking the phone off the night table.

'Hello?'

'Calm down.'

'Donald? Is that you? Where the hell—'

'First thing, don't ever do that again. You'd think from the sound of those messages you were being held at gunpoint. Against your will, Sammy, with fingernails torn out one by one. Nearly gave me a heart attack.'

'What took so long?'

'What do you think, I check my messages every second? I got things to do. Plus, why do I have voice mail? Limited accessibility. If I wanted to be reached twenty-four hours a day I'd get a cell phone. Walk around with the thing strapped on, getting fucking microwaved to death by all the people trying to reach me. Where are you?'

'The Four Palms Motel.'

'The what?'

'The Four Palms.'

'Never heard of it.'

Samson looked around the room. What few clothes he had were strewn across the floor. The sheets had been tugged off the bottom of the bed as if a struggle had taken place. The maid hadn't been in all week.

'It's not the Flamingo, but it's all right. Listen—'

'Stark raving. I had to hold the phone a foot away.' Donald coughed into the receiver. 'What is that in the background? You have people there?'

'It's the weather.'

'What are you listening to the weather for? It's three hundred and sixty days of sunshine a year, Sammy. Like paradise. It's not the fastest-growing city for nothing.'

'So they say.'

'Who says? People don't know this. If they knew, there wouldn't be a single acre left. I got in early. *We* got in early. Don't think your old pop forgot.' The thought of Donald's little barren plot of Zion almost brought tears to Samson's eyes.

'Donald, I need to see you. Where are you?'

'Like Twenty Questions. You wouldn't last a minute with some of the types I know. Curiosity ate the cat, Sammy. I'm in Barstow, if you have to know.'

'What are you doing in Barstow?'

'Jesus H. Christ!'

'Sorry.' Samson made a fist then flexed. He picked up the phone and paced between the beds. 'I'm sorry, right now it's all a little much. Things happened. I left Clearwater. You have no idea the state I've been in.'

'You'll adjust. Who wants to be stuck in that joint longer than necessary? Sure it was nice, but a little dull for my taste. The only thing was the meals. I told my niece, we ate like kings. *Like kings*, I told her. And the toilet paper, every time, folded like new.'

Silence.

'Killed the cat,' Samson said softly, stalled between the unmade beds, having gone as far as the telephone cord would reach, like a man performing at breathtaking heights with only a rope around his waist.

'What? I don't know what you're saying, Sammy. You're talking gibberish.'

Samson exploded. 'For God's sake, Donald, do you realize what they're doing there? Do you have even the slightest notion?'

There was silence and when Donald answered a gulf had opened between them. 'Like I told you, I don't ask questions. I have a job, I do it. They tell me not to talk, I don't talk. Understand?'

The television flickered. Somewhere in the far north of Canada there would be snow, falling soundlessly over the Beaufort Sea, falling over the Arctic without a soul to see it. What kind of weather was that, Samson wondered, and how was one to use such information except as proof that the world was too much to bear? He felt disappointed and foolish for calling, and wondered what to say to Donald. He hadn't expected that Donald would fail to understand, that he would be unable to help – though help with what, Samson didn't know anymore. This was a man whose head he'd been inside, a man who was now inside his head. He knew that as the detonation collapsed, Donald had felt a bolt of love for a girl with red hair.

The weatherman gestured north, in the direction of Canada.

'Where is Newfoundland?' Samson quietly asked aloud. 'Do people know without maps where Newfoundland is?'

Donald's voice softened. 'Sammy, you're a good kid. Go home to your wife. A thousand bucks she misses you. Probably she's waiting for you right now. It's not too late for you, Sammy. Do me a favor and go home.'

'The memory you gave them, I know what it is. All those soldiers, their heads blown back.' His voiced cracked. 'Blood in their eyes, knocked onto the desert floor—'

'Look, I didn't know,' Donald cut him off, his voice lowered. 'It was too late when they told me. I wouldn't have cared except that it was you. Like my own son, Sammy. A man does what he has to do, but if I woulda known . . . Look, all I can say is that it's something between us. Intimate like, you understand? You carrying in your head something that happened to me when I was a kid. They told me never to talk about it and then one day they ask me to talk. I needed the money so I did. If I'd known, it woulda been a different story. But I didn't, you gotta believe that. Who woulda guessed that such a thing was possible?'

Samson felt himself getting dizzy.

'It was an amazing thing, Sammy, you gotta understand. That's what I wanted to tell you. That it scared the living shit outta me, but it was amazing.'

He could hear Donald saying something else but it didn't matter anymore what, because then and there it occurred to him that maybe the emptiness he'd been living with all this time hadn't really been emptiness at all, but loneliness gone unrecognized. How can a mind know how alone it is until it brushes up against some other mind? A single mark had been made, another person's memory imposed onto his mind, and now the magnitude of his own loss was impossible for Samson to ignore. It was breathtaking. He sank to his knees.

'Sammy? I said, are you there?'

It was as if a match had been struck, throwing light on just how dark it was.

He stopped sleeping. He was exhausted but he wanted to remain alert, aware of everything. He felt as if he'd finally been returned to himself. The memory that had been loaded into his mind had broken the spell he'd been under since he'd woken from the operation. It was as if he had lived the past year in a trance. *A fugue state,* he had once heard Lavell say to describe the condition he'd been found in, ignorant of even his own name. Fugue, like fog or fugitive. Like music at a funeral.

He felt foolish, realizing how readily he had allowed himself to be indoctrinated by Ray, how hungrily he had consumed whatever scraps the doctor had thrown him. He had trusted him because he was the only one who seemed to find some beauty, some worth, in his condition. Not the victim of a meaningless tragedy but a man who had somehow been chosen. Samson realized that he knew almost nothing about him. The only proof that he'd known Ray at all was the memory that, unless he deliberately avoided it, kept erupting in his head. It was a relationship struck up in a moment, forged on a proving ground where whatever took place was supposed to be without consequences beyond the scope of the experiment. Ray wasn't a bad man, only a man misled by his visions, one who'd forsaken all culpability in favor of the purchase of a distant, uncertain thing.

Samson checked out of the motel at dawn and walked to the bus station. Since the incident at the hospital he had felt on edge, expecting the police to show up outside his motel room at any moment. He briefly considered going back to L.A. to see Lana, but decided against it. He didn't want to show up, depressed and stinking, to intrude on her and Winn, young and in love, with their whole lives ahead of them. Anyway, what could she do for him now? He thought about going back to California and finding his old street and the house he'd grown up in. He felt sure that it must have been where he was headed when they'd found him a year ago in the desert, and now it seemed right to finish that trip. But when he got to the bus station he lost his conviction and sat listlessly on the bench watching the buses groan to life, the sky snuffing out their headlights as it lightened. He put his head in his hands. His eyes stung from lack of sleep.

There was a dusty Greyhound going directly to Santa Cruz and while the driver was stretching his legs and making small talk in the station, a girl climbed up the steps and peered inside. There was no one on the bus yet and she came back out, looked around, and boarded again as quietly as a thief. She took a seat in the back by the window. When she leaned her head against the glass Samson caught his breath because her small heart-shaped face looked so much like Anna's. He almost could believe that by some mistake in time it *was* Anna, aged eighteen or nineteen, having woken only an hour ago in her childhood bed and hurriedly walked through her house saying good-bye to the rooms one by one. There was so little he knew about his wife. He would have liked to call and hear her voice, but he didn't know how to even begin explaining to her all that had happened and how he felt, and he knew it wasn't fair to keep pulling her back when she seemed to be finally getting on without him. He had left a message while he knew she was at work, explaining that he'd left Clearwater and was probably going to go back to California for a while. The last thing he wanted was for her to have to worry that he'd disappeared again.

A few more passengers followed and then the driver got on and started up the bus. As it coasted out of the lot Samson continued to watch the girl. He was overcome by a need to talk to her. Leaping up, he shouted for the bus to stop. The few people milling in the parking lot watched dumbly as he chased after it, stumbling and waving his arms. Coins fell from his pockets and skittered across the ground. He ran alongside it as it lumbered onto the road, pounding it with his fists, and even after it had come to a full stop, after it was clear that the driver had heard his cry and heeded, Samson continued to pummel the door like the madman he knew he was not, allowing himself the increasingly familiar pleasure of getting carried away. *Making an impression*, he thought to himself, feeling remarkably lucid as the driver slid open the door and stared down at him.

Slowly, theatrically, like a man twice his age, Samson lumbered up the steps. He handed the driver two crumpled twenties – he had no idea how much a ticket was – and the driver's face curled into a scowl. Samson dismissed him with a glance and turned to the rows of seats. The five or six passengers stared at him. He paused at the top of the aisle, allowing them to take him in, to sniff out his suffering like a pack of wild dogs. What did he have to hide? Let them devour him. He met each gaze as he made his way toward the girl, clutching the seats like a wounded man. She was staring at him too, looking bewildered. He slid into the seat next to her, taking off his jacket and calmly arranging it on his lap. The girl turned her face back to the window. An unpleasant smell wafted in from somewhere and Samson realized it was his own, not suffering at all but plain B.O. *Nothing to be done about that now*, he thought, turning with a look of defiance to the driver standing at the top of the aisle. Their eyes met, and for a moment it seemed the whole bus held its breath.

'What?' the girl asked.

Samson hadn't spoken, but he turned and faced the girl now.

'Do you mind if I sit here?'

'Okay.'

She turned back to the window, her hands folded in her lap. But her voice seemed to have settled things, because the driver got back behind the wheel shaking his head and nosed the bus onto the road. Slumped in their seats, the other passengers seemed to forget about Samson. But, because of his nearness, his smell – because he had singled her out among them – the girl could not ignore him. She pressed herself up against the window, but the more she looked away, the more he knew she was considering him. He wanted to talk, try things out on her, to rehearse with one who looked so much like a young vision of his wife.

She wore frayed brown corduroys and a yellow T-shirt that hung on her thin frame. Either they belonged to someone else or she had shrunk drastically from the person she once was. It looked like her last haircut had been done with a saw. She wore a crucifix on a string around her neck.

When Las Vegas dwindled then vanished behind them, she reached down and took a little book out of the backpack at her feet. It was well handled, the pages tattered and folded back. *The Holy Bible* was embossed in gold letters across the cover. The girl cupped the book protectively in her hands, carrying it toward the window light. Samson watched her read, her lips moving soundlessly. He wracked his brain, searching for something, anything, he might remember. He'd been a professor of literature, he must have known the New Testament as well as a Christian does, must have memorized the gory, fanatical deaths of each saint the way a fan knows the knockouts of every boxer, who by fire, who by water, who by a swift jab to the stomach causing internal bleeding.

'Is it any good?'

She turned to him, blinking through the strands of hair that fell unevenly across her face. He had to control the impulse to brush them away. She didn't have the face of a believer; hers was too decidedly suspicious.

'The *Bible*?' she asked.

His ability to disconcert people was something he'd only recently been discovering, though he hadn't been conscious at the time of his greatest, most compelling triumph – disappearing from New York and turning up in the desert without his memory. The shock factor must have been off the scale, and it was Anna alone who'd suffered it.

'The Bible, yes. Do you like it?'

She closed the book and turned to him. Apart from the shape of her face and her dark hair, up close she didn't appear so similar to Anna after all. She had a broad, flat nose that gave her a look of impudence. But there was something – a fragility or perceptiveness maybe – that she shared with his wife.

'Like it? I don't think that's the point, really.' Her nostrils flared as she spoke and she turned and traced a few letters on the grimy window. She had long, thin, aristocratic-looking fingers, though the fingernails were blunt and dirty.

'What *is* the point?'

She looked at him through narrowed eyes, taking him in. She seemed to be struggling to decide whether she should change seats. The desert fled past through the window.

'Salvation. Redemption,' she finally said matter-of-factly. She lifted a slender, ecclesiastical finger to her mouth and delicately gnawed on a hangnail. 'The glory of God. Guidance for the pilgrim's soul.'

Not only were her fingernails grubby; her face looked dirty too. She probably hadn't bathed for days. Samson wondered whether the smell was coming from her rather than him. Or possibly it was both of them, two smelly pilgrims at the back of the bus.

'Great. Read me something.'

'You're serious?'

'Sure. Who doesn't want salvation? Redemption? By all means. Give me glory. I'm starving for glory.'

'If you're being sarcastic—'

'Who's being sarcastic? I just nearly broke my neck running after the bus so I could talk to you. Whatever you want to tell me or read to me is fine. Pick one of your favorite parts. I'd like that. Okay?'

'Why'd you want to talk to me so badly?' She did nothing to disguise her distaste.

'You look like someone I know, that's all. Don't get nervous. I feel a little stupid about it now, so why don't you just read me something from your book.'

'It's not a book, it's the Bible.'

'The *Holy* Bible,' Samson added, leaning his head back and closing his eyes.

A moment of silence.

'You really want me to?'

'I wouldn't have asked.'

He heard her shuffle through the pages. 'Okay, how about this? I read this when I was in India. It was like I'd suddenly woken up after being asleep for years.'

'Perfect.'

'My head was full of all this Hindu stuff, which was all well and good, except I hadn't thought about Jesus since I was a kid and my Sunday school teacher told me Jesus was my only true friend. Which at the time – because I was young and hadn't gone through spiritual bankruptcy yet – seemed mean.'

It was more than Samson had bargained for. The girl continued.

'Here it is. From the Gospel of Matthew: *Come unto me, all ye that labor and are heavy laden, and I will give you rest. Take my yoke upon you, and learn of me; for I am meek and lowly in heart: and ye shall find rest unto your souls.'* Samson thought he heard a tremor in her voice and opened his eyes. 'It's beautiful, isn't it?' she said, looking out the window, her finger still resting on the page.

'Yes. Rest unto your souls. It's very nice. What were you doing in India?'

'Hmm? Oh, you know. What does anyone do in India? Stay at ashrams, read the Upanishads. Try to track down some guru that someone told you is *the one*. Hanging out in Varanasi on the ghats of the Ganges, watching the cremations. Breathing in the smell of sandalwood and burning flesh. Have you ever smelled burning human flesh?'

He paused and pretended to wrack his mind though he was pretty sure that even with full memory capacity he wouldn't have had to hesitate.

'No, I don't believe I have.'

Despite her initial air of suspicion she was surprisingly willing to talk, a practiced wayfarer who seemed to understand another's longing for conversation.

'It's sort of acrid and almost sweet,' she explained. 'They bring the body down wrapped in gold paper. And everyone's happy because a soul is being set free, you know, throwing these pretty flowers, and the boatman takes what's left of the body, takes the ashes out to the middle of the river. And maybe fifteen or twenty feet downriver, someone is squatting in the water washing clothes or brushing their teeth. For them, there's no distinction between life and death; it's just one unbroken circle. And you're sitting there thinking, is that safe? Aren't they going to catch some awful disease? And then you go back to the room you share with like ten other people and you get into your little dirty bed and cry, because you realize you're probably never going to be that spiritually enlightened that you stop caring about germs and disease and just trust in the power of Brahman. Because you grew up in America in a nice clean house with parents that tried to shelter you but ended up fucking you up, and you'll always be branded with that. And no matter how hard you try, you'll never be able to wrap yourself into those yoga positions that even the beggars on the street can do, their legs tucked up behind their heads.'

'Because you're American.'

'And totally inflexible. And so you just sit in your bed and cry, and pretty soon you realize you've been in India for, like, more than a year, and you're totally exhausted and sick of curry and all the filth in the streets and you're lonely as hell.'

'And suddenly it seems like having Jesus as your one true friend is not such a bad idea.'

The girl turned to him, surprised. 'Are you a Christian?'

'No.'

'What are you?'

'Bankrupt.'

She nodded sympathetically.

'So you got on a plane and came back?' he asked.

'Eventually, but it took a while. I had to get

used to the idea that it wasn't going to work out. I'd dropped out of college, sold all my stuff to get enough money together for the trip. My parents loved that. And socially I'd pretty much burned my bridges back home. The only friends I really had were the people I was hanging out with in India, and looking back now I can say that most of them didn't have it all there.' She tapped a finger to her head. 'I used to listen to the radio a lot on a little shortwave my father once gave me. Usually I could get World Service or Voice of America, but I also liked listening to the local stations. Sitars and stuff. There were these soap operas that were in some sort of Hindi, but just the sound of these people swooning and carrying on like that, you know, was fascinating. And one day I was flipping through the stations and I found one, an American voice, and he was talking about God.'

'About Jesus Christ,' Samson added helpfully. It hadn't taken much to get her going, and he didn't want her to clam up now. There was something tentative about her, as if she might cease at any moment, extinguished like a nervous flame.

'He called him Christ Our Savior. I sank to the floor and listened. The man, this preacher, had the most beautiful voice. Very intimate, like he was only talking to me. He leads a group, the Calvary Chapel, and he read from the Book of Job. I listened until he went off the air. By the end I was really crying hard and the next day I went out and found a Bible. I listened to that program every day for three weeks straight and then I came home.'

'Home?'

She looked out the window, squinting her eyes against the harsh light. 'Brookline, Massachusetts.' He could almost hear the greenness of the place in her voice, the grief-stricken autumns and the sweet smell of fresh grass in summer, a place as far from where they now were as India. 'My parents were basically horrified. They hardly recognized me. When they picked me up at the airport my mother just cried and cried. She said I looked like one of those starving children on television. You know, the ones you see while comfortably watching the six o'clock news with a martini? But it wasn't like she was hurrying to embrace me, or anything. I think she was afraid she might catch something. So I hugged her myself and told her she was a child of God. And that made her cry harder.'

Her name was Patricia but everyone called her Pip, something that often happened in WASP families, she explained, the names that had been in the family for years getting replaced in childhood by sporty nicknames, Apple or Kit or Kat. Like Kathleen Kennedy, who of course wasn't Protestant, but in the same spirit was called Kick. Punchy names that rang of a certain brawn, of the ruddiness of coming back from a football game in the early dark, cheeks flushed with autumn and cheer. Pip and Kick and Apple *and Snap and*

Crackle and Pop, Samson added mentally. And Chip and Pebble, Pip went on, like the members of a corny seventies band.

Minutes passed in which they said nothing. Pip drummed her fingers against the window, leaving smudges on the glass. Samson wanted to press her on. He wanted as much from her as she would give.

'Pip,' he said.

'Yes.'

'It's nice.'

'It's all right.'

She'd changed it a few times. For a while she'd called herself Pippalada after the sage who, in the Upanishads, says practice austerity, continence, faith for a year, then ask what questions you wish. When the year was up she changed her name to Laura, after a girl from Minneapolis who'd died in a bus that went over the side of a mountain. This was near Manali, in the north of India. Tibetan monks, refugees in saffron robes, appeared through crevices in the cold, white peaks. Months later, when she walked into her childhood bedroom for the first time in two years, she cried when she saw the framed macramé with the letters *P-I-P* above her bed.

Outside, the desert was brutal, the light high-density. The bus made a pit stop and everyone filed out into the absurd heat. Samson bought two Cokes from a machine and gave one to Pip. He took a few pictures of her leaning up against the bus, as if they were tourists together. She was at ease in front of the camera; probably she had been photographed often as a child.

'I used to take pictures. When I first started traveling I took pictures of everything,' she explained.

'And now?'

'I don't know. I guess I lost my camera at some point.'

She shrugged and twisted the tab on her can back and forth, reciting the letters of the alphabet. It broke off on *K*.

'*K*? Who's *K*? I'm going to fall in love with a person whose name begins with a *K*.' She paused, pressing the frosted can to her forehead. 'I don't even know your name,' she said. He told her. 'Really? You're not making that up?'

'Why would I make it up?'

'I don't know; it's an unusual name. You know the story about Samson, I guess? From the Book of Judges?'

His mother had once told it to him, a man with long hair and great strength. The hair was the secret to his strength, but the woman he loved betrayed him, cutting it as he slept. At the time, the story had not deeply affected him, the young unbiblical Samson.

They climbed back aboard the bus and Pip took out the Bible.

'Tremendous violence,' she said. She didn't open the book, just held it in her palm as if testing its weight. It was all inside her head. In grade school she had been an excellent student, she told him. She could read something twice and recite it back. At her parents' cocktail parties she was asked to perform.

'It's in the Book of Judges. Samson judged Israel for twenty years. First he killed a lion. Then he killed a thousand Philistines with the jawbone of a donkey. The spirit of the Lord rushed on him. That's how the passage goes: it *rushed* on him,' she said. 'His long hair was the symbol of his vows to God, and God was on his side.' She looked out the window. 'Tremendous violence,' she repeated, staring at the alkali flats, the remains of an ocean as old as the Great Flood. 'He fell in love with a woman. Delilah, remember?'

Samson nodded. He was feeling edgy, as if something was welling up in him, threatening to spill over.

'Delilah, of course,' he said.

'He fell in love with her and she betrayed him.'

She could have been telling the story of an Indian soap opera. She could have been a small precocious girl burdened with the gift of recollection, orating the story to her parents' friends, people named Chip and Pebble who laughed and held aloft their dry martinis to toast her. 'She cut off his hair,' she continued, visibly moved, though Samson wondered if perhaps she was performing now. She recited: '*The Philistines are upon you! Delilah said. When Samson awoke from his sleep, he thought, I will go out as at other times, and shake myself free. But he did not know the Lord had left him.* That's how it goes. And then the Philistines storm in and gouge out his eyes.'

It was thrilling, the awful violence, the sheer injustice. Samson could only barely contain the urge he had to let rip a savage shriek, to leap up and run up and down the aisle smacking the heads of each passenger to rouse them from their stupor.

'They gouge out his eyes?' he asked, pitching forward.

Pip tipped her head back.

'They gouge them out and tie him up and throw him in prison.' Her empty hand hovered in the air between them, the fingers slightly arched as if in a question. 'When his hair grows back again he asks the Lord to grant him one more act of strength. And when the Philistines bring him out to entertain them he grabs the pillars of the banquet hall and pulls them down. The roof falls, killing everyone, including Samson. *And those he killed at his death were more than those he had killed during his life.*'

Samson – the latter-day Samson hailing through the desert on his way to Santa Cruz – raised his eyebrows. He wondered if it was a sign, if there was a fate to his name that he should more carefully consider. Pip shifted her eyes away and he thought he saw a fleeting smile, but when she turned back her face was serious.

She was on her way to a mass baptism in the Pacific. She'd heard about it while she'd been at home – *convalescing*, as her mother announced in a loud whisper when anyone called on the phone. At night Pip would go out, saying she was meeting her friend Dina, a dull, unambitious girl she knew from high school who worked at the ice cream shop in town. Instead, Pip drove along the back roads to the Calvary Chapel Fellowship meetings in Boston. One night someone brought pictures in from *Life* magazine. Hundreds, maybe thousands of people gathered on the beach, clapping and singing. Some held tambourines or small, grubby children. A line snaked to the water's edge where a man had just been plunged under and pulled up again, his hands in the air, fists clenched, his head thrown back like a boxer who'd just been hit. It was hard to tell if he was laughing or crying. Small rivulets of water streamed down his face, the sun glinted off him. The man who stood beside him was the preacher whose voice Pip had listened to for three weeks straight before she left India. Behind them the wide-angle ocean expanded, remote and ominous, toward the horizon.

Pip described how after the meeting she'd driven back on the dark roads. As she talked Samson fanatically imagined the scenes, adding details of his own, like her headlights sweeping across the trees. She stopped in town and picked up a pint of ice cream that Dina handed across the counter in a silver insulated bag. At home she put it in the freezer with the others and went up to bed. But she couldn't shake the image of the baptism from her head. The next day she made some inquiries, and a week later she was saying good-bye to her parents again, her mother averting her eyes from the crucified Christ she'd taken to wearing around her neck. Her father, who couldn't hide his disgust, asked if she'd packed her hair shirt. By five that afternoon he would be having drinks at the club, relieved to be able to return to the vision of his daughter bounding across the commons of a New England college to meet a young man with a strong jaw and firm handshake and a name like Pierce.

'Who did you say I remind you of?' she asked, turning away as if she'd already lost interest in the answer. *It was enough that they cut off his hair, but to gouge out his eyes?* Gently he slid his hand into hers. She seemed to take no offense, at ease with the intimacy that from time to time arises between strangers who have no claim on each other.

They emerged from the desert into the vast system of tract housing. Her long fingers twitched, the cuticles were ragged. The sun shone through the dusty window.

She fell asleep, her head slumped forward on her chest and the Bible lodged between her knees. Samson took the slides out of his jacket pocket. He breathed on them and rubbed out the smudges with the corner of his shirt. The delicate samples of tissue were like the fingerprints of the hand of fate. His great-uncle Max had been an amateur artist whose obsession was an Italian city that he drew from an aerial view. Although Max was from

Germany, as a young man he had lived in Italy for a year. Twice or three times he had taken a hot-air-balloon ride there. Years later he began to draw the city he'd lived in, reconstructing it from memory – the streets, churches, and squares rendered with mathematical precision. Samson had admired these drawings as a child, and somehow the specimens with their intricate net of crosshatches reminded him of them.

He studied the flecks of tissue, matter produced by his own brain. There was something uncanny and miraculous about it, he thought now: the dimensionless mind breeding dimension. A year ago he had tumbled down a hole, a trapdoor into a place that seemed to have depth and width, distance and perspective – that seemed *habitable*. He had stumbled and landed in the immaculate geography of the mind. But from the beginning memories had assaulted the emptiness, forcing him back into the world. His mind had filled with the detritus of recollection, and then, as a final humiliation, it had been broken into and vandalized. What Ray had refused to see was that no matter how great the desire is to be understood, the mind cannot abide any presence but its own. To enter another's consciousness and stake a flag there was to break the law of absolute solitude on which that consciousness depends. It was to threaten, and perhaps irrevocably damage, the essential remoteness of the self. This transgression was unforgivable.

Pip stirred in her sleep.

And yet what else does it mean to be loved, Samson wondered, than to be understood? What else but to be profoundly touched by another? He thought about who he had been before the tumor, telling himself the story of his old life like a sad tale. Once there had been a woman he loved whose body he had taken into his own hands, maybe amazed that such touching left no impression. Turning on the bedside lamp, he had found her unmarked. Her name was a sound you could go through, coming out the other side onto an identical place, *Anna*, a mirror image, a double echo in which there was nothing to grasp onto. Maybe he had loved her too much, feeling he was unable to get her close enough; that so long as she remained a separate person, he could get to know her only so well. And because the core of her would always remain elusive, threatening to slip away, he'd switched course and faded away to protect himself from the loss, his voice breaking up, *over and out*, like a pilot's adrift in space.

Or maybe the story had happened differently. Perhaps his love for her had frustrated him, the impossibility of ever getting through. Maybe they had taken drives out of the city, crossing delicate bridges whose steel fibers hummed and swayed imperceptibly in the wind. They traveled north into the country where they imagined a future, passing through small towns with steeples and weather vanes. Anna would take off her shoes and draw her feet up under her. December, a faint snow on the ground, they would come to a crossroads and the dying yellow light would glow under the sky's dark hem. She would be silent, her head tipped against the glass. Then suddenly she would look up, her mouth open, her face changed by an expression he'd never seen before and that made her seem unrecognizable. Maybe he had wanted to rage out against such changes, against the fact that he could not account for her.

Or maybe even before the tumor developed, it was he who had tired of being bound to her. Maybe he had just wanted to get free, having outgrown the person that all along he'd been to her, on whom she depended. How was it possible to wake up every day and be recognizable to another when so often one was barely recognizable to oneself? If Anna was right, if a person was no more than a collection of habits, perhaps the habits were maintained only so as not to disappoint the lover that one slept beside each night. But what chance did that leave for becoming, one fine day, a wholly different being? Maybe it was he, after all, who had not been able to abide being accounted for, who had no longer wanted to be reached.

Once there was a woman he loved. That was how it had begun. But from there the story might have unfolded any number of ways. Only the end was always the same: he had emptied himself of the ballast of memory and lunged weightless into the future. Alone and astonished, attempting to take with him not even a trace. In the end he had betrayed the woman he loved, and who was there who would not judge him for that?

Anna, backward or forward, the name a ghost of itself. If he called her, if he could reach her now, what would there be to say?

Pip gently snored at his side, the sweet, strangled inhalations of a baby. He imagined her as a child at six or seven, her jaw jutting forward and her tongue touching her upper lip in cool defiance. By her side her mother, practically a child herself, her hair parted in the middle and falling loosely over her shoulders, not yet cut, primped, and permed into the unattractive helmet of middle age. Her skin yet unlined by misfortune, by the antics of a daughter who grew up to prefer squalor to her own comfortable home, whose lack of inner peace drove her across the world to be touched by the hands of filthy men in the name of one god, only to return again to be dunked in the Pacific in the name of another. Her heart not yet broken by the lost child.

Samson wondered now whether he and Anna had spoken about children, whether a child of their own with Anna's eyes and his countenance had been waiting up the road in the future that was now lost to them. The thought of it made his heart quake with sorrow and love.

Pip's mother, her days spent in a room with the blinds half-drawn, smoking cigarettes and drinking diet sodas, longing for so many lost things, among them that six-year-old girl, christened Patricia, who so brilliantly entered the world of cocktail glasses under the hearty name of Pip. Ray was right: the misery of others was only an abstraction. And because it is impossible to contemplate, to actually *feel* the suffering of another without reference to one's own, Samson was naturally moved to think of Anna, and then, finally, his own mother. He knew almost nothing of the last twenty years of her life. He could not bear the thought of her having lived out her days alone, perhaps having drawn her own blinds and sat staring into space. Whoever the son was that observed his mother slowly enter middle age; who grew up, left for college, and called her regularly; who moved away and returned from time to time to visit, to register with compassion the small humiliations of old age; who received the phone call that she was ill and flew out to sit by her side and watch as the cancer quickly advanced; whoever it was that saw his mother out of the world and buried her was now as unreachable as she.

And what is a life, Samson wondered now, without a witness?

He felt an overwhelming desire to be close to his mother. He wondered where she was buried. How could he not know where his own mother lay six feet under? She'd never moved from the house he'd grown up in; that much Samson had gathered from Anna. Presumably he'd buried her in a cemetery nearby. How difficult could it be to find her? Were there not records of these things, the grassy plots sons stake out to bury the women who brought them tooth and nail into the world? He would find her grave and when he found it, flesh of her flesh, he would fall to his knees and grieve for her. He would lie down and close his eyes, and pressing his body to the ground, he would bear last witness.

The bus route terminated in a parking lot near the beach. Gulls perched on rusted metal posts, heavyset and unflappable. Samson nudged Pip awake. Her head rolled back and she opened her eyes. He felt the restless fervor of a man who'd been locked up for years, whose recurrent fantasy had been nothing more than an unobstructed view. He wanted to grab Pip and haul her over his head, to jog her down to the ocean and plunge them both under in a briny baptism. Instead he reached out and unceremoniously brushed the hair out of her eyes, tucking it behind one ear. Pip narrowed her eyes but didn't protest.

Outside in the parking lot, they stood blinking in the light, inhaling the coastal, arboreal smell of California, the bracing Pacific where soon Pip would be washed clean of everything but the love of God. From then on she would be called Patricia. The past would live under a different name.

There was someone waiting for her, a woman

with graying pigtails sent by the Chapel. She stood waving in front of a van whose bumper sticker said *I Brake for Miracles*. As a parting gift Pip handed him the Bible, folding down the pages about Samson. The camera was still around his neck, and he took it off and hung it around hers. She smiled and he smiled back, and for a few moments they searched each other's face with the awkward shyness of people suddenly reminded of how little they know one another. Part of him didn't want to let her go, wanted to accompany her, to watch over her sleep and protect her from harm as he had failed to do for Anna. He wanted to take her small-boned body in his arms and carry her safely into a new life.

But he didn't, and finally Pip shrugged and walked to the van. The woman embraced her as if they were old friends. Pip endured the hug, then threw her backpack into the car and climbed in after it. As they pulled away she turned and waved through the window, and Samson lifted his hand in a salute.

There was a thing he liked to do that comforted him when he was a child. Lying in his bed, he would imagine what other people were doing at the same instant. He would allow his mind to drift out the window and down the street, floating above the trees and rooftops as his great-uncle Max had once floated, in his youth, above the Italian city. He would pause outside the upstairs window of the house next door where Mr Shreiner practiced his golf swing bathed in the blue glow of the television. He would continue down the street, past the Sargents, whose oldest son, Chuck, came home from college one winter under mysterious circumstances. Mrs Sargent told people he was writing a play, and Samson would look into Chuck's bedroom to see him in his mother's bathrobe, hunched over a typewriter, his hair freakishly unkempt. Samson would drift through yards that emitted an odor of rotting sweetness. He would linger in front of Jollie Lambird's house, watching as she slept. In his silent sentry Samson would float over the trim lawns and still swimming pools, through the faint blue night of suburbia. He'd sail over the humped foothills with their mossy oaks. His mother would be out on a date, and he would find her wearing her red dress and the black pumps that pinched her toes, laughing like a gypsy with her head thrown back, leaning into the man she was dancing with. Who the man was hardly mattered, a suitor stepped into the spotlight of his mother's attention before receding into obscurity, someone she might have met at a rally, a divorced dentist, a moony artist. His mother never appeared to be deeply affected by the comings or goings of these admirers. Sometimes it seemed to Samson – and maybe also to the men on whom she leaned as she limped up the driveway in her pumps at the end of the night – that she was only biding her time.

This bird's-eye view comforted him, the assurance that beyond the walls of his bedroom the night was also breathing, Mr Shreiner winding up his nine-iron, his mother dreamily spinning across a floor, taken not so much with her dance partner or the band or the pattern of other whirling bodies, but with her own loveliness. He would continue on, pulled by a gentle, watchful gravity, tumbling above mountains and plains, across the patterned country. He would pass over countless lives like the spinning dial of a radio tuning toward the lone signal of one voice.

It was one of his earliest memories, listening to his father speak. Samson had been convinced that he would have been able to recognize his father's voice if he ever heard it again. Once, toward the end of a Little League game, lunging for a ball in the outfield, he was sure he'd heard his father shout his name. The ball landed with a soft thud into his mitt and, heart pounding, he turned triumphantly, holding it in the air. He scanned the bleachers, squinting through the almost submarine light. But there was no sign of anyone who resembled the man in the photographs. He walked back toward the bases still searching the crowd, the ball in his mitt. After the game Samson waited, watching the thinning crowd until the last cars pulled away. When everyone had gone he walked up to the plate and took a few practice swings. He heard the proud crack of the bat meeting the ball and – as the imaginary ball vanished into the inky air above the ballpark – an ecstatic cheer led by his father, whose voice rose buoyantly above the rest. *Atta boy, Sammy. Atta boy!* He made a victory round of the bases and touched home plate. Then he kept running through the empty parking lot and down the street. Later at night, after he'd made his local tour above the rooftops, he fell asleep traveling on toward that voice.

Now he was on his way back, reversing through space. He watched the ocean slip in and out of view from the taxi window. The driver had a sour look on his face and was hunched over the wheel.

296

He had deepset eyes and wore a sweatshirt with the hood pulled up.

Samson had found his great-uncle Max listed in the address book in his bag. Discovering what blows the passage of time had delivered him seemed a wrenching prospect. But aside from Anna, Max was the only person Samson could think of who would know where his mother was buried. He was living, if he was still alive, at a place called Fairview Homes on Monte Rosa Avenue in Menlo Park, and for a hundred and fifty dollars paid in advance, the taxi driver had agreed to take Samson there. He'd handed over the money and the driver had greedily wet his fingertips and counted it out. Then they'd set off, the driver keeping one hand on the radio as he drove, scrupulously adjusting the volume every few seconds. He played the dial as if it were an instrument, a counterpoint to the gas pedal he jerkily pumped. He chortled whenever there was a song he especially liked. Samson wondered whether it had been a good idea to sit up front. He wondered if the man's bludgeoning instruments were in the trunk. He considered taking Pip's Bible out and making a show of reading it. *Come unto me, all ye that labor,* he'd tremulously announce, and if the driver seemed receptive Samson would tell him that he was a pilgrim who had given up all his earthly possessions. In a voice as inspired as the preacher's Pip had heard over the radio, he'd explain how he had given up the woman he'd loved, and not only her but all his memories of her too. He would tell the driver how he'd surrendered his past for a plot of emptiness.

Feeling emboldened, chastened by his own sanctity, Samson took the Bible out and arranged it on his lap. The driver bore down on the road and took no notice, manning the wheel and pumping the gas pedal with disturbing rapture. Samson removed the slides from the other pocket one by one, lining them up on the cover of Pip's Bible. Either the man didn't notice or he didn't care. He twisted the radio up to full pitch. Probably he wouldn't give a hoot if Samson fished a severed finger out of his pocket and laid it down on the dash.

He would tell the driver, should he happen to ask, that he was a pilgrim. He would say that he was on his way home, having been gone for years. This would capture the man's sympathies and he would lower the volume and lean in to hear each word as Samson told him the story of his travails, all ending now as he sped him homeward to his mother. The driver's eyes would fill with tears and he would speak of the importance of his task. To ensure safe passage, Samson would tweak the truth a bit and say that his mother was dying and not already dead.

When they got off the highway at Menlo Park they couldn't find Monte Rosa Avenue. They stopped for directions but got even more lost. The driver's face darkened and he hunched farther over the wheel. He drove like a man possessed, making jerky turns whenever the urge struck him. Samson ignored him. He was consumed by the uncanny spectacle of streets he remembered from his childhood. That they still existed and that he remembered them was exoneration: proof that his memory had served him right. They drove down quiet streets lined with stucco houses. The late-afternoon light fell like dust on the leaves. Samson stuck his head out of the window and felt the warm air. A vertiginous feeling came over him.

Within a few minutes they miraculously found themselves on Monte Rosa Avenue. The nursing home was marked with a discreet sign in gilded script that said *Fairview Homes*, plural despite the singular brick structure perched on a hill set back from the road. The man didn't bother to turn up the drive, just dumped Samson at the curb and reached over to pull the door shut.

'Hey!' Samson flashed his wallet in the window. 'How much for you to wait?'

The driver paused, licking his lips. 'It would cost you.'

'But how much?'

'Depends what we're talking about.'

'Half an hour. An hour tops. Definitely not longer than an hour.'

The man fiddled with the radio.

'How much would that be?' Samson repeated.

'A hundred.'

'Fifty.'

The man snorted and jacked up the volume. Samson leaned in and lowered it.

'Seventy-five,' he said, and before the driver could answer he turned and jogged up the hill. Behind him there was a blast of music, a signal that a deal had been struck.

Sometimes there is an image that outlasts all the others, though one never knows what it will be. He would have been no more than six or seven, standing in the door of Uncle Max's study. A smell of pipe smoke, the light shuttered, falling in slats. The adults were out on the patio; he could hear the occasional glissando of laughter and the clink of cutlery on the plates. The sound of the afternoon passing slowly, according to a design beyond his grasp.

The study was filled with books. Many were in German. Max had escaped to America just before war had broken out and got a job teaching at the university. Samson walked along the wall of shelves, running his finger across the spines. He heard the high pitch of his aunt's voice exclaiming something he couldn't make out. He was aware of the faint pleasure of privacy. He came across an old photograph, unframed. It was black and white, or more yellow than white, printed on thick paper. It showed a family, eight or nine children standing stiffly around the parents. The clothes were high-necked and pompous. He studied the faces with a cruel attentiveness and found them ugly. He had no idea who they were, only that they somehow belonged to Max's past, and this vaguely annoyed him. Max had never mentioned them, and Samson felt a secret had been kept from him. He must have stood there holding it for a while, because then someone was coming down the hall looking for him. When Max walked into the room and saw him holding the picture an inscrutable expression passed across his great-uncle's face. Samson looked at him dully, but in his heart he felt the small irreparable injury of a child whose trust has been broken. Wordlessly he returned the photograph to the shelf. Then he passed Max and walked out of the room into what was left of the afternoon.

At the front desk Samson was told that Max was watching TV in the common room. The attendant, a man in a skinny tie, seemed surprised that the old man had a visitor. Samson had wondered whether the attendant might recognize him – surely he must have been there before to visit Uncle Max, especially when he'd come back to California during his mother's illness. Maybe it was even he who had first brought Max to Fairview. But the man only looked Samson over with suspicion: the last surviving relative who probably looked disheveled and filthy, reeking of sweat and the stink – so disgustingly human – of despair.

Samson warily pushed his license across the desk. The attendant held it pinched between two fingers and studied the picture. He entered Samson's name in the visitors' book.

'I guess you're probably itching to see your—'

'Great-uncle.'

'Your great-uncle. Great-Uncle Max,' the attendant repeated as Samson followed him down the hall. They entered a large sunny room with a linoleum floor. A few residents were seated at one end in front of a large-screen TV on which a woman was demonstrating how to prepare a chicken dish.

'There he is,' the attendant announced cheerfully, as if he were pointing out a rosy newborn and not an old man in a ratty terry-cloth robe. 'Great-Uncle Max!' the attendant sang out, bounding up to the stooped figure in a wheelchair. 'Look who's here to see you!'

With great effort, the old man turned at the waist as if the vertebrae of his neck had been soldered together. The wry expression was clouded by senility, but unmistakable.

Samson had to restrain himself from leaping forward and lying prostrate before the wheelchair, from sideswiping the smug attendant and tackling the old man in an embrace that might crush his brittle, porous bones. Max's thin hair had receded to a scraggly garland around his head, leaving the high dome of his scalp completely bald. The polished shine was extraordinary. The ears that in Max's younger days, when there was still enough hair to frame them, had merely stuck out as if registering dissatisfaction or a lively inner life, now shot out from both sides at an angle well over ninety degrees. They had hinged forward over the years, and while the rest of him had shrunk, the ears had grown in size to reach nothing short of prizewinning.

Max looked the attendant over, then sleepily shifted his gaze to Samson.

Uncle Max had loved children, and could always make them laugh with a trick or a joke, but never had any of his own because of an illness his wife had as a child that had made it impossible for her to conceive. Sitting in his bathrobe was what was left of the man who, after listening to Samson sing the praises of Hunter Froubuck's fishing trip with his father, had made two fishing poles out of sticks, *out of sticks for crying out loud*, strung with fishing line with a brass hook knotted at the end, and taken Samson to a little stagnant body of freshwater. They'd caught nothing but eels.

'Do you recognize this young man?' the attendant asked, raising his eyebrows in mock suspense. In the heavy pause that followed, Samson half expected the attendant to throw wide his arms and announce in a canned baritone, 'Max Kleinzer, *this is yooour life!*' while the geriatrics did jazz fingers in their wheelchairs.

'Who?' Max asked, the sound muffled and inhuman, like the distant query of an owl.

Samson stepped forward in an attempt to cut the attendant off.

'Uncle Max, it's Sammy. Sammy Greene, your nephew. Remember?'

'Sammy Greene!' the attendant boomed, grabbing Max's wheelchair by the handles and rolling him over to the window. Samson trotted after them. Max kept his eyes trained ahead.

'Sammy?' Max said in a groggy voice. 'Sure, I remember.' The attendant whirled Max around and backed him up against the window so that the late-afternoon light streamed in from behind, illuminating the ears like lamps.

'Sammy Greene! Ta-daaa!' the attendant echoed again. Then he turned and made off down the hall before Samson could club him with the jawbone of a donkey.

The old man's hands were clasped stiffly on his lap as if he were waiting for the curtain to go up at a play. They sat in silence, looking at each other.

'Who did you say you were?' Max finally asked.

'Sammy. Beth's son.'

'*Who?*'

'*Beth's son.*'

'Edison?'

'Your great-nephew. *Samson.*'

Max stared at him blankly.

'You remember?' Samson asked.

'Can't say I do.'

He studied Max's face, wondering what his great-uncle saw. He remembered how during the first days back in New York, those clear spring days when the light was thin and impartial, Anna had appeared to him as a distant and indivisible whole, the way a bird is reduced to a spot of blackness in the sky. Even her desire for him to remember her did not lessen this elemental quality of self-containment. But as the days passed, the appearance came unraveled. He began to notice the small details she was made up of: the way she made a small popping noise with her lips when she was about to say something difficult, or played with the ends of her hair when she was watching TV, or drank her coffee with the spoon still in the mug, and so on. Eventually he found he could only see her as a collection of such fragments.

Max's face registered nothing.

A year or so after he'd found the photograph in Max's study, a man from Max's boyhood in Germany had come to visit. He was a little man with a limp and a high-pitched laugh, whose thick hair shone with pomade. Samson was sure he'd never seen him before, but the man embraced him with great affection. He smelled of pine, of a place thickly forested. 'Don't you remember me?' he asked in a grating accent. Everyone turned to Samson, waiting. The man smiled expectantly. A whole minute passed, but Samson could conjure no recollection. Feeling his face flush with shame, he turned and fled the room. He refused to even look at the man during the rest of his visit.

Samson smiled weakly and pulled up a chair. 'How are you, Uncle Max?'

Max seemed relieved to change the subject. 'Fine. I can't complain really. Still can eat. The food is terrible, but I can eat it. To think, all those years Clara – do you know my wife, Clara? – all those years I ate Clara's cooking like an ungrateful wretch. Now I eat, I don't even know what you would call it. A nice word for the food here I can't think of. I watch the cooking show every day on TV. Cordon bleu. What I wouldn't give for a taste of that.'

'I knew Clara,' Samson offered.

'You knew Clara?'

'Sure.'

'You ate her cooking?'

'Plenty of times.'

It was true: she had been a good cook, if a little heavy-handed. Everything she produced had a sort of glazed quality, not greasy but actually appearing as if coated in melted glass or sugar. The roasted chicken, the carrots, the pineapple turnover, all looking hard and shiny as gems.

'Tell me she isn't an excellent cook,' Max said, lost in the twilight of the present tense.

'She was excellent. She was a very good cook.'

'The best.'

'You look good, Max,' Samson lied.

'I feel okay. There was a time you could say I looked good. Back in the day. That's what people used to say. I'd walk into a room and they'd look and say, "Now that's a handsome man." I could have had my pick of the girls.'

Max fell silent and Samson wondered what vision of female beauty his great-uncle had stumbled across in the murkiness of his mind. A submerged moment and then Max surfaced again.

'But I loved Clara. Right off, first time I saw her, I knew she was the one. She was sitting outside in the sun, unwrapping a sandwich from wax paper. Wearing a gray dress.'

'Really.'

'Gray, I said. Cinched at the waist.' Max patted his knee and ebbed back into silence.

It seemed unwise to bully him into remembering, to risk confusion and panic. But if there was any chance at all that Samson was going to discover where his mother was buried he would have to prod Max in the right direction. He pulled his chair closer and laid a hand on Max's, applying a slight pressure. The sun dipped behind a cloud and the old man's ears dimmed and went out.

'You say you knew my wife?' Max asked, looking up.

Samson tried to guide the conversation toward his mother. He reminded Max of how she had been his favorite niece, how they had shared a love for sweet things and also for musicals. His mother would play the piano and Max would accompany her in his rich tenor. They sang duets by Cole Porter, the Gershwin brothers, Rodgers and Hammerstein, entertaining anyone who would listen but mostly themselves. Long after everyone else had turned in they kept at it, the bright chords mingling with their laughter. There had been many nights when Samson had fallen asleep on the couch, his dreams threaded with melodies from *A Chorus Line* or *Anything Goes*. Later his mother would pick him up and carry him to the car, still humming beneath her breath.

'Beth? Sure. Sweet kid. Loves to tap-dance,' Max said.

Samson gave Max's hand an authoritative squeeze, shepherding him back to the present.

'Beth died, Uncle Max. Remember? About five years ago now.'

Max blinked and pulled his hand away. He seemed hurt by this brash statement of the facts.

'You like chocolate?' Max asked in a lowered voice, changing the subject. 'It just so happens that I have some in my room. Not Hershey's, the other kind. I'm not supposed to eat it. High blood pressure. But I happen to have some I won't say how.' Then, as if in retaliation, he added, 'I'll tell you who liked chocolate: my sister-in-law's girl, Beth. She loved chocolate. She had these shoes. What do you call them, Mary Janes. With the little metal taps. You could hear her coming down the hall. She would dance and then I would give her chocolate. Come – you want, I'll give you. Not Hershey's.'

There was something pitiful and moving about the offer of the generic chocolate – not the best stuff, not the all-American candy bar, the one they rained down on starving children after the war, airlifted in cartons the kids ripped open with their teeth, not that one but the other kind, as if there were only Hershey's and the rest, America and the rest. There was something about the meagerness of the offer that made it seem cruel not to accept.

Samson agreed, and taking the handlebars of Max's wheelchair, turned him toward the door. Max turned stiffly, his face clouding over. 'Shhh! Keep your voice down,' he hissed, though Samson had not spoken loudly. 'I don't want any trouble.'

The Max that Samson remembered had had a resistance to authority and made a mockery of it at any cost. Once he had to be bailed out of jail after a small traffic violation because when the police officer had pulled him over he'd handed over the contents of his wallet piece by piece like a Marx Brothers scene – old movie stubs, business cards, his library card – everything except his license. Afterward Max had reenacted the scene to anyone who would listen, laughing uproariously each time. It seemed to Samson now that this pleasure in ridiculing figures of authority was in some way Max's own muted form of protest against the injustice of fate, against the Nazis who had taken his family and destroyed all traces of his former life. Samson felt a jolt of compassion for Max, the singular, sad beauty of kinship. He squeezed his great-uncle's shoulder as he piloted him along, palpating it through the robe as if Max were a wrecked boxer about to make a last appearance in the ring.

On the way to Max's room they passed a glassed-in area where ten or twelve residents stood in front of a cluster of chairs. A plump, animated woman of about sixty, wearing a yellow leotard and tights, stood in front of the room gaily singing 'It's Silver Motion Time! It's Silver Motion Time!' The class joined in with a strangled chorus like roosters trying to keep tune with a fat canary. 'It's Silver Motion Time! Silver Motion Time!' Out in the hall, the old prizefighter brightened up and clapped along.

'That's Ruth Westerman,' Max announced, joining in with the others in a robust and still melodious tenor.

'Now move your head up and down, yes, yes, yes,' Ruth sang out, and the bedraggled troupe nodded their heads yes, yes, yes. 'Beautiful! Now shake your head from side to side, no, no, no,' and like lemmings they followed her, no, no, no. The champ shook his head as well: No Hershey's! No trouble! No I don't remember who you are! 'What else can we move?' Ruth sang out, and a host of suggestions came back, conservative at first – 'Our eyebrows!' 'Our fingers!' – then increasingly bolder – 'Our arms!' 'Our *legs*!' – until finally a booming command – '*OUR PELVIS!*' Ruth Westerman turned to the doorway where the suggestion had come from. Max was still clapping. 'Our pelvis!' he repeated. It took a moment for her to absorb the idea. 'Our pelvis!' she finally called out, raunchily pumping her hips. After a moment of confusion about the new choreography the seniors also joined in, rocking and swaying in assent.

It occurred to Samson that Ruth Westerman, now swiveling her groin ('Stir it! Stir it! Stir it!'), was about the age his mother would have been if she were still alive. That Ruth Westerman should be leading a geriatric dance team in a charade of scandalous motion while his mother lay still for all eternity in a box was too much. All he wanted was to visit her, to pay his respects, to lay his weary head down on her small plot of earth. After that it didn't matter. After that Ruth Westerman could march a whole Silver Motion army over them both for all he cared. He jerked Max's wheelchair around, stripping the class of its second-in-command, who continued to happily thump his thigh as he rolled down the hall.

Max's room was small and cramped. Even with his personal belongings it looked like a hospital room, like the tragically decorated rooms of the terminally ill who've given up paying rent outside. On the wall were four framed views of the Italian city as seen from above. The tiny crosshatched streets and the little churches were all rendered with the tender, compulsive passion of a grieving lover. The strangest and most haunting showed the city as a concave curving around the globe, as if the Italian city of Max's youth was all that remained in the world, its geometry bending to encompass the earth.

Other than the drawings there were mostly books. A set of about ten oversize volumes bound in black leather struck Samson's eye. It looked like they would be a challenge for Max to drag them off the shelf. Examining their German titles, their unabridged girth and uniform darkness, it did not seem impossible to Samson that they contained a lifetime of wisdom, that somehow everything in Max's brain had been meticulously copied down there in tiny print, setting him free to roam the pastures of oblivion.

The room overlooked the front lawn. From the window Samson could see his ride vigorously nodding to the music. He wondered how much time was left before the driver got fed up and drove off without him.

'So you want the chocolate, Max?'

'You have chocolate?'

'I thought *you* did.'

'How did you know?' Max seemed genuinely surprised. 'It just so happens I do. Where I put it, that I don't know. Here you have to hide things. Leave something out in the open and like that, they confiscate it. Gone.' He angrily swiped the air. 'Someone, I don't know who, once sent me cookies. What do you call it, fresh-baked. They let me have a couple and then they took the rest. On account of my high blood pressure. Bastards.'

The remark surprised Samson, delivered in a tone that sounded so distinctly like the Uncle Max he remembered, the wry and contentious man who refused to bend to the petty orders of the traffic police. That he should end up here, ferreting around for a few crumbs of illegal chocolate, seemed a miserable and cruel degradation. Samson let out a sharp sigh. Max turned to him, his eyes keen and focused, and for an instant he seemed to be actually registering his great-nephew's presence. Then the moment vaporized and his face blurred back to infirmity. 'Bastards,' he said again, as if he were repeating something he'd heard someone else say.

Max wanted to take off his robe, and so Samson helped him to his feet and peeled it off. It was spotted with crusty patches like the matted fur of some insufficiently domesticated animal. Underneath Max wore wrinkled pajamas, the bottoms of which ended at his shins.

'Okay.' Max rubbed his hands together. 'Let's go!'

Off they went, Samson gamely moving from shelf to shelf like a child looking for the afikomen – *Warm, warm, warmer!* – while Max coached from his wheelchair: 'Open that little box! That's a music box. You heard that song before? It's a waltz. I got that I don't know where. Maybe Bavaria. Any chocolate in there? No? All right,

314

look behind that book.' *Warmer, warmer,* COLD*!*
'Not that one! The one on the left, the big book.
See if I hid the chocolate behind that. No? Fine.
What about the desk? Maybe I put it there.'

Samson sifted through the tumble of empty
eyeglass cases, uncapped pens, old checkbooks,
and mismatched earrings like an underwater
diver in a flooded city. This was the detritus left
over at the end of a life. He did not really expect
to find the chocolate. It had probably never
existed, or if it had, most likely that had been
decades ago, a long-lost bar of chocolate that in
Max's mind had become the El Dorado of candy.

'Nope, nope, nope. Next,' Max ordered as
Samson opened each drawer and searched
through it.

Samson closed the last drawer. The sky had
begun to turn dark. It saddened him that he
would have to leave Max soon, and for a moment
he forgot why he'd come. He picked up a jar of
salve off the desk and held it up.

'What's this?'

'That? Let me see it.' Max brought it close to
his face, and when he couldn't make out the label
he busily unscrewed the cap and stuck his nose
into it. There was a blast of menthol. He frowned.
'Oh, that. They rub it on my chest sometimes,
when I have trouble breathing.'

'How about I rub some on for you right now?'

'Naaa!' Max hastily screwed the top back on
the jar and tried to shoo Samson away. 'I don't

need it! It smells terrible. What do I need it for? I'm breathing fine. Vicks, I think they call it.'

'Why not put some on before you have trouble breathing? Come on, off with the pajama top.'

Max struggled but Samson grasped him by the shoulders and worked him out of the top. Defeated, shirtless, the champ obediently shuffled over to the bed. Spurred by the medicinal vapors of the Vicks, perhaps Max could produce the name of the cemetery. Samson scooped out a gob of the ointment and began to work it into his uncle's leathery chest. Max seemed unmoved by this sudden act of intimacy. Either he was used to being handled by strangers or he was no longer capable of astonishment. His eyes turned glassy as Samson massaged his wrinkled breasts, the once powerful frame still sinewy.

'How does it feel?'

'Fine. All right. I didn't need it but it feels all right.'

'I need to ask you something, Max. Can you answer something for me?'

'Sure. Okay, I can try.'

'Remember Beth?'

'Sure. Sweet kid. Takes tap lessons—'

'She's dead, Max!' Samson exploded. 'She grew up, she stopped tap-dancing, and she died!'

Max stiffened, and right away Samson felt guilty for having lost his temper. Exhaustion, the pressure of the waiting taxi, and the sadness of not being recognized by Max had made him edgy.

Struggling to regain his composure, he worked the Vicks into his great-uncle's shoulders, kneading the atrophied muscles. Through his fingertips he felt the faint heat of Max's skin.

'There's a lot I'd like to tell you if I had the time and you could understand,' he began. The only sign that Max could hear him at all was a slight relaxation of the shoulders. 'You wouldn't believe the things that happened to me. I'm so tired I could sleep for days. It's not that I feel sorry for myself – I don't. I'd even like to think that one day I might laugh about all this. Sitting in a room, in a house far away from everything. Just sitting by the window watching the leaves outside and suddenly I'd begin to laugh. Because it will all feel so long ago, in another lifetime, like it happened to someone else.'

He was settling into the monologue now, content just to be heard if not understood, like talking over the radio, not knowing if one's voice would reach anyone, but knowing that it was out there nonetheless, traveling the waves.

'I mean, how many someone elses can one claim to be in a life-time? It's not very long a life, is it, Max? You're a kid, it's summer, you blink your eyes and years – *years* – have passed. And you realize that you've become someone else, but that your heart is still caught in that lost kid. That what you're left with beating in your chest is a diminished thing, a shadow of what it was when you were a boy and running under the night sky you felt it was filled to bursting.'

Samson sighed and dropped his hands into his lap. Max sat with his head bent, leaning forward as if in prayer.

'You're lucky, Max, that you remember your wife. Maybe you even remember mine. Her name is Anna, a very beautiful woman. Whenever I think about her now, I'm struck by her beauty. She's the sort of woman who – how can I explain it? – you never know what she's thinking. Or maybe it was only me who didn't know.' He wondered whether Max heard the desperation in his voice. Quickly he got to the point. 'I shouldn't be going on like this, I'm sorry. Look, I just need to know where my mother is buried.'

Max was silent and Samson lifted his hands to his face and pressed his eyelids, forgetting that they were coated in Vicks. The sting was terrible. He rushed to the sink and pushed his face under the tap. When he straightened up, his eyes were bloodshot in the mirror. Over his shoulder he saw a blurred Max struggling to his feet.

'Sit down!' he cried as he stumbled toward the unsteady figure of his great-uncle. He regretted raising his voice as Max collapsed back onto the bed like a puppet and sat with his head hung, blinking. Gently, enunciating each syllable, struggling against forces far greater than himself and Max, than the small room at the end of a life, Samson forged on. 'Is she buried with the others? Next to Aunt Clara, maybe? Where is the cemetery, Max?'

A long silence and then, miraculously, Max answered.

'She's not there,' he muttered.

HOT! You're boiling! Eyes still streaming from the Vicks, Samson began to pump Max's shoulders again, increasing the blood flow to his brain, closing in on the dim glow of recognition.

'Not there? Where? At the cemetery with the rest? Why isn't she there?'

'Not there. Nope.'

Max lunged for the jar of Vicks as if to put a halt to any further interrogation. *Nope, nope, nope. Next.* The lid fell and rolled across the floor. Indignantly he said, 'They don't rub it into my back.'

'They don't do that? Why not? It's good to get the lungs from behind.' Samson pulled over the desk chair and planted himself in front of Max. 'Why isn't she at the cemetery, Max?'

A pained look flashed across Max's face. He patted his leg as if tapping out a distress signal. Samson took him firmly by the shoulders.

'*Please*, I'm begging you. Where is she if she's not at the cemetery?'

Max looked up, his eyes bright and feverish, gripped with sudden lucidity. Without warning, like an illegal blow to the groin, he answered, 'Cremated.'

The old man turned to look out the window. Outside, the light was thin and blue. Stooped, half-naked, embalmed in Vicks, he seemed already of the otherworld.

Samson hadn't slept in about forty-eight hours, not since the day before he'd left Vegas. Had it really only been today that he boarded the bus at dawn? He felt dizzy and weak in the knees. He struggled for air, his breath coming in short gasps. He tried to pry open the window but it was locked shut. It was all a joke, an absurd dream. In his nightly wanderings he had drifted too far. He had been held up, arrested in a stalled moment above the rooftops but soon he would wake again in his own bed, in a world of natural laws and common tasks. He would drowsily grope along the hallway to his mother's bedroom and pushing open the door he would find her asleep, her body under the steady sway of her breath, her red dress crumpled on the chair.

He pressed his forehead against the glass, trying to steady himself. Max might as well have told him that she had been buried in space, launched in a shuttle and set loose, her regulation hospital nightgown floating around her weightless body.

Cremated?

That's what I said.

You're saying they put her in a combustible box with her clothes folded at her feet and slid her into an oven? That I let them pulverize her remains and then accepted a container of what was left, a few handfuls of sooty matter?

Samson turned, but his great-uncle's head was bowed. He seemed terribly still, as if he were listening, and Samson realized that he hadn't spoken at all, that the voice he'd just heard, clear as day, was inside his head.

He tried to compose himself. Cremated? She might as well have been hacked to bits on a mountaintop in the Himalayas and left to be eaten by a horde of ready vultures, this news was so horrifically exotic, so unexpected. She must have wanted it, written it down someplace, because it was impossible to believe that even in the most florid gesture of grief he had taken matters into his own hands and decided to set alight his mother's body. What had he known then of grief?

It was as if some possibility had been foreclosed. Twilight had settled over the room, casting Max's face in shadow. The conversation continued in Samson's head.

And the ashes? What did I do with them? Scattered them in some panoramic spot?

The ashes?

Yes.

You don't remember?

Can't say I do.

At the house.

Our old house? Where other people are living now, total strangers – I left her there?

Nah! You buried her. In the backyard. You put her under that tree, what do you call it.

The magnolia?

Right. The magnolia. You buried her under there.

321

Where we buried the dog? I buried her ashes in the backyard with the dog?
Yeah, with the dog.
This was my idea?
What do I know?
You think this is a joke?
No I don't. Nope. Next.
Do you remember me, Max?
You?

Max was inert, his head resting on his chest. He had fallen asleep. The whole ordeal had exhausted him and he'd simply tucked his head under and checked out.

Samson ran a finger along the spines of the books, trying to steady himself. He thought about what Ray was doing at this very moment, if he was forging on with his project, already picking up a new Output at the airport, driving the man home in his sleek white convertible. Going through the whole act, the house and the thistle tea. Because the truth was that Ray believed in the goodness of his work. He would see the man as a worthy sacrifice for a greater cause; he would make the man feel his worth. For a brief moment Samson considered calling someone – the police, the newspapers – and leading them to the lab in the desert to save the man from harm and expose the whole thing for what it was, not progress at all but a sad and dangerous thing. But who would listen to him? He was half-convinced that if he returned to Clearwater he would find that it had vanished without a trace, dismantled and boxed up overnight so that not even a scrap was left. Where it once stood only the faint hiss of the desert. Maybe one day, a day sometime in the future when his anger had disappeared and he could speak – backed by memory and wisdom – with an eloquence as convincing as Ray's, he would find the doctor and tell him how impossibly wrong he had been.

Samson stopped in front of the set of black volumes. Using both hands he pulled one down and opened it, surprised by its weight. He flipped through the pages of German words arranged in columns. A dictionary, that was all, a strict scholarly edition with the whole immoderate career of each word recorded in full. There was only the hint of an accent in Max's speech, a faint harshness smoothed over like glass blunted by the sea.

A plaintive honk sounded outside, the taxi driver laying into the car horn. Samson replaced the book on the shelf. He began to move as if under command. The horn continued to blare as he went through the motions of helping his great-uncle back into his pajama top and robe. Max's eyes fluttered and his breath caught and struggled for an instant like a drowsy child's.

You?

On the wall the four views of the Italian city were obscured by darkness. The horn ceased now, a hush, the blessing of silence. A drop of saliva appeared at the corner of Max's mouth. Did they take him out from time to time, Samson wondered, for air and light? Did they push him out into the courtyard once a day to feel the sun on his face, to hear the rustle of the leaves and the cooing of doves? Could it really have been he, Samson, who had brought Max to this place? He didn't want to abandon him now, to let him drift alone and obscure toward death. He would have liked to care for Max, to see him through his final days, the two of them living together in a house somewhere where there would be time to talk – time, even, to remember.

The sky was a darkening blue through the window, that passing moment between day and night when the flatness suddenly falls away to reveal infinity. Samson's heart thumped in his chest. His mind was racing and yet he was not aware of any thoughts, only a frenzied whir of consciousness.

He lifted Max in his arms. He was surprised by his lightness, as if his great-uncle had the hollow bones of a bird. Carefully he arranged him in the wheelchair and opened the door. As he hurried down the hall steering a slumbering Max toward a last breath of freedom, he half expected a voice to call out 'Sammy Greene!' But a different attendant was on duty, a woman bent over a book who didn't notice the fugitive pair as they silently sailed past.

Outside, the moon was high and bright. Samson

slalomed Max down the handicap ramp. Slowly, as slowly as a heliotrope turning toward the light, the old man lifted his head. Cheers rose from the taxi's stereo, a wave of ecstatic applause that broke over the empty street.

They drove on through the night, their faces flashing in and out of the sodium light. The driver had asked no questions as Samson unloaded Max into the backseat. He seemed to grasp the gravity of the situation and only pulled his hood tighter over his head. Max was untroubled by the change of scene, accepting it without protest. He stared out the window as if it were a television, his robe fallen open on the seat.

When they pulled up in front of Samson's old house the windows were dark. The garden was overgrown. The front steps that Samson had raced up and down innumerable times, moving through his life with the agile ease of a natural, a creature of instinct, now sagged dangerously. But there were signs of life – a car parked in the garage, a bicycle abandoned on the lawn – its new owners careless but alive enough to trample the grass and fill the garbage bins. The scene could not have been more banal. And yet his heart swelled.

He unloaded the wheelchair. Struggling with the handle, Max opened the door himself and dangled one foot out like a parachuter preparing to jump. Samson jogged around to catch him. Max had lost a slipper in the getaway, and the bare foot hovered above the asphalt like a pitiful question. Samson felt a stab of guilt for having torn him from his familiar surroundings. He lifted Max and held him aloft, the retired boxer with the skeleton of a bird. He lowered him gently into the chair and pulled the robe around him, knotting it at his waist.

Samson had begun to push the wheelchair across the street, staring at the vision of his past before him, when the taxi driver called him back to offer him a flashlight. It was sheathed in rubber, the kind of heavy-duty torch used in violent emergencies, during floods and blackouts, to shine light on terrible accidents, whose weight also recommended it for use as a club. Samson flicked it on. The beam was dull, and the moonlight alone was bright enough to see by, but he accepted it anyway, not wanting to refuse such an uncharacteristic act of charity.

The magnolia tree was around the back of the house. Samson vaulted the wheelchair off the bumpy front path and pushed it soundlessly through the grass. It didn't occur to him to ring the doorbell, as he later told the police in the bright fluorescent station. What would he have said, a foul-smelling vagabond pushing a nonagenarian in a spattered robe? *Hello, sorry to disturb. Don't worry, I won't harm you. Believe me, we have something in common.*

327

I grew up in this house. Seriously. A long time ago, yes. Oh, all kinds of stories! You're too kind, really; a glass of milk sounds lovely. And could I trouble you for a shovel? Oh, nothing, just my mother, who I think I buried under that tree.

He made his way around the side of the house to the green mortuary behind, easing Max over the ruts of the trees, clutching under his arm the official flashlight of rescue missions. Reflected on the branches above he saw the light of a television coming from an upstairs window. Husband and wife, probably brushing up against each other in bed, the children safely down the hall, flushed with sleep.

When the white flowers of the magnolia tree suddenly came into view, his heart froze. The night was dark and complete, locked in a temperate stillness. Max's face was set in the peaceful blank expression of the enlightened, his wheelchair glinting in the moonlight. Samson stood at attention. At a loss for an appropriate gesture, he brushed off his knees and got down on the ground. He began to crawl as if across a delicately frozen pond. There was a slightly sickening smell as he made his way around the tree, some base ripeness coming from the rotting magnolia flowers or the thick grass.

With the dog there didn't seem any reason to mark the spot. The magnolia was enough, a reminder each spring with its first bloom, a white and rising echo. But a person? Surely the resting place of a human being demanded some form of memorial, however modest. He held the flashlight with one hand and felt along the ground with the other. He made a full circle around the trunk but found nothing, and was about to give up when the dim beam of light caught on something inscribed in the bark. He brought his face closer. Carved in bold, deep strokes were her initials: B.S.G. No dates or epigrams, just the undecorated facts and all at once he understood that she had asked this of him – at some point before she died, her mind sharply focused by the pain, she had asked him to bury her in her own backyard, without ceremony, released from the extravagance of death. To bury her in a familiar place, under the magnolia, which – of course, how could he have forgotten? – had always been her favorite tree. A place where, should a man who looked like Cary Grant in a bright white suit ever come looking for her, he could find her.

Max was elsewhere, his face tipped skyward like a child's in a snowstorm.

Samson took out the slides and lined them up in the grass. Using both hands he began to dig a hole, and when it was sufficiently deep he dropped them in and covered them with dirt. He felt exhaustion seeping in. He laid his head down in the grass, flattening his body against the ground. He tried to imagine the sensation of being dead. To remain unmoving under the magnolia tree through days and nights, washed by the rains until he himself turned to weather. He imagined himself settled in for the long haul, his mother beneath him, above him the breathing black dome of sky.

Somewhere many miles away, in the heart of the desert, a man was recording memories, preserving them as another desert air once preserved scrolls of parchment. Creating a vast library of human memory, and so that that library should not be lost – so that it should not combust in fire or vanish into dust and light – he was learning how to inscribe those memories in the one place they were ensured survival: in the minds of other people. A purely scientific project, but off the record he would say that he believed he had found the key to human compassion. *To step into another man's skin.* He would say he believed he had found a way to inspire empathy, a sense of cosmic belonging, that at some near point in the future human beings could be immunized against alienation as they were once vaccinated for smallpox, polio. Yes, he was aware of the dangers. But what knowledge cannot be used for greater stupidities, for greater evils, he would ask, and if we allowed such fears to stop us, where would we be? Human knowledge advances regardless, pulled forward by its own inevitable momentum. Either you ride its crest or someone else does. This man, a doctor, was doing what he had to do.

And somewhere maybe someone else was forgetting everything he ever knew, giving up the ghost of an old life, entering a new emptiness. A man halfway through his life, putting his book facedown on the desk, turning a corner, and disappearing into the future. And the doctor would learn of this man. When the time was right, he would call him. And the man who forgot everything, even his own wife, would come. Knowledge was seductive and emptiness was perishable, and he couldn't stop his mind from filling again, the way a can left outside fills with rain. The man wanted, again, to be worthy, and so he would surrender himself up, and the transferred memory would come through, shattering the silence forever. And then the man would open his eyes, shell-shocked and betrayed.

In a room near the beach, there was a girl waiting to be baptized in the ocean. Standing by the window, her tapered fingers obscuring her face as she moved her lips, preparing to enter the future under a different name. And between that beach and Las Vegas, in some desert town, there was a man near the end of his life, who when he went would leave behind nothing but a memory and a plot of useless land in his name.

And somewhere, too, was Anna.

Samson's cheek was pressed against the grass as if he had fallen from the sky. The idea of ever getting up again seemed absurd. The flashlight lying at his side was still on, a dim ray of accidental light grazing Max's bare foot. It was like a little devotional scene, a tragedy happened and passed and the quiet setting in now, lit up by the flashlight used to rescue. It seemed that in time they would be washed by weather, found years from now by a boy who had lost a ball, running through a future landscape, the rusted wheelchair still intact, and a skull in the grass that showed signs of having been split open and broken into long ago.

He closed his eyes. Sounds that had only been at the furthest margin of his consciousness, the pinpricks of each moving leaf and the ocean rush of a distant car, made a point of themselves, each a tiny argument against nothingness. It was the world minutely insisting on itself, making it impossible for Samson to believe that this was all a dream outside of time, that when he opened his eyes again he would be lying in bed next to Anna, that he would wake up with a gasp, a sudden rush of air filling his lungs, and reach out and press her body against his, saying *forgive me.*

And then there was a sound he thought was in his own head until it became too loud to ignore, a sound steadily rising. It took a few moments for him to register the words but then he did. Something from deep within him rose up to meet the familiar song—

Start spreading the news! I'm leaving today! I'm gonna be a part of it!

It was Max, singing what must have been one of their songs, making it clear that he understood where they were, that they had come to pay their respects, to remember, and, Max's song implied, to rejoice.

If I can make it there! I'll make it anywhere! he

yelped, belting out the notes as best he could. Samson half expected him to start beating his arms or pumping his hips in a flurry of Silver Motion, but Max only rocked slightly as he sang, hammering the air with one hand as if hitting a cymbal. Rapidly he moved toward the finale until finally, hailing glory, he arrived—

It's! Up! To! You! New! York! New Yoooork!

But the song didn't end there, for Max started again from the top, his voice unstoppable, rising from deep within, loud enough that it awakened the neighbor's dog that began to bark, and the lights came on in the upstairs window of the house, and the new owners peered anxiously out, so loud that Samson feared Max might have a heart attack, that sheer volume alone would be the cause of his death as he went out in a last blast of life.

But it was not so. The performance ended as suddenly as it had begun and Max continued to rock to and fro as the dog barked steadily on, as tears of joy filled Samson's eyes, and a police siren sounded its approach.

PART IV

APRIL 2002

He stood waiting on the corner. He had arrived early, and now he glanced down at his watch and saw that it was past two o'clock. The air was cool and he shivered in his sweater. It had rained earlier and the sidewalk was wet.

When he looked up again she was walking toward him, a small figure in a light green coat. He had not seen her for a year, and his heart thumped in his chest. A few feet away from him she stopped, her face calm and still, pale in its frame of dark hair. He had often imagined the moment, had given it weather and latitude and a scripted exchange, but now all of that scattered, replaced by the irrepressible singularity of happening.

He smiled and stepped toward her.

Anna, he said.

They walked along Amsterdam Avenue. She had given up their apartment and was living elsewhere, but they had decided to meet in their old neighborhood just the same. It felt like a long time ago that they had lived there, and he was surprised to find nothing changed.

You look good.

You too.

They laughed, relieved that the first nervous moments had passed. They walked slowly, passing familiar shops and restaurants they had probably eaten in together more times than either of them could remember.

Are you hungry? she asked. They stopped in front of a small Italian place with a blue striped awning. Through the window they saw the diners inside, a couple sitting by the window, a man talking as a woman lifted her glass of wine. They stood on the sidewalk and looked at the menu, and for a moment they might have been such a couple. They might have gone in and taken a table, with time enough to talk about what to eat and drink, to discuss what they had read in the morning paper. Lifting the wine-glass, moving onto more obscure topics, the climate in Norway, the conversation following the natural path of their joined effort. A couple with years of conversation between them so that now a single word stood in for vast themes, and small noises were sufficient to communicate subtleties of mood, and after all the talking they could lapse again into the mutual silence that was the foundation of their life together, at ease, the only sound being the clink of silverware against the plates.

But they were not such a couple, and so they turned away from the restaurant and walked on.

The sun came in and out from behind the clouds. They headed east toward the park, moving side by side under the trees. The first green buds had already come out on the black branches. Conversation came slowly, the words they had planned to say replaced by the things they said. She had left her job and gone back to school. He was living in California, working in a library, renting a small house not far from the ocean.

You should come visit sometime.

Many times he had imagined it, walking with her along the beach or showing her the view from Windy Top. But he knew now with certainty that it would not happen, and he felt the hope gently part from him like an escaped balloon floating up into the afternoon.

They walked for a long time, and then they stopped and sat on a bench. The clouds had gathered and turned dark, but neither of them moved to leave. The things they spoke of were of little importance. He had not imagined that it would be this way; he had thought that there would be many difficult things to explain and feelings to confess. But it was not so, and he realized now that he was glad for this, to sit and talk of things of little importance, as if they had all of the time in the world. He had imagined telling her that he loved her, but now he realized the declaration would sound flat, a wrong note struck in a simple song. To say it would be to disturb the care and stillness of what was unspoken between them.

The rain began in heavy drops.

Here, he said, offering her his sweater. *Put it over your head.*

She shook her head.

You'll get wet.

So will you.

They rose and walked without hurrying. It was coming down hard now; the air held the smell of earth. When they reached the street she turned to face him. Her hair was wet and a drop of water ran down her temple. He took her in his arms and for a long while they stood like that, the taxis splashing past in the street. Then she stepped back, arms hanging at her sides. Her face shone in the muted light.

Take care, she said.

There was so much he had not asked her, and something in him wanted to call out to hold her back. But the moment had gotten ahead of him, and he had no power to strain against it.

You too.

She nodded and her smile was soft. Then she turned to go. He watched her green coat disappear into the distance. The wind picked up and the traffic lights changed. He put his hands into his pockets, and with his face tilted down against the rain he walked away, a man with a past like any other.

EPILOGUE

I used to walk down stairs and imagine myself falling and breaking my teeth. I actually pictured this, the hapless tumble and the blood in my mouth. On the subway platform I imagined the violent push that would come from behind and saw my body flung onto the tracks. If Samson were five minutes late to meet me I would start reciting catastrophes like the rosary. Whenever he took a plane flight I pictured the crash, rescue men pausing to lean against each other among the charred remains. It never occurred to me to mention these thoughts to anybody. It was a reflex, a protective measure as banal as knocking on wood. When Samson didn't come home that first night, I felt surprisingly composed; I'd been rehearsing for this my whole life. And yet when it was all over – once they'd found him in the desert and he had the operation, once I'd brought him home and it became clear that the person I'd known wasn't coming back – I felt disappointed to discover that I had survived. The disaster I'd always feared had finally come to pass and still I was standing, so how could I go on in the old way?

343

One image that outlasts the others. One never knows what it will be. There was a day, six or seven months before he disappeared, one of those perfect days in late autumn, a championship of light. Already the leaves were almost gone, only a few stabs of color in the trees or scattered on the ground. We had borrowed a house for the weekend from one of Samson's colleagues, a white clapboard cottage upstate with a view onto a lake. You could see it from the kitchen, a furrowed reflection of the sky. Samson poured himself a glass of orange juice and drank it down slowly, looking out the window. I came up and stood behind him. It was always, even then, a question of should I touch him. Something had to be crossed to get there. We watched one sturdy crow and then another land on the lawn. Otherwise there was nothing to disturb the stillness.

We took a drive and stopped by a path on the side of the road. There was a No Trespassing sign, but we ignored it. The sound of a hunter's gunshots broke the distance. We ducked into a silo – you could see the sky through the gaps in the tin roof, and there were birds up there. Everything, parts I couldn't have imagined would care, ached for some physical remark of his love. His mouth was cold and tasted metallic, like the season itself, if that's possible. To me he always seemed like that, autumnal. Painfully earnest, with an awkward swiftness to the way he moved, a physical remoteness like he was already receding. I don't

344

remember who kissed whom. It was one of those lucid days in which you can see your whole life like a promise before you.

Later that afternoon we were lying in bed. We had just made love, him touching me as if he'd suddenly remembered that I existed and couldn't get enough. The way he looked at me, his eyes as blue as I'd seen them. I remember feeling then that I would forgive him anything. Afterward we were lying wrapped in the sheets. He was holding me, his face turned to the window, and neither one of us had to say that the moment possessed the indelible weight of beauty. He said he wouldn't mind always remembering this, lying with me and looking out at the lake. A wind had come up in the trees, and the branches were bending nervously.